REVENGE OF THE WANNABES

CLIQUE novels by Lisi Harrison:

THE CLIQUE

BEST FRIENDS FOR NEVER

REVENGE OF THE WANNABES

REVENGE OF THE WANNABES

A CLIQUE NOVEL BY
LISI HARRISON

LITTLE, BROWN AND COMPANY
New York ∿ Boston

Little, Brown and Company
Time Warner Book Group
1271 Avenue of the Americas, New York, NY 10020
Visit our Web site at www.lb-teens.com

First Edition: March 2005

The characters and events in this book are fictitious. Any similarity to real persons, living or dead, is coincidental and not intended by the author.

 Produced by Alloy Entertainment
151 West 26th Street, New York, NY 10001

10 9 8 7 6 5 4 3 2 1
CWO
Printed in the United States of America

Library of Congress Cataloging-in-Publication Data
Harrison, Lisi.
Revenge of the wannabes : a Clique novel / by Lisi Harrison.— 1st ed.
    p. cm.
Summary: Friendships are tested when Alicia, a seventh grader at Octavian Country Day School, decides to break away from the exclusive clique led by her best friend to start her own group.
ISBN 0-316-70133-5 (alk. paper)
[1. Interpersonal relations—Fiction. 2. Cliques (Sociology)—Fiction. 3. Friendship—Fiction. 4. Middle schools—Fiction. 5. Schools—Fiction. 6. Westchester (N.Y.)—Fiction.] I. Title.
PZ7.H2527Re 2005
[Fic]—dc22

                                    2004026409

For B. J. and Carly

Alicia Rivera usually thought sweating was a sign of weakness. But today she flaunted her shiny forehead like a badge of honor. It proved how hard she had just danced and would remind every girl in the class that she was the best.

Alicia lived for Thursdays at 4:30 PM. She craved the clean, lemony smell of the studio's wood floors and felt reborn the second she inhaled the clean, crisp air that hummed from the ceiling vents. She loved being surrounded by mirrors and pretending that she was a professional dancer in a music video. But the main reason Alicia took modern jazz lessons was because Massie Block didn't. And that meant every week, for one whole hour, Alicia Rivera was the most popular girl in the room.

"This is the final combination of the day, so make it count." Sondra, the no-nonsense instructor, pinched the waist of her low-rise Capezio pants and folded them over twice, revealing her perfectly sculpted six-pack.

"You don't get abs like these watching the WB." She slapped her stomach. "Do you, ladies?"

The room was silent as fourteen girls caught their breath.

"*DO* YOU?" she asked again.

Alicia saluted Sondra and shouted back, "No, sir!"

"What was that?" Sondra looked around the room.

Alicia immediately regretted talking back to her teacher until she heard Catherine Carlisle let out a snort. Then a few other girls snickered too. Alicia focused on the ground, trying to look sorry, but she loved being the center of attention, and it was written all over her face. She lined up her head with Olivia Ryan's, hoping her friend's blond ringlets would hide her smile from Sondra. But it didn't work.

Sondra aimed her piercing green cat eyes in Alicia's direction and stared for what felt like nine lives. Alicia could feel her insides starting to shake from all the nervous laughter she was trying to suppress and willed her teacher to look away before she exploded.

"Ms. Rivera," Sondra finally said.

Alicia craned her neck out from behind Olivia. She widened her brown eyes, hoping to look innocent, and ran her hands over the top of her head, where her glossy black hair had been slicked back into a high ponytail. "Yes?"

"Please come to the front of the class."

Her stern yet steady tone made Alicia even more nervous, and she pinched the back of Olivia's elbow in a silent cry for help.

Olivia casually turned around and used her big navy blue eyes to let Alicia know she was wishing her luck.

Alicia lifted her chin and lowered her shoulders to demonstrate perfect "jazz posture" before she started to make her way to the front of the class. It was one thing to get in trouble for a funny comeback, but getting busted for bad form would have been mortifying.

Alicia took her time slowly weaving her way through rows of Lycra-covered bodies. Her father always told her she was "an exotic beauty" and a "special girl, well worth waiting for," and so Alicia had decided never to rush for anyone. Not even angry dance teachers.

The girls stood completely still, watching Alicia's every move in the studio mirror, wondering what was going to happen next.

When Alicia finally arrived, Sondra smiled and sighed. "You are like poetry in motion." She put her lean, muscular arm around Alicia's shoulders and turned to face the class. "Girls, I want all eyes on Alicia for this last combination. She's going to lead. Not only does she have a dancer's attitude, or dare I say, 'bad-itude'"—Sondra paused briefly and grinned, appreciating her own cleverness—"but she is the only one who seems to fully *get* this routine." Sondra began clapping, and everyone felt obliged to join her.

Amid the applause, Alicia locked eyes with Olivia and giggled softly. She hadn't expected this.

Alicia pulled the red elastic band out of her hair and retied her ponytail as tight as she could to show the girls that she was up for the challenge. The hours she had spent practicing at home were about to pay off, and she found herself wishing Massie was there to witness her big moment in the spotlight. Maybe then she'd realize she couldn't *always* be number one.

"Ah-five, ah-six, ah-five, six, se-vaan, eight," Alicia called the eight count and led for the entire length of the Black Eyed Peas' song "Let's Get It Started," which was blaring from the stereo. For the next three minutes and thirty-five seconds Alicia understood what it felt like have a roomful of girls copying her every move. She understood what it was like to be Massie Block.

When the song ended, Alicia quickly turned to Sondra and asked, "Can we do that again?"

The exhausted girls let out a collective moan.

"We're out of time." Suze Charskey pointed to the clock on the back wall.

"Yeah," another girl panted.

"It *is* getting late," Sondra said to Alicia with a sympathetic grin. "We'll pick it back up next week."

"Can I lead again?" Alicia asked quietly while the other girls raced for their bottles of Glaceau mineral water.

Sondra crouched down and popped the CD out of the stereo. She slid it into one of the clear sleeves of her black Case Logic before she answered.

"I should probably give someone else a chance," she said as she zipped up the case.

"But you said I was good," Alicia heard herself whine.

"You *were*," Sondra reassured her as she stood up and slipped into her floor-length baby blue puffy coat. "You're one of my best." Sondra waved and said good night as she hurried toward the studio exit, but Alicia couldn't respond. She wanted to be *the* best.

The other dancers had run to get the only shower with strong water pressure while Alicia just stood there in the dance studio, facing the mirror. At five-foot four, she was taller than a lot of girls in her grade and above average when it came to her big boobs. At school socials or bar mitzvah parties, boys always asked her to dance, and she got e-mails from different guys all the time asking her if she wanted to hang out after school. But she usually turned them down because she had more fun with her best friends: Massie, Kristen, and Dylan.

Being told she looked like a "hotter version of Penelope Cruz with a better nose" used to make her happy. But lately Alicia wanted more. She was tired of being known as Massie Block's beautiful friend. And today, for the length of an entire song, she'd been "Alicia Rivera: the best dancer in the class." But now that song was over.

Alicia took a deep breath and rolled her shoulders back before she turned to join the others in the locker room.

Meredith Phillips turned off her hair dryer when she saw Alicia saunter through the door. "You were really on today."

Alicia peeled off her black Nuala yoga pants, covered herself in a towel, and then wiggled out of her racer back tank top. "You *think*?"

"Beyond," Meredith said before turning the hair dryer back on. "I wish you could lead every week," she shouted as she ran a comb through her stringy beige bob.

Normally Alicia wouldn't have cared what Meredith the Mouse thought. Her tiny bland features and her oatmeal-colored skin made her hard to notice, even when she was the only other person in the room. But at that moment Alicia thought Meredith's opinion was just as important as a pretty person's.

"Me too," Alicia replied to her red toenails as she padded across the cold tiles toward the showers. "Maybe you could say something to Sondra."

"I totally will," Meredith said. "I promise."

And that gave Alicia hope.

While she washed her hair with Glisten shampoo, Alicia made a mental note to try and convince the other girls in her class to speak to Sondra too. She was determined to lead again.

Alicia took her time drying off, knowing Olivia would wait for her.

"You were *better* than J.Lo," Olivia said when Alicia walked over to her locker. Alicia was surprised to see that she was still wrapped in a towel, tugging on her silver lock. Olivia turned the dial again and yanked down, but it wouldn't open. "Ugh! I am spacing on the combination. This totally sucks."

"You really think I was good?" Alicia asked, towel-drying her hair.

"Do cows *fly?*" Olivia said, letting go of her lock and looking at Alicia with a warm smile.

Alicia stopped drying her hair and raised her eyebrows. "No."

"Oh." Olivia looked confused. "Wait, I got that wrong. What I meant was *yes.* You were awesome."

Alicia exhaled and opened her locker.

"You had perfect timing and you didn't miss a step," Olivia said, still tugging on her lock.

"And what about how you called Sondra 'sir'?" Catherine butted in, then snorted at the thought. She had huge dimples and a cute round face that reminded Alicia of a cherub. "Rivera, this class would *so* suck without you."

Alicia put her hand on her heart and shook her head slowly. She wanted her public to know that she was truly grateful for their support.

"Heeelp," Olivia whimpered. "I can't re-mem-ber my locker combo."

Alicia reached for her yellow quilted Chanel makeup bag, unzipped it, and pulled out a folded piece of paper. "Here." She handed it to Olivia.

"What's this?" Olivia smiled, forgetting her lock for a minute. "A secret note?"

The other girls stopped dressing and watched Olivia with curiosity and envy. She turned her back to them and quickly unfolded the paper.

Olivia glanced down and saw a series of numbers, then lifted her head and smiled at Alicia. "What would I do without you?" She turned to face her lock, spun the pink dial three times, pulled it down, and snapped it open.

Meredith, Catherine, and a few other girls started clapping and cheering. Alicia climbed up on one of the wood changing benches and bowed.

When Alicia stepped down, Olivia gave her a big hug and said, "You really are my friend, aren't you?"

Alicia reached into the deep outside pocket on her green alligator Prada bag and pulled out a sheet of stickers from *Lucky* magazine. She ran her Vagabond Red nails along the *no*s and then *maybe*s, knowing Olivia was anxiously awaiting her response. After a few more moments of playful teasing, Alicia peeled off a *yes* and stuck it to Olivia's arm.

"Yes! I'm a *yes*," she said, holding her arm out for everyone to see. "Does this mean I can start going to Massie's Friday night sleepovers?"

Olivia's question hurt more than an eyebrow wax. Alicia wondered if all this time Olivia was using her just to get in with Massie.

"Massie has a strict GLU policy for her sleepovers and there's nothing I can do about it," Alicia said, avoiding Olivia's hopeful eyes.

"What's a GLU policy?" Olivia asked.

Most of the other girls had their jackets on and were leaving, but Alicia noticed Meredith and Catherine lingering by their lockers, hoping to hear her explanation.

"A GLU is a Girl Like Us," Alicia responded, sounding bored.

"How does someone become a GLU?" Olivia pressed down on the *yes* sticker before sliding her arm inside her navy peacoat.

Meredith and Catherine stopped masking their interest and moved in closer.

"You can't *become* one," Alicia snapped. "Massie, Kristen, Dylan, and me are the only GLUs."

"Who made up *that* stupid rule?" Meredith squeaked.

"Massie," Alicia said, then slammed her locker shut.

"Well, don't you have any say in who you hang out with?" Catherine asked.

Alicia stuffed her pink knit scarf and hat into her bag and quickly put on her gray wool coat. She was desperate to get away from their questions, because she didn't like the answers any more than they did. "It's Massie's party, so I guess she gets to decide who goes, okay?"

"Then why don't *you* have the party?" Olivia said, rubbing Burt's Bees lip balm across her pouty lips. "Then we can all go."

It sounded like a simple solution, but it was beyond complicated. Everyone knew Massie owned Friday nights in the same way that MTV owned the Ten Spot. She had claimed the night; therefore it was hers.

"It's so funny, 'cause I always thought *you* were the one that made all of the rules." Catherine zipped her ski jacket. "Not *Massie.*"

Alicia should have been surprised that Catherine and Meredith knew so much about her best friend, considering they didn't even go to Octavian Country Day School, but she wasn't. Everyone knew Massie.

"Why?" Alicia wasn't sure if she had just been complimented or insulted.

"Well, you're prettier, you have a ton of friends, your clothes are all designer, the Briarwood boys are in love with you, and you're an amazing dancer," Meredith said, running her fingers through her limp hair.

"It's true," Catherine added. "I bet if you had sleepovers, they'd be so awesome. I always tell my friends about the funny things you say in class and they all want to meet you."

"And your house is way bigger than Massie's," Olivia added.

Alicia's heart felt like it was beating faster than a hummingbird's and her armpits started to sweat. "You know, maybe I haven't been living up to my full potential," she said out loud, more to herself than to the others.

"Not even close." Olivia threw her arm around Alicia.

"Hmmm," was all Alicia could say.

Had she been eclipsed by Massie's shadow all these years? Was the world waiting for her to step out on her own and shine?

"Why *shouldn't* I be able to have my own sleepover?"

It was the first time Alicia had considered doing something new on a Friday night. She smiled to herself when she thought of how jealous Dylan and Kristen would be for not thinking of it first. "You know, now that I think about it . . ." Alicia tapped her chin with her index finger. "It's not natural for *anyone* to stay 'in' for more than three years. Even Burberry's out again."

The girls jumped up and down and hugged each other, excited to be in on the start of something so new.

"And how cool is it that some of us go to different schools?" Catherine said. "That's never been done before."

"What should we plan for our first night?" Meredith asked Alicia. "Name something you've always wanted to do."

Alicia clapped. "How 'bout we give you a makeover?"

Meredith leaned in toward the mirror and examined her face, but Alicia was too excited to notice. "My mother was just in Spain visiting my grandparents and she brought back a ton of European makeup. You should see my bathroom right now. It's so Sephora."

"Are you going to invite Massie?" Olivia asked.

"Oh my Gawd, how much fun would *that* be?" Meredith said.

"It would be great. Massie is sooo good at putting on makeup. Have you ever seen her at the MAC counter?"

Alicia rolled her eyes. She couldn't believe they were talking about Massie again.

"No, I wish," Meredith said. "Have you?"

"No," Olivia admitted. "But I *heard* she's even better than the people that work there."

"Didn't they ask her to quit school so she could work with them?" Catherine said.

"That's what I heard."

"Why are you guys so ob-*sessed* with Massie Block?" Alicia asked. What she really wanted to say was, "Why are you guys more obsessed with Massie Block than you are with me?" But she stormed out of the locker room instead.

The girls chased after her.

"What's wrong?" Olivia called. "What did we do?"

Alicia poured herself a glass of cucumber-infused water from the pitcher by the receptionist's desk and waited for Catherine and Meredith to catch up. She was only going to say this once.

As soon as Meredith and Catherine arrived, Alicia spoke. Her voice was crisp and controlled, but on the inside she was shaking.

"I am about to put my social life on the line to host a sleepover party for you and all you can talk about is Massie Block," she announced, tossing the cup full of water into the trash. "News flash, I'm not the head of her fan club, okay?" Then she took off again.

The sound of the girls' feet following her lightened Alicia's mood.

"We're sorry—we'll never mention *her* again," Meredith shouted.

"Yeah, never," Catherine said.

"Come on, wait up," Olivia pleaded.

Alicia stopped, then sighed and turned to them with a forgiving smile that said, "Your begging worked."

The girls apologized one last time for hurting her feelings before they said their goodbyes.

"Call and let us know what time to be at your house tomorrow night," Meredith said.

"Wait," Olivia said. "Don't we have the *Teen People* interview tomorrow?"

"Oh my Gawd, I almost forgot." Alicia fluffed up her hair. "We're going to New York City tomorrow. The fashion editor at *Teen People* is doing a big story on us because we won a uniform design contest at our school last week."

"I know," Meredith said. "We heard all about it. That's sooo cool."

"Does this mean the sleepover is off?" Catherine asked, her dimples slowly fading.

"No, it just means we'll have tons of great stories to tell you when we get back."

Catherine's dimples popped back on her face and Meredith put her hands over her mouth and jumped up and down.

"Don't forget to call us later," they called back to Alicia as they pushed through the heavy glass doors and ran outside to meet their parents.

"I won't." Alicia waved goodbye to her dance friends.

A gust of freezing winter air smacked her cheeks and made her eyes water. She was relieved to see her father's driver, Dean, waiting in their limo. It meant she didn't have to stand alone in the cold thinking about what she had just done.

Alicia still felt chilled a half hour later when she sat down to dinner with her parents. The six-bedroom estate often felt big and lonely, especially when Alicia's cousins and grandmother weren't visiting from Spain. The staff had the night off and it was one of those rare occasions where Alicia, her mother, Nadia, and her father, Len, were alone in the house. Nadia had done her best to make the big house feel like a home with music, cinnamon-scented candles, and authentic Spanish cuisine.

"What *is* this?" Alicia slid a dark, salty chunk of meat across her gold plate with the side of her knife.

"*Cordero asado* and *escalivada Catalan,*" Nadia said.

"Ohhh." Len sounded impressed. "It's delicious."

"What is *that?*" Alicia asked.

"Roast lamb and roast vegetables." Nadia smiled with pride. Her perfectly white teeth looked like pearls against her dark olive skin and her red lipstick made them seem even brighter. She hadn't modeled since she'd left Spain and moved to Westchester, fifteen years ago, but Alicia thought she still could.

"It's good." Alicia tried to be polite, but she had no appetite. Every chunk of dead meat on her plate was a reminder of what she would be when Massie found out about the sleepover.

They sat around the rectangular glass-and-cast-iron table, eating to the frenzied rhythm of Spanish music Nadia had brought back from her last trip to Barcelona. The singer's voice sounded like a groggier version of Ricky Martin's. She knew her father felt the same way when he casually pressed the bottom arrow on the remote control to lower the volume.

"I know what you're doing," Nadia said to Len.

"What?" Len smiled. "I love this song." He winked at Alicia.

"Can I be excused?" Alicia said. She forced a piece of roast zucchini down her throat. "I'm full."

"Homework?" Len asked, his face becoming serious. The flecks of gray in his full black hair made him look handsome, not old.

"Yeah, I think a few girls from dance are going to sleep over tomorrow night, so I want to get my room ready."

Alicia pushed her chair away from the table and tossed her napkin on her plate. She wanted to escape before they could ask her the one question she was hoping to avoid.

"Why are you doing that *now?*" Nadia asked, looking at the clock on the microwave.

Alicia was relieved. That wasn't the question she was afraid of.

"Because I have the *Teen People* interview tomorrow, so I won't have time to set up before they get here." Alicia turned to leave.

"Wait, isn't tomorrow Massie's sleepover?" Nadia asked. Faced with the dreaded question, Alicia tried to look casual by picking invisible pieces of lint off her black cashmere turtleneck.

"She isn't sick, is she?"

"No." Alicia turned to face her mother but spoke to the bottle of red wine in the center of the table instead.

"Is she jealous because you beat her in the uniform design contest and you're going to *Teen People* without her? I bet she is and she's giving you a hard time, right?" Nadia raised her wineglass and toasted herself. "If there's one thing I know, it's catty women."

"Puh-lease, she's not *jealous.* This has nothing to do with the design contest."

Alicia had been haunted for days by what she and Olivia had done to Massie and Claire during that contest. She felt a little guilty for switching the ballot boxes moments before the judges tallied the scores, but she had been desperate to win. She was tired of taking second place and wanted to know what it felt like to be number one.

And it felt great.

Since then Alicia wondered if Massie suspected what they had done. Every night she would lie awake in bed and relive the day's events in her mind, analyzing every word Massie said and every gesture she made, desperate to figure out how much she knew. Massie had been acting completely normal, though, so after nearly a week of nerve-racking days and restless nights Alicia figured she had gotten away with it. But every now and then she had to wonder, because Massie always had a way of finding these things out.

"This has nothing to do with Massie, okay?" Alicia folded her arms across her chest. "I should be *allowed* to have my own sleepover if I want."

"No one is stopping you." Nadia smirked and shook her head. "Go from it."

Len chuckled and immediately put his hand over his mouth.

Alicia knew her mother meant to say "go for it," but she sometimes mixed up American expressions. Alicia stood up from her chair and hurried to the winding staircase.

When she got to her bedroom, she closed the door and locked it. Ever since her room had been redecorated two years earlier, it had been her favorite place on the planet. She'd wanted it to look like the kind of bedroom Jasmin would have in *Aladdin* and it did . . . only Alicia's also had a walk-in closet and a private bathroom.

The walls were painted deep red and orange and the canopy that hung over her bed was gold. Her CDs were tucked away in tall wood cases that looked like towers, and multicolored "magic carpets" were spread out across the floor. But nothing topped the cozy "reading nook" in the far corner of her room. It was piled high with Moroccan pillows and cashmere blankets. It was perfect for long phone conversations. Alicia flipped open her brand-new Motorola picture phone and flopped down on a stack of velvet cushions. She had five new messages.

1. "Hey, Leesh, it's Massie. Just wanted to let you know what tomorrow's Sleepover Activity is. READY?" [a second of pause] "I was thinking we could decorate our jeans. How *ah-dorable,* right? I'm getting special paint and rhinestones and glitter and a bunch of patterns, so bring a few pairs of Sevens or something. 'Kay? Laytah."

2. "Hey, Alicia, it's Catherine. Wondering what time we should come over tomorrow night. My mom is trying to coordinate a carpool with Meredith's mom. Call me. Bye."

3. "Hey, Alicia, it's Meredith. Just wanted to find out what time you want to make me over tomorrow night. My mom is trying to coordinate a carpool with Catherine's mom. Call me. Bye."

4. "Hi, my name is Dan Sir Scout. I heard you were an amazing dancer and I would like to recruit you for my troupe. We will be traveling to hot boys' schools around the country in a stretch Hummer and—[burst of laughter] Okay,

just kidding, it's me. Olivia. Just checking in to make sure you were still alive after you told Massie you weren't going to her sleepover. Call me. Oh, and you were *ah-mazing* today in dance. 'Kay. Bye."

5."Hey, Leesh, it's Kristen. Just wondering if you happen to have an extra pair of old Sevens or something. My mom will kill me if I come back from Massie's sleepover with paint on my jeans. Dylan said I could use a pair of hers, but they'd probably be too big on me. So let me know if that's cool. 'Kay? Thanks. See ya tomorrow."

Alicia felt like she couldn't breathe. Her mouth went dry and her throat tightened. Too many thoughts were racing through her head and she didn't know what to do first. Call Massie? Cancel the sleepover? Find jeans for Kristen? Leave town?

She stood up, hurried over to the silver mini-fridge under her desk, and pulled out a diet root beer. She twisted off the cap on the cold glass bottle and took a long drink. The rush of fizz woke her senses and helped her think straight. After the second sip, Alicia knew what she needed to do. She slammed the bottle down on her Formica desk, stepped into the bathroom, and locked the door behind her.

The walls and ceiling were covered in gold and sea green tiles. The rest of the bathroom was decorated in art deco antiques her mother had collected over the years.

Alicia's favorite was an old makeup vanity that had origi-nally been part of a 1940s hair salon. A tall oval-shaped mirror was attached to the far side of the marble countertop and rose into the air like a peacock's feathers. A beat-up Honda motorcycle seat from one of her father's old Hogs served as the seat. For the last year it had become much more than a place for Alicia to apply her mascara. It was her newsroom.

She sat down on the motorcycle seat and faced the mirror. Then she opened the vanity's only drawer and pulled out an old karaoke microphone.

"How much time do I have, Phil?" Alicia asked as she fluffed up her hair.

She imagined Phil saying, "You're on in five seconds . . . four . . . three . . . two . . ." and then giving her the hand signal to let her know she was live and on the air.

"Good evening, Westchester," Alicia said to her reflection. "We interrupt your regularly scheduled program to bring you this breaking news story. Alicia Rivera, the new *Teen People* sensation, wants to throw her own Friday night sleepover party tomorrow night. Will Massie Block understand, or will it be the end of their friendship as we know it? Alicia is too nervous to comment but wants it known that she means no harm to Massie or her other best friends, Kristen and Dylan. She isn't looking for trouble; in fact, she hopes Massie and the others will join her as she gives Meredith the Mouse a makeover. If anyone has any advice for Alicia on how to tell Massie about this new development, please call the hotline number at the bottom of your screen. Alicia, our prayers are with you. Thanks and good night."

Alicia placed the microphone back in its drawer and

unlocked her bedroom door. She always felt better after a newscast. There was nothing she liked more than reporting gossip, and being an anchorwoman was the most respectable way to do it.

Alicia was thinking more clearly now and powered up her eMAC so she could send Massie an IM.

HOLAGURRL: DON'T PICK ME UP 2MORROW. DEAN
IS TAKING ME 2 SCHOOL CUZ I
HAVE 2 GO 2 THE DR.
HOLAGURRL HAS SIGNED OFF AT 8:57 PM.

By passing up her usual seat in Massie's carpool, Alicia would be able to delay an awkward confrontation with her by at least thirty minutes.

The next morning Alicia felt lightheaded and slightly nauseous. She declined her English muffin with raspberry jelly for two sips of apple juice. She was too nervous to eat.

"What is wrong with you?" Nadia asked as Joyce, their live-in housekeeper, scraped Alicia's uneaten food into the garbage. "Are you anxious about *Teen People?* You shouldn't be. You look beautiful."

"Thanks, Mom," Alicia replied, knowing that she'd made the right choice by going with the camel Ralph Lauren suede cargo pants, turquoise-and-brown argyle V-necked sweater, and brown nubby Nanette Lepore blazer with the flirty turquoise flower on the lapel.

Alicia was glad she'd had the foresight to plan her outfit days in advance, because she was too stressed about Massie and the sleepover to give it the proper attention.

"I told you, I'm worried about my history quiz," Alicia said, avoiding eye contact with her mother. "That's why I asked Dean to take me early. I want to go over my notes one more time before class."

She grabbed her Prada bag and headed toward the door.

"Good luck today." Nadia kissed her daughter's forehead.

"Thanks, I'll need it."

Alicia's real plan was to get her books and hide out in math class until the first-period bell rang. She knew she couldn't avoid Massie forever but thought it was a good idea to lay low until she could think of the best way to tell her about the sleepover. But a traffic accident slowed down the morning commute and Alicia arrived at her locker the same exact time as Massie.

"I like your outfit today," Alicia said to Massie as Massie took off her black wool coat.

Massie adjusted the thick black leather belt so it hung perfectly around her emerald green drop-waist jersey dress. "I got it last night after school." The dress had cap sleeves and Massie was wearing a long-sleeved gray shirt underneath, paired with matching gray tights and black wedge ankle boots.

Alicia wished they could trade outfits. Massie looked way more *Teen People* than Alicia did. "Well, I think it looks great," she said, aware of her own shaky voice.

"Cool." Massie smiled, but her eyes stayed fixed.

Alicia looked away. Did Massie already know?

"Gawd," Massie said, looking down the long hall. "Where are Kristen and Dylan with my chai latte? I would have asked them to get you one, but I thought you had a doctor's appointment."

Alicia crouched on the floor and pretended to search her bag for something important, her face protected by a wall of shiny black hair. "It was canceled. He had an emergency surgery."

Alicia peeked through a space in her hair to see if Massie was buying it; so far, so good. Massie was rifling through her pencil case.

"I can't find my favorite fuzzy purple pen."

Alicia exhaled for the first time all morning. Maybe Massie believed her.

"What's wrong with you, by the way?" Massie asked.

"Huh?" Alicia became aware of her quickening heartbeat.

"Why did you have to go to the doctor?"

"Oh, uh, 'cause—"

"There you are," Olivia interrupted. "What's up with the sleepover tonight? Catherine and Meredith keep calling me for a time." Her white-blond hair was twisted into a ballerina bun on top of her head and her big navy blue eyes looked wide and innocent. "It would be so much easier if they just went to this school. Maybe they'll transfer next semester."

Alicia's olive skin turned gray. Then white.

Massie turned to Olivia. "Who are Catherine and Meredith and why do they think they are coming to my sleepover?"

"We're back!" A clump of Dylan's long red hair was stuck to her lip gloss. "Help," she said, trying to remove it by lifting her shoulder to her mouth. "Someone help me; my hands are full." She was barely balancing a to-go box of lattes.

Kristen dropped her book of crossword puzzles on the floor and stood on her toes to pull the hair away for Dylan.

"Thank you," she said before turning to Massie. "The line at Starbucks was in-sane."

"I say we try that new Dr. Juice place that opened up

across the street. Starbucks is so September," Massie said.

"Great idea," Dylan said, wiping her tea-soaked hands on her Citizen of Humanity jeans. "I'm over this."

Alicia prayed for a fire drill.

"Hey, Leesh, what are you doing here? Didn't you have a doctor's appointment?" Kristen said as she took a cup out of the box and handed it to Massie. But Massie ignored her, refusing to take her amber eyes off Olivia. Kristen handed the cup to Dylan.

"What?" Olivia took a few steps back. "Why are you staring at me?"

"You were talking about my sleepover," Massie said, hooking a piece of dark brown hair behind her ear.

"No, I wasn't," Olivia said with an understanding smile. "I was talking about Alicia's. But you're going to come, right?"

"I don't remember getting an invitation," Massie shot at Alicia.

"It's so funny, I was just about to explain when—"

"When what? When you decided it would just be easier to steal my identity?" Massie put her hands on her hips and stuck out her neck so her face was a little closer to Alicia's. "What is this, *Freaky Friday*?"

"I wasn't trying to steal your identity," Alicia said, not exactly sure *what* she was trying to do.

Massie rolled her eyes and looked at Kristen and Dylan. The two girls tilted their heads and looked at Alicia. Dylan broke the tension by burping the words *Freaky Friday*. Kristen and Olivia busted out laughing.

Alicia wanted desperately to laugh with them. She wished she had never thought of hosting her own sleepover party and wanted her friends back. But Massie's scowl reminded her that she was in too deep to just walk away without a scratch.

"Look," Alicia said, trying to stay calm. "This girl from jazz asked if I would give her a makeover and this was the only night she could do it." She noticed Massie's face starting to soften and Alicia thought that everything was going to be okay. "We're going to eat tapas and drink virgin sangria and I would love it if you guys came—"

"Puh-lease," Massie said. "Spare me the whole European act. You are more fake than Olivia's nose."

Kristen and Dylan giggled and Olivia turned bright red. Alicia widened her eyes and gasped.

"Don't look so surprised. I know all about your father being Fannish," Massie said.

"What?"

"Fake Spanish?" Massie said, as if everyone should have known what *Fannish* meant. "I happen to know his real name is Len *Rivers*, NOT Len Rivera. He's from Brooklyn, not Barcelona, and he made up that last name so your grandmother would bless their marriage. So please stop trying to impress us."

"Ehmagawd," Kristen said. "I need a six-letter word for *scandal* starting with *g*."

Alicia was usually the first one to try and guess Kristen's word games, but she wasn't in the mood for games.

"Gossip," Massie shouted. "Gossip, gossip, gossip!"

"How did you know—" Alicia started to ask. But Massie wasn't through with her yet.

"Face it, Alicia, you are an Eternal Wannabe, or EW, as I like to call them." Massie put her hands on her hips and stuck her neck out. "You are never going to *be me* and your dad is never going to be from Spain, no matter how hard you both try."

At one point Alicia had been prepared to apologize, but not anymore. She had an overwhelming urge to rip Massie's diamond studs out of her ears but didn't want to arrive at *Teen People* with bloodstained clothes. So she pressed her lips together and kept her anger inside.

"Hey, EW, have fun at your little fiesta tonight," Massie called over her shoulder as she headed down the hall. Dylan and Kristen followed right behind her, giggling.

Alicia gathered up her books and twisted her hair into a low ponytail. Her cheeks were flushed red and it felt like her stomach was on fire. She tried her hardest not to cry. The last thing she needed was puffy eyes. Alicia turned on the heels of her brown Cole Haan square-toed boots and started walking in the other direction. Olivia scurried to catch up.

"Hey, Leesh." Kristen stopped walking and called back to her. "Did you by any chance remember to bring me a pair of jeans?"

Before Alicia could say "yes," Massie tugged Kristen's arm and pulled her down the hall.

Alicia froze. She had no idea what to do next.

┌───┐
│   │
│   OCTAVIAN COUNTRY DAY SCHOOL   │
│   HISTORY CLASS   │
│   11:18 AM   │
│   November 14th   │
│   │
└───┘

While Joel Morris droned on endlessly about the Roman Empire, Massie tilted her Chanel compact mirror so she could see Alicia in the seat behind her. Was her mascara smudged from crying? Were her eyes all red and puffy? How much of her morning was spent sobbing in the bathroom? But Alicia's eyes looked the same as always: brown, bright, and beautiful. Why wasn't she devastated by their fight?

Massie had known for days that Friday, November 14, was going to be a bad Alicia day. It was the official date of Alicia's *Teen People* interview, a coveted prize that really belonged to Massie and Claire Lyons. And now everyone in school was congratulating *Alicia*, wishing *her* luck and telling her how badly they wished they were her.

Massie kept telling herself that the right time for revenge would be obvious. She just had to be patient. But now her Friday night sleepovers were threatened and Massie couldn't sit still any longer. Alicia had woken the sleeping giant and the giant was pissed!

"As I was saying, Ms. Block," Joel said, and Massie jumped. "Caesar made his way to office by 62 BC, but many of the Senate thought he was a dangerous, ambitious man. Sooooo, they deprived him of a triumph after his command in

Spain and did their best to keep him out of the consulship. . . ."

"*ZZZZZZZZZ.*" Massie turned to Amanda Levine as soon as Joel rested his beady eyes on someone else. Amanda tapped her palm against her mouth and fake-yawned. Massie smiled, then looked around the room. The entire seventh-grade history class was one useless fact away from slipping into a coma. It was the perfect time to start working on a Christmas shopping list. Massie flipped to a blank page in her notebook and began. . . .

MASSIE'S CHRISTMAS LIST

Name	Gift	Naughty	Nice
Parents:			
Kendra & William	Spa weekend		👍
Dog:			
Bean	Fur booties & cashmere poncho (white?)		👍
Horse:			
Brownie	Plaid Ralph Lauren blanket		👍
Driver:			
Isaac	Armani driving gloves		👍
Housekeeper:			
Inez	Chanel snow boots		👍
Best friend:			
Kristen	Walkie-talkie		👍
Best friend:			
Dylan	Walkie-talkie		👍
New friend:			
Claire	Cell phone (Nokia vs. good one?)		👍
New crush:			
Cam Fisher	Headphones vs. new leather jacket		👍
Ex-friend:			
Alicia	☠	☠	☠

For the first time ever, Cam Fisher made the list. She'd first noticed the ultra-*ah*-dorable seventh grader exactly fifteen days ago, at her boy-girl Halloween party, and hadn't stopped thinking about him since. She had always heard the name "Cam Fisher" because he was one of the best soccer players at Briarwood Academy, but Massie had never been into team sports, so that didn't carry a lot of weight. What she liked about Cam were his eyes. One was green and the other was blue, and that made him rarer than a vintage Hermès handbag.

When it came to Cam's gift, Massie was torn. Should she play it safe and get him a cool pair of headphones for his iPod, or buy him a brand-new leather jacket so he could finally stop wearing his older brother's ripped hand-me-down?

Massie tickled the bottom of her chin with her fuzzy pen while she deliberated.

Everyone knows how much he loves that beat-up coat, she thought. *He even wears it in the summer. And it would be so embarrassing if I gave him something he never used. People would think he didn't like* me.

Massie knew she had to find a clever way to convince him that a new one would be much cooler. All she had to do was spend a little quality time with him . . . which was exactly why she'd made plans to attend her first Briarwood soccer game very soon.

Massie imagined giving Cam a big rectangular box wrapped in red paper and tied with a big green bow. Cam would tear open the box and look at her lovingly with his one blue and his one green eye. Then he would try on the jacket and say, "Massie, I love my new Hugo Boss leather jacket—but not half as much as I love you."

Massie would smile shyly and would somehow know that he thought she looked beautiful.

"How can I possibly thank you?" he'd ask.

"I'll show you," she would say with a suggestive wink.

Massie would take his hand and lead him up the stairs to her bedroom.

"What about your mother?" Cam would ask.

What a considerate guy, Massie would think while turning the glass knob on her bedroom door.

"She won't be home for another hour," Massie would say, pushing the door open and revealing her immaculately clean all-white room.

"This is perfect," Cam would say as he started to take off his leather jacket.

"No, leave it on," Massie would say.

He would smile appreciatively.

"Are you ready to do this?" Massie would ask.

"I can't wait," Cam would say.

"Awesome, let's go."

Cam would plug his iPod into her speakers and blast some Strokes song that Massie had never heard before. But she would bob her head and pretend to love it anyway. Then Massie and Cam would start pulling the books off her bookshelf and hurling them on the floor. They would tear the goose feathers out of her down comforter and throw them at each other like they were having a snowball fight. They would toss her CDs around like Frisbees and yank the evenly folded sweaters out of her walk-in closet and lob them into the air, giving each other points every time one of them landed on top of the white shade of her floor lamp. They would wrap toilet paper around her mannequin and write their names with lipstick on her bay window. They would be laughing so hard Massie's stomach would start to feel like she had just done a thousand crunches. But she would ignore the pain because she'd be having too much fun. She was so tired of her mother nagging to her keep her room "spotless" and couldn't think of anyone she'd rather mess it up with than Cam Fisher, the cutest boy in . . .

The familiar smell of chocolate, spices, and vanilla filled the air and pulled Massie out of her fantasy. She was no longer laughing with Cam. She was back in Joel's mind-numbing history class and Alicia Rivera was standing in front of her, reeking of Angel perfume.

Massie refused to look up. Instead she moved her fuzzy purple pen vigorously across the lined pages of her Claire Fontaine notebook so Joel would think she was taking notes. She could feel Alicia glaring and knew it was time to remind the EW who she was dealing with. Massie was about to stand up and confront her when Alicia swatted Massie's pen out of her hand. It looked like a purple fuzzy dart as it shot through the air and landed on the light brown carpeting two rows away. Massie looked straight into Alicia's eyes, trying her hardest not to let the rage she was feeling show on her face. She stuck her leg out in front so she could drag the pen toward her with the wedge heel of her new boots. But Alicia beat her to it. She stepped on the pen and twisted her toe into it like she was grinding out a cigarette. Massie leaned forward in her chair and pushed Alicia's leg, but Alicia was too quick for her. She hooked her thin fingers around the chunky gold chain of Massie's charm bracelet and closed her fist around it. Massie struggled to pull away, but Alicia was stronger than usual. Massie took a deep breath in and counted silently in her head. . . . *One . . . two . . . THREE.* On the final count Massie pulled back as hard as she could, but Alicia held on with all her might and ripped the bracelet right off Massie's wrist.

The tiny bell, the Eiffel Tower, the miniature black pug, the white-gold horse, three stars, and her favorite charm of all, the diamond-encrusted gold crown, scattered and bounced across the carpet like a handful of dice. Massie fell to her hands and knees. She needed to get that crown back.

Massie could hear the girls in the class snickering but didn't dare look up. She was too humiliated. Why wasn't Joel getting involved? Why was Alicia *doing* this to her? Why wouldn't everyone stop laughing?

"Looking for this?" Alicia said, standing over Massie. She slowly opened her fist and revealed a sparkly gold crown in the center of her palm. Massie reached for it, but Alicia closed her fist and stuffed it in the front pocket of her Ralph

Lauren suede pants. She let out a maniacal laugh, grabbed the Prada shoulder bag off the back of her chair, and strolled out of the classroom, looking calm and confident.

Massie was still on her hands and knees gathering her charms when all eighteen girls stood up and applauded for Alicia. Even Joel was clapping.

"Why are you taking *her* side?" Massie shouted. "She started this."

But everyone kept clapping.

Massie tilted her neck back, hoping the tears would fall back inside her head, but they were coming too quickly now and couldn't be stopped. When the first one managed to escape and roll down her cheek, Massie surrendered. She had no choice. She curled up on the floor and broke into loud sobs in front of the entire class.

Suddenly she felt a light tickle on the back of her neck, but she refused to react. It could be a trap. But when Massie felt it again, she looked up. For some odd reason, she was back in her seat.

"What?" she snapped.

"You dropped this on the floor when you nodded off," Joel hissed. He was holding Massie's fuzzy purple pen between his fingertips like it was a dirty pair of underwear from the lost and found. "I'll try to make things more interesting for you next time, Ms. Block."

"Thanks," Massie said as she took it. "You know, for the pen, not for making class more interesting."

The girls in the class burst out laughing. They didn't

realize she was being sincere, but Massie didn't care. At least they were laughing with her, not at her.

Joel shook his head and then walked away. Massie curled in toward her desk and examined the pen like she was on *CSI Westchester.* There were no signs of it getting crushed under Alicia's boots or dragged across the carpet by Massie's heel. It was in perfect condition.

Massie grabbed her wrist and instantly breathed a sigh of relief. The diamond-encrusted crown was exactly where it was supposed to be, on her charm bracelet right between the pug and the stars. It was all just a dream. . . .

Or was it an omen? Massie rolled her pen between her palms, thinking about Alicia and how to keep that dream from becoming a reality.

Finally the bell rang, marking the end of history and the beginning of World War III.

┌───┐
│   │
│   OCTAVIAN COUNTRY DAY SCHOOL   │
│   LUNCHTIME   │
│   12:30 PM   │
│   November 14th   │
│   │
└───┘

The minute the lunch bell rang, Alicia gathered her books and bolted out of history class. She couldn't handle another nasty confrontation with Massie. She'd tried her best not to cry after Massie called her an EW and even managed to put on a happy face while Massie was spying on her with her compact mirror. But she didn't know how much longer she could keep her cool. Thankfully it was time for her to meet Olivia and head into Manhattan for the *Teen People* interview. She needed to get out of OCD for a while.

"How was history?" Olivia asked when Alicia arrived at their meeting spot by the alumni photos. "Did you talk to her?"

"Nope, now let's go before we see her. She always goes by here on her way to the Café."

"Let's go out the back," Olivia said.

"Done." Alicia put her gray wool coat on while they zig-zagged through the bustling lunchtime crowd, avoiding anyone who might have heard about the fight.

"What's up, gang?" a voice bleated over the school's intercom system. *"Deena Geyser here with your afternoon news brief."*

Alicia and Olivia rolled their eyes the minute they heard Deena's voice.

"Is she chewing gum?" Alicia said. "She always *does* that. It's sooo unprofessional."

"Is that what that slurping noise is? I always thought she had a speech peppermint."

Alicia stopped walking and looked at Olivia with a puzzled look on her face. "You mean a speech *impediment?*"

"Really? You think she has *both?*" Olivia said, her blue eyes filled with pity.

"Probably." Alicia didn't bother correcting her.

"But before I get started," Deena continued, *"I have a few announcements to make. . . . Since I like to put humor in my daily broadcasts, I am officially changing my name from Deena to Comma Dee. Funny, right? And the best part is I can spell it with just a comma and the letter* D*. . . . I'd show you, but this isn't television, people; use your imaginations. . . ."*

Alicia heard gasps and giggles from every girl she passed.

"I would also like to say congratulations to Alicia Rivera and Olivia Ryan once again for winning the OCD Fashion Week Uniform Contest last week. . . ."

A round of applause erupted in the halls.

Olivia started jumping up and down. "That's us!" she screamed. But all Alicia could do was look over her shoulder for signs of Massie.

"They are about to leave for their big interview with Teen People, *so if you would like to see them off, please head over to the parking lot ASAP. . . ."*

Everyone they passed in the halls looked at them with envy in their eyes. Alicia unbuttoned her coat so they could get a good look her new suede pants, argyle sweater, and nubby blazer. She slowed down to her regular leisurely pace, deciding to enjoy this red carpet moment.

"Why are they looking at us funny?" Olivia whispered out of the side of her mouth. She tucked a white-blond strand of hair behind her ear and looked uncomfortably at the ground. After a second she shot her head back up and looked straight into Alicia's big brown eyes. "They must have heard about your fight with Massie."

"This has *nothing* to do with *Massie,*" Alicia snapped while managing to keep her head up, shoulders back, and eyes fixed on the Exit sign at the end of the hall. "They wish they were the ones getting interviewed by *Teen People* this afternoon. They want to be us."

"Really?" Olivia covered her mouth and widened her eyes. "You mean they're actually jealous of me?"

"And *me,*" Alicia reminded her.

"Maybe they'll come back with the inside scoop on some new trends. . . ."

Alicia knew her fake broadcasts were ten times better than "Dee's" real ones, but she wasn't going to trash her. Alicia needed the publicity.

". . . and speaking of trends, it seems like Massie Block's infamous charm bracelet has started a phenomenon. I've been seeing charm belts, charm necklaces, and even charm key chains hanging off some of your pocketbooks. . . . I guess this is turning into a real CHARM SCHOOL. . . ." Deena started laughing at her own joke.

"She makes it seem like Massie invented *jewelry*," Alicia said as she pushed open the heavy wood doors that opened onto the school's parking lot.

"Oh. My. Gawd," Olivia said, her wide eyes fixed on the crowd.

Alicia froze too. She couldn't believe how many girls had skipped lunch to see them off. "I bet there are at least fifty people here."

"What are they doing on the other side of the parking lot?" Olivia asked.

"No one expected us to sneak out the back door," Alicia said. "If anyone asks, we did it to avoid Principal Burns, NOT Massie, okay? Let's go."

Alicia moved across the cracked gray cement in the parking lot with ease and confidence. Olivia was a few paces ahead.

As she got closer, Alicia could see that everyone was bundled up in their puffy winter jackets, hats, and scarves, but she was too excited to notice the biting wind and left her coat unbuttoned.

"Look," Cindy Bennett shouted when she saw Alicia and Olivia coming toward her. "There they are!" The crowd of girls ran across the parking lot to greet them.

"Oh my Gawd." Cindy tried to catch her breath. "You are so lucky." She pushed her way through the crowd and stood right beside them. "If you see Orlando Bloom, pleeease take a picture of him for me?" Cindy handed Alicia a silver Sony camera. "He was on last month's cover. I have it up in my locker right now."

Alicia took the camera and dropped it in her Prada bag, "No problem."

"You guys look incredible," Denver Gold shouted. "Smile!" She snapped their picture. "Don't forget us when you're famous."

"We'll do our best." Alicia kissed her hand and waved back. She had never been happier in her entire life. For once everyone was there for *her.* Massie who?

Ann Fox smothered them both with a hug, "Great outfits," she said, throwing her arms around them. When she released her grip, she gave them a more thorough scan. "Alicia, those suede pants are to die for. And Olivia, I love your winter white cords. And that's a *fab* poncho. Is it real rabbit fur or faux fur?"

"F—"

"It's real," Alicia interrupted. She pulled Olivia by the arm and led her toward the stretch limo that was waiting for them in front of the school's entrance. Dean, her family's driver, stood patiently beside it, his hands folded behind his back.

"Sorry about the pulling," Alicia said once they were away from the crowd. "But you almost told Ann your poncho was fake. *Never* admit to a fake unless you're dealing with a member of PETA."

Olivia touched her index finger to her temple and said, "Got it."

"Ready, ladies?" Dean asked when the girls got to the limo. His smile accentuated the tiny wrinkles around his eyes.

"Yeah," Alicia said. But she didn't move toward the open door. Instead she looked back at her adoring fans and waved goodbye. She noticed Claire's friend Layne Abeley, standing off to the side of the crowd with her two Gwen Stefani–wannabe friends Heather and Meena. Layne wasn't wearing a jacket, just a T-shirt that said BORED WITH BRITNEY and a pair of secondhand plaid pants.

"Did Layne say anything to you?" Olivia asked. "Like congratulations or anything?

"No, why?"

"Because she didn't say a word to me. All she did was stand off to the side and whisper with Meena and Heather."

"I bet she just came out to make fun of our fans," Alicia said, blowing air kisses to everyone. "Ugh, that's so Layne. She thinks she's so above everyone because she has the guts to wear those used clothes."

Olivia shrugged.

"Yeah, who cares." Alicia stepped into the car and slid across the buttery leather seats and Olivia followed. Dean had turned on the seat heaters, so their butts were warm and toasty the minute they sat down.

As the limo pulled out of the parking lot, Alicia scanned the crowd one last time. After today's fight Alicia didn't expect Massie, but Kristen and Dylan had no excuse, unless of course they knew she cheated. . . .

Alicia felt a quick pang of guilt when she remembered what she had done to her friends but waved it away like a bad smell. It was time to have some fun.

Once they were on the road, Alicia cranked up the volume on the stereo and the girls sang along to Avril Lavigne's latest song.

When they got to a red light, Alicia opened the sunroof, stood up on her seat, and sang the rest of the song with her head sticking out of the top of the limo. Olivia popped up beside her.

"SIT DOWN!" Dean shouted. "I am not moving this car until you SIT."

The girls couldn't hear him over the loud music and assumed the symphony of honking horns meant everyone was in love with their performance. They sang louder and waved their arms in the air.

Dean shut off the music and craned his head out the window. He slapped the outside of the door, then looked up at the girls. "Hey, ladies, these people don't sound like they want to wait much longer." His small brown eyes looked tired and puffy.

"Then drive! The light is *green*," Alicia said.

"SIT!"

The girls quickly ducked back into the car, hysterically laughing. Tears ran down their faces as they rocked back and forth, holding their stomachs. Olivia started pointing at the seat across from her but was too breathless to speak.

"What?" Alicia said, wiping her eyes.

Olivia pointed again. "What is *that?*" she finally managed to say.

A white envelope wrapped in a red bow had been placed

on the leather cushion. Alicia was about to sit on it. *For my Teen People—have fun today. Love, Dad* had been written in black marker on the outside.

"I don't know," Alicia said, grabbing it out of Olivia's hand. She gently pulled one end of the ribbon.

"Hurry," Olivia said. She was bouncing up and down on the edge of the seat. "Gawd, you are *so* slow."

Alicia purposely moved even slower. Once the bow was undone, she rested the sealed envelope on her lap and turned to face the window. She knew the anticipation was killing Olivia and thought it would be funny to milk it.

"Gimme that," Olivia said, swiping the envelope and tearing it open. She reached inside and pulled out three concert tickets. She held them in front of her face like a hand of cards. "BEYONCÉ! TONIGHT! MADISON SQUARE GARDEN!"

"Yes!" they heard Dean say all the way from the front seat. He reached his arm into the backseat and plucked one of the tickets out of Olivia's hand. "This one is mine."

Alicia grabbed the other two. "Box seats! Perfect!"

"You know this means we'll have to call off the sleepover with Catherine and Meredith," Olivia said.

"Given," Alicia said, trying not to sound upset that she had ruined her friendship with Massie for basically no reason.

"How did your dad *get* these?" Olivia asked. "I heard Jay-Z couldn't even get tickets."

"His law firm has gotten like a million celebrities out of jail, so he has tons of connections," Alicia dropped nonchalantly. "He can get me into *anything*, even Fashion Week."

"The only way this day could possibly get any better is if I suddenly grow boobs," Olivia said.

Alicia smiled and folded her arms across her chest. She would have gladly given Olivia hers if she could.

In less than two hours Alicia and Olivia were standing in midtown Manhattan staring up at 1271 Avenue of the Americas. The *Teen People* building took up an entire city block and Alicia couldn't wait to see the inside.

"Look, it's one of those hot dog guys. They're always in movies about New York." Olivia pointed to the heavily mustached man standing in front of a silver cart. "I *have* to buy something. This is so cool."

"What's so cool about a hot dog?" Alicia asked quietly, trying not to offend the guy.

"It means we're in New York City." Olivia reached inside her Dooney & Bourke hearts bag and pulled out a matching wallet. "Look, he even has those big soft pretzels."

Alicia rolled her eyes. "Olivia, we have to go; we'll get something after." But Olivia ignored her.

"One pretzel and one orange soda, please." She looked back at Alicia and smiled excitedly.

"Want one?" Olivia waved a five-dollar bill in the air.

Alicia shook her head and turned away, wondering if Olivia would have obeyed Massie. "I'm not hungry."

"It's almost three," Dean said, checking his gold Rolex. The watch was last year's Christmas gift from the Riveras, and Alicia saw him check it at least fifty times a day. "We should head on up."

Alicia shellacked her mouth with a fresh coat of clear M·A·C Lipglass and checked her side part in the reflection of Dean's sunglasses.

"That's okay, Dean, you don't have to come with us." Alicia reached up and put her hand on his shoulder. "Why don't you get a coffee at Au Bon Pain? We'll meet you there when we're done."

"I promised your mothers I would go with you," he said. "If I don't go, you don't go."

"Puh-lease, we don't need a babysitter, do we, Olivia?"

Olivia licked a blob of mustard off her thumb and shook her head.

Alicia put her hands on her hips and looked up at Dean with her big brown eyes. She had *I told you* written all over her face. While Alicia stared at Dean, she couldn't help noticing his bushy unibrow. It was just one more reason why she didn't want to be seen with him at *Teen People*. But the piercing sirens of a rush of passing police cars startled Alicia and she heard herself scream.

"Lead the way," she said to Dean, forgetting all about his embarrassing facial hair.

Alicia walked in between Olivia and Dean as they fought their way through the sea of fast walkers that scurried by.

"Look at this revolving door. It's huge!" Olivia gasped. "All three of us can fit in at the same time."

"It's just a door," Alicia said, but she was secretly relieved they wouldn't have to separate even for a second.

The door spit them out into the massive lobby of the

building. The walls and floors were made of the same shiny white marble and the ceiling seemed a mile high.

"I feel like we're in heaven," Alicia said, looking up at the gigantic Christmas tree that towered above her head.

"You will be if you don't watch where you're going." Dean put his arm in front of Alicia to keep a husky man in a business suit from banging into her.

Alicia pinched the sleeve of Dean's itchy blue wool coat so she could continue looking around and stay safe.

She passed a newsstand that had a huge display of glossy fashion magazines all around it.

"I haven't heard of *half* of these," Alicia said to Olivia when they walked by.

"Me either," Olivia said. "What's up with that one?" She was pointing to *Vogue Italia.* "They totally ripped off *Vogue's* name. That's so cheesy."

Alicia wanted to laugh but bit her lip instead. There was so much to look at, she didn't have time to explain the facts of life.

"This way," Dean said, leading the girls through a maze of people. He stopped in front of the security desk.

"Names and ID, please," said the guard. He was seated behind a console of TV monitors and telephones.

Alicia and Olivia took out their OCD cards and Dean took out his New York State driver's license.

"Who are you seeing?" the guard asked, grabbing their cards with his chalky old fingers.

"Lucinda Hill at *Teen People,*" Alicia said, applying a fresh coat of pink gloss.

The security guard typed their names into a computer, and three badges slid out of his printer. Their ID pictures were on them.

"We're being interviewed," Olivia said, hooking a long strand of blond hair behind her ear. "And photographed."

"Yeah, for *Teen People*," Alicia said with a proud smile.

"Thirty-fifth floor," the guard said, handing them their badges.

"They're doing a whole story on us," Olivia said, leaning over his desk and peeking at his high-tech setup.

The guard used his coffee-stained clipboard to push her elbows off his desk. "Elevators are to your left," he said, replacing the clipboard with a roast beef on rye. He lifted the sandwich to his mouth and took a bite. "Next," he called with his mouth full, and the bike messenger who was in line behind them stepped forward.

Once they were on the crowded elevator, Alicia let out a huge sigh. Everything finally felt still. She squeezed past the woman in a navy sweater set and caught her own reflection in the thin band of brass that separated the black leather panels on the walls. She fished around the inside of her purse for a brush. Her hair looked healthy and shiny despite the dry winter air and her side part had held up nicely despite the strong winds. Alicia winked at her image. She didn't need the brush after all.

"I am totally saving this," Olivia said, admiring the badge that was clipped to the bottom of her poncho. "I bet I could get a fortune for it on eBay."

A few of the adults in the elevator snickered when Olivia said that and Alicia was embarrassed.

"She's just kidding," Alicia said to the panel of numbers that lit up above their heads . . . 25 . . . 26 . . . 27. . . .

"No, I wasn't," Olivia insisted.

Alicia widened her eyes and looked right at Olivia, hoping her friend would start acting less like an amateur.

The elevators opened up on the thirty-fifth floor, and a girl in her twenties was there to greet them. She had short brown hair that had been combed to the side and still looked a little wet. The boys in Alicia's grade styled their hair the same way for dances. The girl had huge blue eyes and her skin was porcelain white. Her bright red lipstick provided the only dash of color she needed, because she was one of those girls who looked good pale. She reminded Alicia of an airbrushed photograph of a New York model.

"You're the OCD girls, right?" she asked when she saw them. "I'm Lucinda Hill, fashion editor at *Teen People.*" She smiled with her mouth closed and extended her right hand. The stack of thin gold bangles on her arm swayed and clanged together. Alicia studied them, trying to think of a store in Westchester that might sell them. She could tell Olivia was thinking the same thing, because she was staring too. Dean was the only one who realized Lucinda was waiting for them to shake her hand.

"I'm Dean, the Riveras' family driver," he said, flashing his new professionally bleached teeth. "This is Alicia Rivera and Olivia Ryan."

Both girls followed Dean's lead and shook the woman's hand.

"Super, well, let's go," Lucinda said in a pinched tone. "Follow me." She led them toward a maze of cubicles and offices.

Alicia and Olivia started giggling when they realized they had to trot if they were going to keep up with her manic pace.

"Everything okay back there?" Lucinda asked when she heard them laughing. But she didn't turn around, because she was typing an e-mail into her BlackBerry. "Ugh, my inbox is flooded. Not a good day for my assistant's grandmother to die, you know?"

A gaggle of trendy girls dressed in a variety of different-colored ballet flats, tank tops, and miniskirts raced by carrying brown paper bags overflowing with clothes.

"Aren't they chilly?" Olivia whispered to Alicia. "It's freezing outside."

"It's more important to *look* hot than to feel hot," Lucinda said to her BlackBerry.

Alicia studied the back of Lucinda's head and wondered how she could have possibly heard Olivia. It must be the short hair—there was nothing covering her ears.

Lucinda was a different kind of beautiful than Alicia was used to. Her nose was bold and her eyes were slightly bugged out. Yet it was these imperfections that Alicia found so interesting and attractive. She even admired Lucinda's outfit—gray wide-legged suit pants, a tight lime green

T-shirt with cap sleeves, and a brown leather cowboy belt with a big round buckle that said EARL on it. Not one bit of it was designer. Alicia tried to get a look at her boots, but she didn't want Lucinda to notice her giving the obvious once-over, so she decided to sneak a peek later.

"How 'bout a super-speedy tour before the interview?" Lucinda spoke even faster than she walked.

"Yay!" Olivia clapped and jumped up and down.

"Well, aren't you excitable," Lucinda said. "If my assistant were here, I'd send her out to get you some Ritalin ASAP."

"That's okay." Olivia rubbed her tummy. "I had a gi-normous pretzel before I got here."

"Ritalin isn't a food; it's the drug my parents used to force-feed me when I was seven." Lucinda contorted her face as if she had just been forced to swallow another pill. "It's for hyper kids."

"That's so coool," Olivia said, as if Lucinda had just invented the flatiron.

"I guess, if you like spending your eighth birthday in a psychiatrist's office," Lucinda said.

"What's that?" Alicia asked, pointing straight ahead. She had no idea how to break the tension and found herself missing Massie. She always knew how to fix an awkward situation.

"Uh, it's our hall," Lucinda said. She led them down a long corridor with hot pink carpeting and red glitter splattered on the walls. Every *Teen People* had been blown up, framed, and hung.

"This was our first issue ever." Lucida pointed to a picture of Jennifer Love Hewitt.

"Cute," Alicia said flatly. She wanted Lucinda to think she visited magazines every day. But there was so much to look at, Alicia had no idea where to turn next. Glossy framed pictures of Josh Hartnett, Usher, Mary-Kate and Ashley, and Hilary Duff fought for her attention.

"Here's our autograph box." With the antenna of her cell phone Lucinda tapped a Lucite box that had been mounted on the wall. "We have signatures from every celebrity we've ever worked with in here."

"My brother keeps his World Series tickets in a case exactly like that," Olivia said.

"Really?" Lucinda said to her BlackBerry.

"I bet you could sell that for quite a pretty penny," Dean said, pressing his bulbous nose against the box. The plastic fogged up from his breath.

"Ew, stand back, Dean." Alicia was looking at Lucinda when she spoke. "You'll melt it."

"Seriously," Lucinda said.

Alicia rolled her eyes and mouthed the word *sorry*. Gawd forbid the editor thought Alicia approved of her driver's gauche behavior.

"Okay, who's ready to see The Closet?" Lucinda led them down another sparkle-filled corridor.

Alicia and Olivia's hands shot straight up into the air.

Everyone at school had heard of the mythical fashion paradise called The Closet, but no one could prove its existence. Some said it was magazine folklore. Others claimed to have cousins or friends of cousins who had seen it. But either way, Alicia was about to discover the truth.

They stopped in front of a big door that looked more like a full-length mirror. *The Closet* was written across the top in red lipstick.

Alicia dug into her purse and quickly applied a fresh coat of gloss. She adjusted her side part and pinched her cheeks for some extra color. She could feel her palms sweat with anticipation.

"Excuse me." Lucinda reached into her shirt and pulled a long gold chain out of her cleavage. An old-fashioned key dangled off the end. She lowered her neck and stuck the key in the lock of The Closet's door. Her hand disappeared inside. "Voila," she said, flicking on the light switch.

"Ehmagawd," Alicia and Olivia declared at the same time. It was twenty times bigger than Alicia's walk-in and it smelled as sweet as the perfume counter at Bergdorf's.

The Closet was set up to look like a runway show. A long catwalk with flashing lights divided the room, and mannequins were positioned to look like they were walking it during a show.

"Look at those models." Olivia was pointing to the seven mannequins dressed in the latest trends: colorful ponchos, blazers dotted with sparkly brooches, Juicy sweats in brand-new colors, ballet flats with fuzzy pom-poms, and knee-high Uggs with miniskirts. It was like looking into a fashion crystal ball.

"Are any of those ladies single?" Dean asked with a playful smile.

No one bothered to answer.

Alicia was speechless. All she could do was slap Olivia on the shoulder and point to the different racks of clothes that lined both sides of the runway.

Olivia ran straight to the trendy cartoon T-shirts. "Look," she said, sliding the hangers across the bar. "They have Elmo, Barbie, and Strawberry Shortcake. These are ah-dora-ball!"

"Those are super-big for spring," Lucinda said. "So are these super-skinny straight-legged jeans." She pointed to a tower of denim in a rainbow of different washes. "Esti, our photo editor, tried a pair of these on without taking her shoes off and we almost had to amputate."

Stacks of leather belts, piles of bright bead necklaces, and boxes of handbags were everywhere. Wedge-heeled boots, strappy sandals, and metallic clogs in pink, silver, and gold hung in wire baskets suspended from the ceiling. It looked like it was raining shoes.

"What's that?" Alicia asked, pointing to an outfit that had been tacked to a giant *Teen People* magazine cover made entirely of cork.

"Oh, Avril's wearing that tomorrow for her cover shoot," Lucinda said. She popped a piece of Nicorette gum into her mouth and started chomping. "This reminds me, I still have to find a new makeup artist." She flipped open her cell phone and started dialing. "It's like everyone decided to have a death in the family the day before my shoot."

While Lucinda barked orders into her phone, Alicia and Olivia walked closer to the board.

"I can so see Avril in this," Alicia whispered, running her fingers across a boat-neck cashmere black-and-white-striped sweater. They had it paired with a pair of deep red, ultra-straight-legged cords that were covered in zippers. Vintage combat boots and a black velvet riding blazer were there to complete the look.

Olivia pulled what appeared to be a black mesh tube top off the corkboard. "Alicia, what do you think *this* is for?"

"That is *theee* latest accessory," Lucinda said quietly, covering the mouthpiece of her cell phone before deciding to just hang up on the person she was talking to. "And Avril's going to break it on *our* cover. It's going to be bigger than her tie obsession in 2002." She signaled for the girls to join her behind the pyramid of straw hats to avoid being overheard. "There are fifty-eight different ways to work it," she whispered. "But Avril's manager told me she wants to wear it *over* the cords, like a big wide butt belt. How brilliant is *that?* It's called a Dixon."

"I love it!" Alicia said, unable to contain her excitement.

"Want one?" Lucinda asked, handing them each a circle of black mesh fabric. "Be the first ones in Winnchester to wear them."

Alicia was so grateful she didn't bother correcting Lucinda.

"What's Winnchester?" Olivia giggled. "We live in West—"

Alicia elbowed her friend in the ribs. "Thanks so much, we love these," she said.

"Hey, where's *my* Dixon?" Dean asked, pretending to look offended. "Can't forty-year-old men use them too? I could use it to drain my pasta."

"Have this instead." Lucinda handed Dean a black wallet. It had a thick silver chain hanging off it with a clasp on the end so it could be attached to his belt loop. "I've never seen a girl look cute wearing one of these yet, and it's been here since the late nineties."

"Awesome! Thanks!" Dean said, mocking Alicia and Olivia's enthusiasm.

All three girls responded with eye rolls.

"Let's move on." Lucinda turned off the lights in The Closet. She led them back down the hall. "I have a five o'clock with Ashlee Simpson's camp and her agent hates it when I'm late."

"Is Ashlee going to be here?" Olivia asked.

"Unfortunately." Lucinda groaned. "Hey, Olivia, is that poncho real rabbit?" She reached over and rubbed a tuft of white fur between her thumb and index finger. "*J'adore* rabbit."

"N— Yeah, it's real." Olivia winked at Alicia. "Don't tell Peter."

Alicia wanted to scream, "It's PETA! People for the Ethical Treatment of Animals!!! Not PETER." But she didn't. Instead she pretended she hadn't heard Olivia, a trick she learned from Massie.

"And your boots are so retro," Lucinda said to Alicia. "I haven't seen square toed since my babysitter rented *Young Frankenstein* for me, like, ten years ago."

Alicia felt the blood rush to her face. She wanted to sue

Saks for selling her a pair of old-fashioned Frankenstein boots.

"Oh, these are from Spain," Alicia lied. "They are very IN there. My mom just brought them back for me. They aren't even out in America yet."

"Kewel," Lucinda said. She actually sounded excited. "You girls are pretty cool. I swear, you're never going to believe this, but when I was in the seventh grade, I was a total beast. And I had *no* boobs."

Alicia folded her arms across her chest when she noticed Lucinda checking her out.

"How much did you pay for those?" Lucinda asked. "I bet they were at least five grand a pop."

"I didn't *pay* for these; I would never—"

"Hey, Barnaby, come look at this girl's boob job; it's perfect," Lucinda said to a guy who was walking toward them in the hall. He was wearing tight white pants, moccasins, and an off-the-shoulder cable-knit sweater.

"This is Barnaby, our staff photographer. Paolo, our other photog, is on assignment in Bora Bora."

"Hay-ayyy." Barnaby waved. "Those are fierce," he said to Alicia's boobs.

She smiled politely and put her Prada bag in front of her chest.

"I paid for my nose," Olivia offered.

Normally Alicia would have been mortified, but she was grateful for the distraction.

"O-M-G, so did I." Lucinda lifted her palm in the air and high-fived Olivia.

After their laughter died down, Lucinda's expression suddenly became serious.

"Have you two ever modeled before?"

"Sure," Alicia lied.

"Genius!" Lucinda clapped. "Not that it matters, because you're both gor-jusss." Without warning she stopped walking and leaned against the wall. Her head rested on a picture of Britney Spears's navel. Her eyes shifted back and forth and she tapped her fingernail against her bottom teeth.

"Here's the deal. We're looking for pretty-in-a-real-sort-of-way girls to model in our Christmas holiday issue. I envision a scene of girls dressed in this year's hottest holiday fashions, holding tons of bags and waiting on line to get their photos taken with a mall Santa. How fun is that?"

"So fun," Alicia said.

Dean smiled politely.

"Would you girls be interested?"

"Ehmagawd. Given." This time Alicia couldn't mask her excitement.

Barnaby put his hands on his hips and sighed. "Luce, Nina will so have you fired if you put them in the same issue twice."

"Ugh! I hate you, Barn," Lucinda pouted. "Not only is your waist smaller than mine, but you're always right."

"We don't have to do the interview thing," Alicia said, throwing her bag over her shoulder. "We totally heart modeling." She drew an air heart with her two index fingers and Lucinda smiled.

"Oh, good." Lucinda threw her hands up. "And I *heart* you guys." She drew an air heart of her own.

"I'll have to check with their mothers, but I'm sure it won't be a problem," Dean said.

The girls rolled their eyes once again.

Lucinda walked at high speed as she led them back to the elevators. "I need six models total, so e-mail pictures of your pretty-in-a-real-sort-of-way friends, 'kay?"

"Sure," Alicia said. But she'd sooner donate her new Prada raffia handbag to the annual OCD holiday gift drive than include Massie, Kristen, and Dylan in her modeling debut. This was going to be all about her. "I'll see what I can do."

The elevator door opened and Alicia and Olivia were suddenly face-to-face with Ashlee Simpson and her people.

"Ash," Lucinda said, double-kissing her. "Grrreat to see you."

"Heyyyyy, honey," Ashlee said, double-kissing back. "This is my mom-slash-manager, Linda; my agent, Seth; my makeup artist, Kristy; my stylist, Naomi; my trainer, Marcus; and my label rep, Vince."

"Given," Lucinda said with a huge smile.

"No way, I say given too," Alicia said.

"Cute," Lucinda said, holding the elevator door open for Alicia, Olivia, and Dean. "Thanks for coming. I'll have my assistant, Franka, call you if she ever gets back from her stupid funeral."

"Thanks for the tour, babe," Alicia said, trying to sound cool in front of Ashlee. The girls hugged Lucinda goodbye and promised to have their parents call ASAP so they could get started on the arrangements.

Alicia took one last look at Ashlee and her outfit before she stepped onto the elevator. "Hate the black hair, love the black leather mini, double-love the denim blazer, detest the flower Doc Martens, adore the green eye shadow," she said once the doors closed.

"Agreed," Olivia said.

It was dark outside when they stepped out of the revolving door. The city streets were even busier than they had been earlier. Hordes of people rushed by carrying briefcases and heavy shopping bags from Bergdorf's, Bloomingdale's, and Saks. Everyone they passed had lowered their necks into their coat collars to shield themselves from the howling wind. But Alicia and Olivia were oblivious to the cold.

"This is the best day ever," Olivia said. "Who should we tell first?"

"Where to begin, dahhh-ling?" Alicia did her best diva impersonation. "Where to begin?" She brought two fingers to her lips like she was taking a drag off a cigarette and exhaled. Her warm breath mixed with the freezing air looked like a puff cloud of smoke. They burst out laughing and walked the rest of the way to the limo with their arms linked through Dean's, pretending to smoke.

"Who wants Chinese?" Dean asked as he turned out of the underground parking lot onto 50th Street.

"Meee," shouted the girls. Now that they were no longer

in the presence of magazine greatness, Alicia felt free to act as excited as she felt.

"I know a great place in Times Square called Ruby Foo's." And off they went.

Their black lacquer table was covered in plates of glistening food: sweet-and-sour chicken, shrimp dumplings, moo shu pork, short ribs, wontons, and seven different dipping sauces. But the girls barely ate a thing. They were too busy trying to guess the fifty-eight different ways to wear their Dixons. They had come up with thirty-two by the time the check had arrived.

"How about we do a little exploring?" Dean reached across the hostess stand and grabbed a handful of toothpicks on their way out the door.

"What about the concert?" Alicia asked. She broke into an impression of Beyoncé's famous booty shake, right in the middle of Broadway. Olivia laughed so hard she burped.

"Why don't we walk?" Dean stuck a toothpick between his two front teeth and Alicia looked away in disgust. "It's only twenty short blocks. We can explore."

Alicia and Olivia were already walking toward a guy wrapped in a wool blanket selling bootleg DVDs.

"I guess that means you're up for it?" Dean said, following the girls to the wooden card table.

"Given," Alicia said as they made their way downtown.

"Oh. My. God." Olivia pointed to a man on the corner of 44th Street. He was standing behind a fold-out table just like the DVD guy's, only his was covered in scarves. "Look at all of those Louis Vuittons!"

Stacks of white silk scarves dotted with green, red, purple, orange, blue, and black *LV*s were on display. A sign tacked to the edge of the table said LOUIS VUITON SCARVES $15.00.

"Fifteen dollars?" Olivia screeched. "Those are like three hundred bucks at home."

"Are you serious?" Alicia said. She raised the corner of her upper lip to show her utter repulsion. "Oliv-i-ahhh, those are fake."

Alicia reached into her purse and pulled out a sheet of *Lucky* stickers. She peeled off a *no* and stuck it on one of the scarves.

Olivia immediately tore off the sticker. "Why would you *say* that?"

"Look." Alicia flicked the cardboard sign. "For starters, *this* Louis Vuitton spells his last name with one *t*, not two." Alicia paused so Olivia could absorb the information. "And they're only fifteen dollars."

"So, they *look* real," Olivia said.

"But they're NOT!"

Alicia glanced at Dean for backup, but he shrugged and shook his head. He'd learned the hard way to stay out of Alicia's shopping disputes.

"No one will ever know," Olivia whispered. "I could give them away as holiday gifts. My shopping would be done before Thanksgiving."

"I'll give you a special deal," said the guy behind the

table. "Just for you, pretty lady." He rubbed his black beard and squinted. He looked like he was giving this "special deal" some serious thought. "Ten for one hundred dollars."

"Don't do it," Alicia said from the side of her mouth. "It's a sin to give knockoffs at such a holy time of year."

"Puh-lease," Olivia said. "You're just jealous 'cause you didn't think of it first." She handed five twenties to the guy in exchange for a handful of fake scarves.

"Whatevs," Alicia said, tightening her grip around her Prada handbag. "Maybe we'll go plastic Christmas tree shopping next."

"Very funny."

"I'm going to start calling you Faux-livia from now on because everything you have is fake."

"Oh, really, Alicia RIVERS," Olivia fired back.

Alicia felt her stomach drop. "Thanks a lot. I was finally starting to forget about Massie."

"Sorry," Olivia said, looking down at the sidewalk. "I was just kidding."

"It's okay. I can't wait to tell her we're going to be models. She'll regret every mean thing she's ever said to me."

"How are you going to tell her? I thought you weren't talking."

"Oh, I'll find a way," Alicia said, the corners of her lips curling up into a devious smile. "I always do."

"I read that in California you have to be eighteen to go to a tanning salon," Kristen said, braiding a small clump of light blond hair by her face. "You have to show ID and everything."

"That's only if you want to fake 'n' bake." Massie took every opportunity she could to correct her know-it-all friend. "Which *no* one does anymore." She pulled off her gray tights and stuffed them in her boots. "Spray tans are much more *aujourd'hui.* Trust me, Kristen, you're gonna love it."

"What does *oh jor dwi* mean?" Dylan asked while pushing her red hair into a paper shower cap.

"Five-letter word for 'in this day,'" Kristen said.

"Today," Massie said.

Dylan stomped her foot. "You never let *me* guess."

"We don't have time," Massie told her. "We only have this booth until six-thirty PM."

"Are you sure this spray tanning isn't poisonous?" Kristen pushed the instructional video back in the VCR so she could watch it again.

"Stop." Massie hit eject and grabbed the tape. "This is so easy. The only thing you have to worry about is the Lohan tan."

"What?" Kristen shrieked. "I'm not doing this." She

grabbed her Miss Sixty jeans off the changing room floor and started getting dressed.

"Relax." Dylan laughed and pulled the jeans off Kristen's leg. "You won't get it unless you're an obsessive spray tanner like Lindsay Lohan. She is so orange, I swear she must have self-tanner coming out of her shower nozzle."

"Just make sure you rub everything in and you'll be fine," Massie said. Kristen reached for the video, but Massie pulled her arm back before she could get it in the VCR again. "It couldn't be easier. Watch me."

Kristen, Dylan, and Massie squeezed into one of the narrow silver cylinders and forced the accordion-shaped door shut. The space outside the actual spray area was no bigger than a phone booth, but Massie didn't mind the cramped quarters if it would get Kristen to put a little color on her pale body. The holiday parties were quickly approaching and it was important to Massie that they look better than anyone else in the room.

Massie dropped her towel and hit the big green On button outside the glass door. She waved goodbye to her friends and stepped inside. One second later she was blasted by a smelly cold brown mist. When the spray stopped, she turned around and let the second batch coat her back.

"That's all there is to it," she said, reaching for her towel so she could rub the muddy solution into her legs. She didn't even stop to answer her phone.

"Can you grab that?" Massie asked Dylan. "My hands are sticky."

Dylan pulled Massie's phone out of her black leather Coach bag and checked the caller ID.

"It's Alicia," she said. "Should I hit ignore?"

"No, I bet she's having a guilt moment at *Teen People* and wants to beg for my forgiveness." Massie grabbed the Motorola out of Dylan's hand and flipped it open. One of the purple rhinestones Massie had glued to her phone fell off and bounced along the tin floor of the booth. She was instantly reminded of the way her charms had scattered across the classroom in her daydream. Massie squeezed her eyes shut to squash the memory. Her phone continued to ring.

"You think Alicia knows my mom's been trying to put a stop to the uniform thing?" Dylan asked.

"There's only one way to find out," Massie said. "Lean in." Once their three heads were pressed together, Massie hit talk.

"Hullo," she said.

"Hey, it's Alicia. I'm in New York City. . . ."

Massie rolled her eyes.

"I know you're mad at me, but I just wanted to let you know I'm not having the sleepover party anymore."

"And you want to get invited back to mine, right? Well, it's too late. It starts in two hours—you'll never make it back from '*New York City.*'" Massie did her best to imitate Alicia's obnoxious tone.

Dylan put her hand over her mouth to keep from laughing out loud.

"Relax, Massie," Alicia snapped. "I don't want to go to

your lame sleepover. If I wanted to spend my night doing arts and crafts, I'd babysit a six-year-old. Besides, Olivia and I are going to the Beyoncé concert tonight."

"No fair," Kristen mouthed.

"Alicia, do I sell fertilizer?" Massie asked.

"No, why?" Alicia fell for Massie's setup.

"Then why do you think I care?"

Dylan and Kristen burst out laughing. Massie heard Alicia let out a frustrated sigh.

"I'm calling because I want my Calvin Klein winter white blazer back," Alicia said.

"Why? Are you packing up? Is the Rivers family finally moving back to Brooklyn?"

Kristen and Dylan laughed even harder this time and Massie pushed them away from the phone.

Alicia ignored the dig. "I was asked to model for *Teen People*'s holiday issue and I may want to wear it."

Massie suddenly felt like she was falling down a well. There was a loud ringing in her ears and she felt dizzy. Was this really happening? Alicia cheated and now she was being *rewarded* for it? Would Kristen and Dylan like Alicia more now that she was a model? Would the rest of the school?

Massie knew her expression must have changed to one of sheer horror, because Kristen and Dylan looked at her and mouthed, "What?" over and over again.

"Nothing," Massie mouthed back.

"Look, I gotta go, the concert is about to start," Alicia

shouted over the screaming fans in the background. "Bring the blazer to school on Monday, 'kay?"

"Sorry, I can't hear you," Massie said. "What? What?" Then she hung up her phone. Her entire nervous system was in a state of shock.

"Share, please," Dylan pleaded as she opened the door to the booth. "What did she say?"

"Oh, nothing, just that she got a job MODELING FOR *TEEN PEOPLE!*"

"Huh?" Kristen screeched. "How?"

"I have no idea." Massie was so furious, she put her green dress on inside out.

"Maybe she's just a hand model or something," Dylan offered.

"That should have been *us,*" Massie said. "If we'd won the contest, *we* would have been at *Teen People* this afternoon and *we* would have been asked to model. Not *her.*"

"It's not fair." Dylan pressed the on button outside the tanning chamber and stepped inside. She closed her eyes and waited for the spray.

Massie was so blind with rage, she didn't notice that Kristen was fully dressed. Suddenly her problems were much bigger than showing up at a holiday party with a pale friend. Her entire reputation was in jeopardy. What would people say when they found out Alicia was asked to model and she wasn't?

Massie was silent for the next fifteen minutes. Once they were in the Blocks' Range Rover, she finally said, "The time is now."

"Huh?" Dylan said, grabbing a bowl of low-sodium cashews out of the minibar.

"Payback."

"You mean we can finally stop being snakes that lie in the weeds?" Dylan said, recalling Massie's strategy.

"Yup, let's pounce."

"Thank God." Kristen sat up in her seat. "Can I get a seven-letter word for *vengeance?*" She threw her palm in the air and the others high-fived it.

"What's the plan?" Dylan asked.

"I'll tell you at the sleepover tonight," Massie said. She needed time to think.

Isaac stopped the Range Rover in front of the luxurious Montador building.

"This is me." Kristen opened the car door and waved to her doorman. "I'll see you after dinner." The overhead light in the car popped on. "Massie, what's wrong with your face?"

Massie reached in her bag and pulled out her Chanel compact.

"Ehmagawd," she screamed. "Alicia got me so pissed, I never finished rubbing in my tan."

Dylan and Kristen immediately started laughing.

"It's not funny," Massie said, wiping her face. She pulled her dress away from her body and looked down at her stomach. "I'm all stripy. I look like a candy cane!"

"'Tis the season," Kristen said.

"That's even worse than the Lohan," Dylan said.

"Isaac, we have to stop at Dr. Juice," Massie barked

toward the front seat. "I need a large Calm immediately. Then drop me off at home so I can exfoliate."

"What about me?" Dylan asked.

"Isaac will take you last," Massie said, examining her uneven arms. "This is an emergency."

Kristen slammed the door and the car sped off down the street.

After the stop at Dr. Juice, Isaac pulled into the circular driveway in front of the Block estate and for the first time ever Massie wished she lived on a smaller piece of property. Suddenly the distance between the Range Rover and her shower seemed endless.

"See ya later," Massie said to Dylan as she jumped out of the SUV with her bag in one hand and her banana, strawberry, and kava kava juice in the other.

She ran across the gravel of their circular driveway through the grass, and up the stone steps that led to the tall oak doors. Too frantic to search for her keys, Massie dropped her bag so she could pound the iron knocker and ring the bell with her elbow at the same time.

"What is it?" she could hear Kendra, her mother, shouting as she raced down the steps.

Inez beat her to it and opened the door.

"Look at me," Massie wailed when she saw them.

"Your dress is on inside out," Kendra said.

"No, my skin. My skin!" Massie said. "I'm uneven."

Inez waved her hands in the air. "I have to check on dinner," she said. This was a problem for Kendra, not her.

Massie felt her mother's arm around her shoulders. She was gently being led into the sitting room, just off the front hallway. "Honey," Kendra said softly when they were alone, "do you mind keeping it down? The women from my self-help book club are meeting in the upstairs parlor." Kendra pinched the pink diamond on her necklace and slid it back and forth along her gold chain. "We're reading *Power of Now* and trying to stay in a state of inner peace for just ten more minutes. Can we talk about it over supper?"

Massie opened her mouth to explain that there was nothing to talk about when a voice from upstairs shouted, "Kendra, honey, is everything okay?"

"Yes, Sudie, everything's fine," Kendra yelled softly.

"Well, then come back up—Mimi has something she'd like to share."

"Coming." Kendra placed her manicured hand on the top of Massie's head. "Go use my new loofah; it's in the closet beside the sauna. If that doesn't help, I'll take you to my aesthetician in the morning."

"Where's Dad?" Massie asked.

"Late meeting, he'll be home after dinner."

"Fine," Massie said as she ran up the stairs ahead of her mother.

Once Massie was in her bathroom, she tore the plastic wrapper off her mother's loofah and stepped into the steaming hot shower. She rubbed a bar of L'Occitaine shea butter soap all over her body and scrubbed.

Once Massie dried off, she combed her shoulder-length

hair and slipped on her Michael Stars hot pink boy shorts and matching tank top. She sat down on her white duvet and pulled out her PalmPilot. It was time to record the day's events.

CURRENT STATE OF THE UNION	
IN	**OUT**
Dr. Juice	Starbucks
Loofahs	Spray tans
Rivers	Riveras
Q: Seven-letter word for vengeance	Q: Eleven-letter word for mercy
A: Revenge	A: Forgiveness

When Massie finished typing, she looked down at her raw, red hands. Alicia had gotten the best of her this time. But the battle had just begun. And Massie was ready to fight.

After almost three long months of living in the guesthouse on the Blocks' estate, Claire Lyons had finally started to feel at home. It was a smaller, more rustic version of the grand stone mansion Massie and her family lived in. And Kendra had used the cottage to store antiques and paintings that weren't impressive enough to display in the main house. But Claire didn't think there was anything second rate about it. In fact, now she liked her new home even more than her old one in Orlando. Suddenly they were reclining in cushy leather chairs—no more stiff wicker. They could sip root beer floats from heavy crystal fountain glasses instead of mismatched plastic ones. And family game night no longer felt like a tired tradition. It was an event.

"Todd, it's your turn to pick," Judi Lyons said to her son as she burst through the swinging kitchen door and joined her family in the living room.

Claire heard the soothing hum of the dishwasher in the background and knew that meant her mother was finally ready to play.

Todd put his root beer float down on the glass card table and wiped his sticky hands on his Hulk Hogan pajama bottoms.

"Gross," Claire said.

"Oh, please, I just saw you wipe the sugar from your sours on the chair," Todd said. "Why don't you take them out of your back pocket and share them with the rest of us?"

"I have no idea what you're talking about," Claire said, feeling the bag of candy under her butt as she shifted in her seat.

"I know why you're hoarding them," Todd said.

Claire felt her face turn red. She prayed that for once in his life, her brother would be cool and keep his mouth shut.

"Because Cam Fisher gave them to you." Todd made kissing sounds and started rolling around on the couch. "Oh, Cam, I love you sooo much. I will protect your sours with my life. . . ."

Claire lifted her leg, ready to kick Todd off the couch, but quickly changed her mind. Instead she crossed it over her knee and tugged her shoelace. She was defenseless, and had been for the last week, ever since Cam stopped Todd at Briarwood Academy's bike rack and asked if he was Claire's brother. When Todd said yes, Cam made him his trusted delivery boy, the guy responsible for bringing mix CDs and candies home for Claire. And the last thing Claire wanted to do was kick the messenger in case he walked off the job. All she could do was roll her eyes and pray for the moment to pass.

"So when are we going to meet this Cam?" Jay asked, removing his wire glasses and sticking them in the front pocket of his blue Brooks Brothers shirt.

"I dunno, whenever," Claire said. "It's not like we hang out every day after school or anything. We just e-mail each other and stuff. We're just friends."

Claire wished there was more to it than that, because Cam was the sweetest, most thoughtful boy she had ever met. But they never actually hung out alone and sometimes Claire wondered if maybe there was some other girl he liked better.

Claire slapped the scoop of ice cream in her float with the back of her spoon. "So what game are we playing?"

"Hey, Dad, what do you feel like playing?" Todd said as he walked over to the oak armoire where they kept the board games.

"Anything—I'm feeling lucky," Jay said, rubbing his chubby hands together.

"Cranium?" Todd held the purple box over his head.

"No, you always pick that," Claire said, brushing the blonde bangs out of her eyes. "Let's play Trivial Pursuit."

"Claire, I'm ten," he said. "The only trivia I know is who got kicked off last night's *Survivor.*"

Claire watched her parents crack up.

"Cranium it is," Jay said, stuffing a handful of popcorn into his mouth. A clear brown kernel shell stuck to his cheek and Claire watched it bob up and down while he chewed. It finally fell off and landed on his sweatshirt.

In Orlando, Jay and Judi were thought of as attractive. They both had bright blue eyes, big warm smiles, and deep tans. But ever since they moved to Westchester, Claire had become aware of their imperfections. She noticed that her mother and father were relatively short and that they dressed too casually and were both about ten pounds over-weight. When Claire found out Massie's parents had personal trainers and nutritionists, she was ashamed hers still got excited every time Ben & Jerry's came out with a new ice cream flavor. But in time she learned to appreciate their shameless snacking habits, because they were the only people in Westchester who didn't give her dirty looks when she ate a bit of junk food.

"Who wants more ice cream?" Todd said, jumping to his feet.

They had been playing for two hours and Claire and Judi were one right answer away from winning.

"You always do that when you're about to lose," Claire said to her brother.

"Do not."

"Do."

"Fine," Todd said. "Go." He turned the hourglass over as quickly as he could, clearly hoping to catch them off guard.

But Claire refused to let him intimidate her. "Okay, Mom." The whole game was riding on Judi's ability to sketch a picture with her eyes closed. She picked up her tiny pencil and started drawing.

"Belly button," Claire shouted.

Judi shook her head.

"Stomach woman!"

"No," Judi said. She shut her eyes tighter and drew faster.

"Belly mover. Belly button shaker. Stomach dancer. BELLY DANCER!"

"Yes!" Judi screamed. She pulled Claire into a hug.

Claire smiled brightly. Beating Todd at Cranium was the

only way to put him in his place these days. "Losers clean up," she announced. She couldn't wait to escape the mess of candy wrappers and empty froth-stained root beer glasses that Todd and her father were obligated to clean. All she wanted to do was take off her orange Old Navy cargo pants, slip into her flannel Power Puff Girls pj's, and return Cam's e-mail.

Suddenly Claire heard the front door open.

"Who's here?" she asked her mother.

"No idea," Judi said with a trace of fear in her eyes. "Jay? You expecting anyone?"

"What, dear?" he called from the kitchen.

Claire's stomach clenched with nervousness and excitement when the mystery guest walked into the living room. "H-hey, what's up? What are you doing here?" she asked.

Judi brought her hand to her heart and slowly shook her head. "Massie, you scared us."

"Sorry." Massie pulled her black cable-knit poncho over her head and draped it over the back of the corduroy couch. She was wearing a red velour sweat suit and sheepskin slippers. "Sometimes I forget I have to knock. I guess I'm still used to walking into this house whenever I feel like it."

"That's totally understandable," Judi said with a nervous chuckle. "Did you need something?"

Before Massie could answer, Todd barged through the kitchen door wearing an apron and yellow rubber gloves. "Massie, want a root beer float? I can make you one."

"No thanks, I ate already," Massie said. "But thanks for offering."

Claire knew Massie was just being nice to Todd because her mother was in the room. Normally Massie would have said something about too many fat grams or not wanting his booger-stained hands touching her food.

"I just got *The Sims 2*. Wanna start a family together?" Todd asked, his brown eyes flickering with hope.

Massie looked at Claire and tilted her head toward the staircase. "Normally I'd be all over that, but I have to talk to your sister." She turned away from Todd and looked straight into Claire's eyes. "Now," she mouthed.

"'Kay." Claire couldn't help feeling like she was about to get in trouble for something and wondered if anyone could hear her heart pounding. "Let's go to my room," she said, avoiding her mother's suspicious glare.

"Perf," Massie said as she walked toward the staircase.

Claire followed Massie up the stairs. While they were walking, Claire reached into the back pocket of her orange pants and pulled a sour out of the plastic bag as quietly as she could. She popped it in her mouth while Massie's back was to her.

"Why do you eat those?" Massie asked, without turning around. She sounded disgusted. "They're all sugar."

"I know." Claire was ashamed and tried to swallow the red worm as quickly as she could. "I'm over them. That was my last one."

When they entered Claire's bedroom, Massie closed the door.

Claire was so uncomfortable she walked over to her

window and looked outside, hoping the spacious lawn below might make her feel less trapped.

"What's going on down there?" Claire pointed to the woodpile outside the old horse barn that hadn't been there in the morning.

"My parents are turning the barn into a state-of-the-art home gym," Massie said, sounding utterly unimpressed.

"Phew," Claire said with a smile. "I thought another family was moving in."

"No, you guys are more than enough," Massie said. "By the way, when are you leaving? I thought this situation was quote 'temporary,' end quote."

Claire looked at her pink-and-white-striped socks, suddenly aware of how ridiculous they looked with her orange pants.

"It *is* temporary," Claire explained. "My parents look at houses every day." She actually had no idea how much longer they'd be staying and had stopped asking her parents when she and Massie had started getting along, barely a month ago.

"Relax, Kuh-laire. I was joking. I actually don't mind having you here anymore."

"Oh," Claire said, lifting her eyes to meet Massie's. "Sorry."

"It's okay." Massie smiled.

Claire was desperate to ask Massie why she was there but thought it might be better to act as though the surprise visit was normal. Maybe that way it would happen more often.

"What's *this?*"

Claire hoped Massie was talking about the e-mail on her computer screen from Cam. She had been dying to share the details of her secret crush with Massie but could never catch her alone. Maybe tonight . . .

But Massie was pointing to the digital pictures on her wall. Every shot was of Claire standing in front of her closet wearing a different outfit.

Claire felt her face getting hot. "Oh, that's nothing."

"It looks like you're stalking yourself," Massie said.

Claire couldn't help laughing.

"What is it? Come on, I won't tell anyone."

"Yeah, right," Claire said, enjoying the moment. Finally Massie Block wanted to know something about her.

"I promise." Massie held out her pinky. Claire held out hers. They looked each other in the eye and then locked fingers.

"Fine," Claire said, letting go. She paused and took a deep breath. "I hang those pictures up to keep track of my outfits. You know, so I don't wear the same thing twice."

Massie widened her amber eyes. Claire instantly regretted confessing.

"That's brilliant," Massie said.

"Seriously?"

"Yeah. Mind if I copy you?"

"Not at all," Claire replied, sweeping her bangs to the side of her forehead. She couldn't believe how well things were going and decided *this* was the perfect time to show Massie the note Cam sent her the night of the OCD Fashion Week Uniform Contest.

Claire reached for the mesh pocket inside her backpack and pinched the worn paper between her fingers.

"Kuh-laire, we have to talk," Massie said.

Claire released the paper and watched it fall to the bottom of her bag.

"It's go time." Massie pushed on the bedroom door to make sure it was completely shut.

"Huh?"

Massie went into a detailed description of Alicia's sleepover party, the phone call she got while she was spray tanning, the candy cane tan that she blamed on that phone call, and the *Teen People* modeling job.

"What are you going to do?" Claire felt just as cheated by Alicia as Massie did but wasn't quite as bloodthirsty. Maybe because she knew how awful Massie made *her* life when she moved to Westchester and refused to wish that on anyone, even Alicia.

"Let's destroy her," Massie said, looking deep into Claire's eyes.

Claire felt paralyzed, like the breath just got sucked out of her body.

Massie dived stomach first onto the middle of Claire's unmade bed. The mattress squeaked under her weight. "Here's the plan."

Claire stayed on the very edge with her feet planted firmly on the ground while Massie explained.

"So are you in?" Massie asked when she had finished.

Claire thought about it.

"Well?" Massie pressed.

Claire nodded, deciding a little guilt was better than making Massie angry.

"Good."

Massie lifted the olive green rotary phone off the dark wood night table and handed it to Claire. "This is so heavy, I don't know how Grammy used to lift it."

"I know, my arm gets stiff after one phone call," Claire said, trying to lighten the mood.

"You *have* to get a cell phone."

"Four more years," Claire said, remembering her parents' rule.

"Brutal," Massie responded as she flipped open her cell phone, pulled up a number, and hit Send. She hit Speaker Phone before anyone answered.

"Can you hear it ringing?" Massie whispered.

Claire nodded.

Massie covered the mouthpiece. "We'll probably have to leave a message because it's late—"

"Lucinda Hill's office," a voice answered.

Claire gasped and Massie raised a finger to her lips.

"Sorry," Claire mouthed. She dug into her back pocket and popped a yellow sour in her mouth.

"Uh, yeah, uh, is Lucinda Hill there, please?"

"Who's speaking?"

Massie stood up and started pacing. "It's Ma— It's Alicia Rivera and Olivia Ryan."

"Hold."

"Hey, gorgeous, make my day and tell me you got permission to do the holiday shoot," a different voice then said. Claire assumed it was Lucinda.

"Mmmm, not yet," Massie replied.

Claire sat perfectly still on the edge of the bed, trying not to make a sound. She didn't want to miss a single word.

"That's not why I'm calling." Massie faced the window, reminding Claire of a high-powered executive on an important business call.

"What, then?" Lucinda sounded annoyed.

"I have a confession to make and I can't handle the guilt anymore."

"Yup," Lucida said, hurrying her along.

"Olivia and I cheated during the OCD Fashion Week Uniform Contest. We didn't really win. Massie Block and Claire Lyons did. We switched the ballot boxes because we're such losers and we've never won anything before and we were desperate."

Claire's mouth hung wide open. "Nice," she mouthed enthusiastically, giving Massie a thumbs-up.

Massie returned the gesture and Claire felt a surge of warmth rush through her entire body. They were a team.

The two girls looked at each other, their eyes wide open, wondering what Lucinda would say next. Would she sue Alicia and Olivia for fraud? Would she call all the newspapers and expose their lies? Would she blacklist Alicia from every store in Manhattan?

"And . . ." Lucinda said.

"And what?" Massie said. "How are you going to punish us?"

"I'm not a priest," she said. "I don't care if you cheated."

Claire raised her eyebrows in shock.

Massie opened her mouth to speak, but Lucinda cut her off.

"All I care about is that you stay gorgeous. Gain a pound between now and the shoot and I'll take a Town Car straight to Winnchester and kick your butt."

"Uh, okay," Massie said.

"Now what?" Claire mouthed.

Massie shrugged and Claire could hear Lucinda's fingers clacking away on a keyboard in the background.

When the typing stopped, Lucinda said, "Alicia, you still there?"

"Uh, yeah, bad connection, sorry," Massie said.

"When can you get me those pictures of your friends?"

"Huh?"

Lucinda sighed. "I need pictures of your pretty-in-a-real-sort-of-way friends because we're still looking for four more models."

Massie mouthed, "Yes!" and Claire got so excited, she jumped up on her bed. But the phone cord was so short, she had to sit back down to continue listening.

"Oh, right," Massie said. "Sorry, I forgot. I'm a total airhead."

Claire covered her mouth to conceal her laughter.

"What's your e-mail address? I'll have my friend Massie send those to you right now. She's gorgeous; you'll love her."

As soon as Massie hung up the phone, she hopped on

Claire's bed and started jumping. "We are *totally* going to crash Alicia's modeling party."

Claire put the green phone on the floor and started jumping too. They bounced and giggled and held on to each other to keep from falling.

"I have to stop," Massie panted. She fell onto the bed, rolled off, and stood up. Her hair was a tangled mess and her cheeks were flushed. "Can I take one of these?" Massie asked. She was pointing to the row of pictures on the wall.

Claire's knees buckled. She stopped jumping and folded her arms across her chest. "You promised you wouldn't tell anyone."

"I won't. I just want to scan a picture of you so I can send it to Lucinda," Massie said.

"Oh," Claire said. "Cool." She jumped off the bed and landed on the floor with a thud. "Let me get you a better one."

Claire pulled a shoe box out of her closet, tore off the lid, and quickly flipped through a stack of pictures. She couldn't believe Massie thought she was pretty enough to model. Her hands shook with excitement.

"Here, send this one." Claire held out a shot of herself sitting on the hood of a red convertible. She was hugging her knees to her chest and smiling brightly. Her legs were golden brown and her blond overgrown bangs were falling in her eyes. It was her favorite picture.

"Thanks," Massie said. "I have some good ones of me, Kristen, and Dylan back in my room. I'll go send them now."

"Good luck," Claire said.

"Bye!" Massie called, slamming the door behind her.

The minute Claire was alone, she went straight for her computer and read Cam's latest e-mail one more time . . .

C,

U COMING TO MY SOCCER GAME 2MORROW? IF U DO, LOOK UNDER SEAT #27. THERE WILL B A SWEET SURPRISE WAITING THERE 4 U. OH, THANKS FOR SENDING THAT PICTURE OF YOUR TOE. . . . AND NO, I DON'T THINK IT LOOKS LIKE A FAT MAN'S THUMB.

—C

Claire wasted no time writing back.

C,

I'LL BE IN SEAT #27. BTW—THNX FOR THE SOURS. I 8 THEM ALL. ☺

—C

Claire was bursting to tell Cam she and Massie were going to be models but held off. She wasn't quite ready to stop accepting his sugary candy.

The glare from the stadium lights blinded Alicia and kept her from seeing Briarwood score the winning goal. But she heard all about it from the announcer.

"The Tomahawks kick butt once again thanks to their star forward, Derrick Harrington," a man's voice bellowed through the speaker towers. Everyone jumped to their feet and waved their orange-and-blue flags. Alicia and Faux-livia waved their pink knit mittens.

"Whoo-hoo!" Derrick shouted. His teammates lifted him up and carried him toward the bleachers. They rubbed his shaggy blond hair and sprayed him with Evian water. When they put him on the ground, Derrick turned his back to the crowd and pulled off his shirt. They cheered and hollered while he stuck out his tongue like a rock star.

"That makes standing out here in the freezing cold almost worth it," Alicia said, putting her mitten back on her hand.

"I don't care how immature everyone says he is—*I* think he's cute," Faux-livia said.

"He *could* be if he stopped wearing shorts all the time." Alicia sat down on the cold metal bleachers. "I've never seen him in long pants. Not even at dances. His knees are *purple* from the cold."

Faux-livia sat down and stuffed her hands in the pockets of her red puffy coat.

"He reminds me of my old yellow Lab, Smash," Faux-livia said. "I think it's the brown eyes and the blond hair. . . ."

"Probably." Alicia never asked Olivia to clarify. It usually just confused her more. Besides, Derrick was walking up the cement steps and she didn't want to miss her chance to greet the star player.

Alicia crouched down, pretending to pick something off the ground, and swiped a quick coat of light pink gloss across her lips. "Nice game!" she called out when she resurfaced.

"Yeah, you were so *on* today, Derrington," Faux-livia shouted.

Alicia quickly elbowed her in the ribs.

"Ow," Faux-livia said.

"You're lucky you're wearing that coat or it really would have hurt," Alicia whispered.

"Why'd ya elbow me?"

"He doesn't *know* we call him *Derrington*," Alicia said through her teeth. "When you're talking to him, use his *real* name."

"Sorry." Faux-livia rubbed her side. "I thought he'd think it was funny how we blended his first and last name together."

Alicia knew Faux was right. But Massie made up Derrington, and Alicia didn't want Olivia to get credit for it. Of course she could have lied and said the nickname was her idea, but Massie would find out. She always did.

"Yes!" Alicia murmured when Derrington and three of his teammates stopped in front of their seats. "You guys were sooo Beckham-y today." She tilted her head and smiled sweetly.

"Thanks, Alicia," Chris Plovert said as he lifted a bottle of Gatorade to his mouth. A line of blue juice dribbled down his chin.

"Hey, Alicia, look," Danny Robbins said, pointing at Chris's face. "He likes you so much he's drooling."

Chris punched Danny's lanky arm, then used the sleeve of his team jersey to wipe it away. "You're the one who's always looking for her in the stands," he said.

"It's your older sister I'm looking for," Danny said, flashing a mouthful of silver braces.

The two boys started giggling and punching each other. A few other guys on the team heard them joking around and forced their way into the tight circle.

Alicia was enjoying the rush of confidence that always came from so much boy attention. That, combined with her recent experience at *Teen People,* made her feel unstoppable. She scanned the bleachers to make sure Massie, Claire, Dylan, and Kristen were still there. They were. And they were looking straight at her. *Perfect!*

"Relax, boys, you're too old for her," Derrington mumbled. He put his sweaty arm around Alicia.

"The eighth grade is so *not* too old for me." Alicia wiggled to free herself from his grip. She ran her fingers along the inside of her pink knit cap and casually loosened a few strands of black hair. She knew they'd look sexy blowing around her face.

"What about the eleventh grade?" Harris Fisher asked.

Alicia reached into her bag and peeled off a *yes* sticker. She pressed it against the sleeve of his leather jacket.

"We love eleventh graders." Faux-livia's navy blue eyes stayed fixed on Harris.

The boys giggled and punched each other all over again.

Cam rolled his two different-colored eyes. "Ignore him. He's a complete stranger."

Alicia smiled and looked down at the gray cement. There wasn't a girl at OCD who hadn't heard of Harris Fisher. He was Cam's *hot* older brother. He had *two* gorgeous green eyes, whereas Cam only had the one.

"What about Massie? Does she like older guys too?" Derrington asked.

Alicia pretended she didn't hear Derrington's question and quickly changed the subject.

"You better be nice to us because we may not be around for much longer," Alicia said. She casually unbuttoned her gray coat so they could see the Dixon she was wearing around the top of her jeans.

"Why, where are you going?" Derrington mumbled, not noticing that her butt was wrapped in black mesh.

"Yeah, where are you going?" Faux-livia asked. Her eyes were wide with panic.

Alicia squeezed Faux-livia's hand. "We got a modeling contract with *Teen People* and they might want us to drop out of school and move to Manhattan." She tried to sound blasé.

"Really?" Derrington sat down on the bleacher beside Alicia and put his arm around her. "Did Massie get one too?"

"*What* is your obsession?" Alicia snapped. "This has *nothing* to do with Massie."

"Sorry." Derrington jumped to his feet. "I just thought because you're such good friends—"

"Well, you thought wrong." Alicia folded her arms across her chest.

"She *is* pretty enough to be a model," Cam chimed in.

Harris followed his brother's gaze down five rows of bleachers and straight to Massie Block. She was surrounded by a group of girls who were taking turns holding her black pug. Both Massie and the dog wore white scarves and fluffy earmuffs. Her cheeks were rosy from the cold. She looked like a beautiful snow angel under the hazy glow of the stadium lights.

"I second that," Harris said. "She could definitely model."

"Hey, Alicia," Faux-livia said. "You should send Lucinda Maooie's picture. Didn't she say she was looking for more—"

Alicia stepped on Faux-livia's toe with the heel of her boot.

"Ow!" Faux-livia screeched.

"You guys are freaks." Cam shook his head. He stuffed his hands in the pockets of his beat-up leather jacket. "I'll be right back."

"You're the one with two different-colored eyes," Alicia shouted after him.

Cam turned around and smiled. "Sure, make fun of the eyes, that's sooooo original."

"Whatevs." Alicia watched him hop from one metal bench to the next. He stopped when he got to Massie, Claire, Kristen, and Dylan. What made *them* so interesting? Why wasn't Alicia enough? Why did everyone choose Massie?

Alicia tried to seem interested while Chris, Danny, and Derrington recapped the boring details of their winning goal. But she was distracted by Massie. She *did* look pretty. Her hair was even glossier than usual and Alicia couldn't help wondering if there was someone special she was trying to impress.

The minute she saw Massie whack Cam with her signature roundhouse kick, Alicia had her answer. All the signs were there . . . the ultra-glossy hair, matching outfits with Bean, and, most importantly, the kick-boxing moves she'd learned from her mother's old Taebo workout DVDs.

Oh my God, Massie likes Cam!

"Can you talk to her for me?" Derrington mumbled in Alicia's ear. He had seen her roundhouse kick.

"What?" Alicia said, annoyed. "You have to speak up."

"Can you tell Massie to go out with me?" Derrington said louder. "Come on, you're her best friend. She'll listen to you."

Alicia didn't want to tell Derrington that she and Massie weren't speaking. Then he'd take sides. And she knew exactly whose side he'd take.

"Sure," Alicia said to the cement. When she looked up again, she caught Harris sneaking a peek at her boobs.

"When did it get so cold?" Alicia buttoned her coat and folded her arms across her chest.

"Six weeks ago." Harris flashed a big toothy smile. "The Strokes just canceled their Chicago show because of a snowstorm." He tilted his head back and looked up at the late afternoon sky.

Alicia did the same, even though she had no idea why. It wasn't dark enough yet to see any stars.

"I swear if that happens when they come here, I'll freak." Harris returned his gaze to Alicia.

His green eyes were so intense, Alicia had to look away. "Are you going to their concert?" she asked.

"I wish. I'm still trying to get tickets. They always sell out when they play in New York. I even tried eBay." Harris ran his hands through his shaggy brown hair. "I'll probably have to buy from scalpers."

"How many tickets do you need?" Alicia asked.

"Two." He sighed

"Done," Alicia said.

Chris and Derrington laughed.

"Yeah, right," Derrington said.

"I'm serious," Alicia said.

Harris's green eyes flickered with amusement. "There's no way you could actually get those tickets," he said. "Could you?"

"Given," Alicia said. She waved her hand through the air to show him how ridiculous he was being. "My dad has the ultimate hookup. We just saw Beyoncé last night."

"Why?" Derrington mumbled.

"He's a lawyer and he knows *everyone.*"

"No," Derrington said, "why did you see *Beyoncé*?"

Chris Plovert busted out laughing. They high-fived each other.

Alicia turned to Harris. "Do you want the tickets or not?"

"Hell, yeah." Harris threw his arm around Alicia and she caught a whiff of his new leather jacket. It smelled fishy, but Alicia didn't mind. It meant the leather was real.

"Who's the other ticket for?" Alicia forced herself to stare straight into Harris's pupils, because her cousin Nina told her boys got turned on by direct eye contact.

Harris smiled and raised his eyebrows. He didn't speak, but his green eyes seemed to say, "It could be yours if you play your cards right."

Alicia felt prickly heat spread through her entire body. She immediately looked toward the soccer field.

"Hey, Cam." Harris cupped his hands over his mouth and called again, "Cam, time to boogie."

Alicia watched Cam say goodbye to her ex-friends and felt a little pang of envy. It wasn't fair that he got to hang out with them when she couldn't.

"Why. Are. They. Calling. You an EW?" Cam panted. He was out of breath from running up the bleachers.

Alicia stepped away from Harris and lowered her voice. "They didn't tell you?" she whispered to Cam's shoulder.

"No, they said you'd tell me."

"Come on, Cam, I have to get Mom's car home," Harris

said. Then he turned back to Alicia one last time. "Call me as soon as you find out about those tickets."

"Given." Alicia looked around to see if anyone heard Harris ask her to call him. But it was getting dark and almost everyone had cleared out.

"Cam, I'll be waiting in the car." Harris lifted the collar on his jacket to block the wind and walked away.

"Okay, *one minute*," Cam said. "I just have to talk to Alicia about something."

Alicia prayed silently while Cam led her to a bleacher. He sat down. *Please, God, don't let him ask me why they are calling me an EW. PLEASE!*

"Aren't you going to sit down?" Cam asked.

"No, I'm fine," Alicia said.

Cam stood up. Alicia could smell his Drakkar Noir mixed with dried sweat. It smelled better than his brother's fishy jacket, but she still liked Harris more.

"Alicia, will you talk to your friend for me?" he asked softly.

"What's with everyone?" Alicia snapped. "Do I look like the host of *The Bachelorette*? Go talk to Massie yourself if you like her so much."

"I don't," Cam said through the side of his mouth. "I like hair."

"What?" Alicia crinkled her eyebrows. "Are you looking for a stylist?"

"NO, I like Claire," Cam said, raising his voice. "CLAIRE." He quickly looked at his friends, who were busy helping Faux-livia decide if she should tattoo her ankle or her lower back. "But I never get a chance to talk to her alone. Massie's always interrupting."

Alicia looked at the dark sky and winked a thanks at God for this small miracle. Massie liked Cam. And Cam liked Claire. Alicia couldn't *wait* to spread the news.

"I'd be psyched to talk to Claire for you," Alicia blurted. Cam shushed her immediately. Then she whispered, "But you have to do something for me in return."

"Anything," Cam said. He was looking at Claire in the distance. She was sharing a bag of candy with Dylan. For some reason that made him grin.

"Tell your brother to take me to the Strokes concert," Alicia said.

"Can't you just get more tickets?" Cam asked.

"That's *not* the point."

"Don't tell me you're a Harris groupie too." Cam sounded disappointed. "That's disgusting. He's like four years older than you." Then his eyes lit up. "Ohhh, wait," he said, throwing his hands in the air and slapping his thighs. "So *that's* why they call you an EW. Right? 'Cause that's gross?"

Alicia stuffed her hands in the pocket of her coat. "Yeah, that's why."

"Fine, I'll talk to him. But you *have* to talk to Claire." Cam stuck out his right hand. "Deal?"

Alicia grabbed his hand and shook it. "Deal."

Cam jumped to his feet and Alicia watched him walk away with Derrington and Chris.

"Congrats again on a great game," Alicia called after them.

"Go, Hawks!" Faux-livia shouted.

"Let's go," Alicia said. "Massie's packing up and I want to beat her to the parking lot."

"Let's walk across the soccer field," Faux-livia said. "It's faster."

"Done." Alicia led the way.

It was windy on the field and the two girls were walking fast. "So I think he's going to invite me to the Strokes concert," she announced, tightening the pink scarf around her neck.

"What are you going to wear?" Faux-livia asked. "Hopefully something that shows off your tan."

Alicia punched Faux on the arm. "Gross! Shut up! Why would you say that?"

"I saw him checking you out." Faux-livia laughed.

"Puh-lease, he was not," Alicia insisted. "Was he?" This time they both laughed.

"You should totally wear your Dixon," Faux said.

"Too daytime," Alicia said. "I'm thinking more Miu Miu with a splash of Calvin."

"You always know exactly what to do when it comes to boys."

"I learned a lot from my older cousins. You should come to Spain next summer and hang out with us. They'll teach you *everything*."

"If I did, would that make me your beta?" Faux-livia asked.

"Huh?" Alicia stopped walking and looked her friend in the eye. The cold temperature turned her breath into white puffs of air that came out of her mouth when she spoke.

"Well, didn't you once spend the summer with Massie and her family in the Hamptons?" Faux-livia asked.

"Yeah, so?" Alicia wondered when the Massie comments would end.

"So isn't that when you became her beta? 'Cause when you came back, she was the alpha and you were like her second in command."

"Yeah, but I am so over being a second," Alicia said softly.

"Then be an alpha," Faux-livia said. "And I'll be your beta. I've always wanted to be one."

"Are you serious?" Alicia asked, still not moving.

"Totally. Betas have it made. They don't have the pressure of leading, but they still get the status."

"No, I meant about me being an alpha," Alicia said.

"Given," Faux-livia said. "I mean, you're as good as going to the Strokes concert with *Harris Fisher*. Only a true alpha could have pulled that off. You're a natural."

Alicia peeled off a *yes* sticker and stuck it to Faux-livia's cheek. For the first time ever, the ditzy girl actually said something right.

Massie couldn't bring herself to take another bite of the turkey burger that was on her lap. Every time she tried, a glob of ketchup fell onto her True Religion pre-ripped jeans and she couldn't stand to keep them in harm's way any longer.

She stood up from the head seat of table 18 and chucked the half-eaten burger in the trash.

"We have to clean up this mess," Massie said to the piles of wrapping paper, ribbons, and mini–holiday cards that had taken over their regular lunch table in the Café. "There's no room to eat."

"But the gift exchange is only ten minutes away," Dylan said. She pointed to the Jessica Simpson CD beside Massie. "And your gift isn't even wrapped yet."

"Who cares—this whole thing is stupid." Massie gathered up a heap of paper scraps and bunched them up into a tight ball. "Our school is the only one on the planet that does a Secret Santa before Thanksgiving. Principal Burns smells."

"Can someone give me a five-letter word for *grouch*, starting with *g*," Kristen said, perfecting the bow on her gift. She was the first one ready.

"Grouch," Dylan shouted, shoving the last bite of her turkey burger in her mouth.

"That's six letters," Kristen said, using the Scotch tape to pull blond hair off her black cardigan.

"*Groaner?*" Claire teased.

Kristen rolled her eyes and giggled.

"I'm not being a *grump*," Massie said. "I just don't like when things are messy, okay?" She started straightening up the area around her, wondering why Alicia hadn't tried to make up with her yet. Was she really having more fun with Olivia? Why didn't Alicia miss her?

"There's a piece of salad caught in your ribbon," Dylan said, tugging on the leaf inside Kristen's red bow.

Kristen slapped her hand. "That's holly. It's decorative. Don't eat it."

"I wasn't going to *eat* it." Dylan sounded offended. "I hate salad. Maybe that's why I gained five pounds since Halloween." She pushed up the bell sleeve of her burgundy Diane von Furstenberg dress and reached her arm across Kristen's plate. She pinched a few of Kristen's uneaten soy chips, then dropped them in her mouth.

"Mmmm," Dylan said, letting small pieces of soy fall out of her mouth. "Why not use that on your present too?" She pointed to the crumbs on her thighs.

Kristen shoved a bunch of chips in her own mouth. "Because I'd rather use these," she said as the crumbs sprayed all over the table.

"Gross." Claire giggled. She snapped a picture of the girls with her digital camera.

"How's that low-carb diet going, Dylan?" Massie

asked, cutting into a piece of smiley face wrapping paper.

Dylan's bright green eyes turned flat and dull. "Great." She smirked. She looked down and flicked a piece of chip off her lap.

"Ewww!" Kristen and Claire screamed. It landed on the edge of Kristen's Diet Coke can.

"Speaking of EW." Massie sat up a little taller in her seat. "The plan for revenge on Alicia has been set into motion."

"Tell us everything." Dylan pushed her half-wrapped gift aside and leaned forward.

"Yeah, don't leave one thing out," Kristen said, twirling a strand of blonde hair around her index finger.

Massie and Claire took turns telling the girls about their phone call with Lucinda, how they pretended to be Alicia and Olivia, the photos they sent in, and the possibility of crashing the *Teen People* modeling shoot. Massie hadn't wanted to tell her friends about the plan until she'd spent the weekend finalizing it.

"Lucinda just has to approve our pictures and we're IN," Massie said. She couldn't wait to hear them scream.

"What picture did you send of me?" Dylan said. She was stabbing the leftover sesame seeds on Kristen's plate with her fingernail.

"That's all you have to say?" Massie ripped a piece of tape off the spool and stuck it haphazardly to the CD she was wrapping.

"Well, I don't want them to think I'm faaat," Dylan said.

"Puh-lease. Do you think I'm a total amateur?" Massie

said. "Of course I Photoshopped the pictures before I sent them. We all look ah-mazing."

"When is the shoot?" Kristen asked. "It's not on a school night, is it?"

"We thought you'd be excited about this," Claire said.

Massie was impressed with Claire for chiming in. Obviously she was way more loyal than Alicia.

"I'm *fully* excited," Kristen said with a genuine smile. "It's just that I kinda got this after-school job. . . ." Her voice drifted off. She gently nudged the holly on her present until it was in the perfect position.

"What? Why do you have an after-school job?" asked Dylan. "What are you *doing?*"

Kristen displayed her gift like a game show hostess. "Gift wrapping at the mall. It's just until New Year's."

"*Why?* It's not like you need the money." Massie licked a green envelope and sealed her card inside. "Your dad is one of the richest art dealers in the country."

"It's not about money; it's about building *character,*" Kristen said as she squirmed in her chair, then sat on her hands. "At least that's what my parents say."

"My dad says things like that all the time," Claire said to Kristen.

Kristen winked at Claire, like they shared some kind of secret, but Massie quickly dismissed it. She refused to let her fight with Alicia make her paranoid.

"Your parents can be so ah-nnoying," Massie said.

Kristen shrugged.

"So Massie, don't we get two hundred dollars if they pick us?" Claire asked.

"Oh yeah," Massie said. "I forgot all about that."

"That will help your *character* even more, won't it, Kristen?" Dylan said.

"At least the job taught me how to wrap," Kristen said, looking at the crumpled lump of metallic red paper on Dylan's lunch tray. It looked more like Massie's sloppy turkey burger than a candle.

Massie was suddenly overcome by a strong whiff of perfume. She leaned across the table and sniffed Dylan's candle to see if maybe it was scented.

"Get your hands off my present, you big molester," Dylan said, pinching Massie's hand.

"Ouch." Massie laughed, but she wouldn't let go.

"What's going on here?" Alicia stood facing Massie at the opposite end of the table. Olivia was beside her and they were both holding a plate of California rolls.

"That explains the stench," Massie said, taking her hand off Dylan's present and sitting back in her seat.

Alicia was wearing a tight pink V-necked sweater, a pair of ultra-low-rise Frankie B. jeans, and a ridiculous black mesh tube top around her waist. Olivia was dressed the exact same, only her V-neck was baby blue.

"We should keep wrapping." Claire looked down at the sparkly orange pencil case on her lap. "The gift exchange is in five minutes."

"Oops, I totally spaced," Alicia said. She pulled a chair

over from another table and forced her way between Claire and Kristen. She tapped the seat as if to say, "Come share," and Olivia squeezed in beside her.

Massie was itching to ask them what they were wearing around their butts, but she refused to speak to Alicia until she apologized. She angled her chair so she faced the window behind her.

"Mind if I use some of this?" Olivia asked.

Massie didn't like not being able to see what Olivia was talking about, so she opened her Chanel compact mirror and acted like she was touching up her cheek tint.

"Go ahead," Claire said, handing her the tape.

"Thanks." Olivia pulled a fake Louis Vuitton scarf out of her knockoff Hermès Birkin bag and tossed it on the table.

"Faux-livia," Alicia said. "Do you have another one of those scarves? I don't have anything to give—" She pulled an index card out of her pocket and read the name that was written on it. "Emily Esbin."

"Why don't you give her that stupid girdle you're wearing?" Kristen said.

Massie laughed with the others.

"FYI, this is a Dixon. We got them from the fashion editor at *Teen People*. Avril will be wearing one on the February cover. You'll see—they're going to be huge." Alicia poked her pinky through one of the holes in the mesh.

"There are fifty-eight ways to wear it," Olivia added.

"Fifty-nine if you count stuffing it up your butt," Dylan said.

Everyone laughed again, but Alicia ignored their jabs.

"Of course, you would know all of this if any one of you bothered asking me how our interview was," Alicia said, popping one of her California rolls in her mouth.

No one asked for a single detail. Not even Claire, and Massie was grateful. Why give Alicia the satisfaction?

"So Faux-livia, can I have one of those scarves?" Alicia asked.

Massie's ears perked up. Why was Alicia calling Olivia "Faux-livia"? Was it an inside joke? How close *were* they?

"I only have one," Olivia said to Alicia. "The rest are at home."

"Can I have yours?" Alicia asked sweetly.

"No! I have to give it to Thao Luu."

"I'll tell everyone why you're called Faux-livia," Alicia threatened. "Then no one will want your scarves."

"You wouldn't! Would you?"

Alicia raised her eyebrows and nodded, yes.

Olivia dropped the scarf on Alicia's lap, then slid down the back of her chair. Massie couldn't believe Alicia bossed Olivia around like that. Bossing was *her* thing.

Alicia reached across the table and grabbed the plastic salt and pepper shakers. She slammed them down in front of Olivia. "Here, give *these* to Thao."

Faux took the shakers and without saying a word began rolling them up in a long strip of wrapping paper.

"You look like you're making sushi," Alicia said with a giggle. Olivia ignored her and kept trying to wrap the oblong shakers, but every time she moved them, little hills of salt and pepper would fall out.

"Ugh!" she shouted. "Ugh! Ugh! Ugh!"

"Stop whining!" Kristen grabbed the shakers away from Olivia. She covered the holes with a piece of tape, then finished the wrapping job herself.

"Have you been hanging with 50 Cent lately?" Alicia asked Kristen.

"No."

"Then where did you learn to rap?" Alicia leaned back and locked her hands behind her head.

Olivia and Claire laughed. Kristen rolled her eyes and Massie felt her spine stiffen. It was one thing for Alicia to steal first prize in the uniform contest or to start her own Friday night sleepovers, but copying Massie's humor was inexcusable.

"Alicia, are you a poor dressmaker?" Massie asked without turning around.

"No," Alicia said.

"Then why are you ripping off my material?"

Kristen and Dylan burst out laughing. Claire giggled softly.

Alicia ignored them. "So Kuh-laire, where's Layne Abeley? Don't you usually eat at her table?"

Massie wasn't surprised Alicia was attacking Claire. She was the weakest in the group and an obvious choice. It was what she would have done.

"Layne is at the orthodontist," Claire said softly. "So Massie said I could sit here today."

"Oh, well, I'm glad," Alicia said. "Because I have some gossip for you. It's worth at least twenty-five points."

Massie stopped breathing for a second. No one ever got *that* many points for one piece of gossip. This had to be big.

"You know Cam Fisher? The cute Briarwood boy with the two different-colored eyes?"

"Yeah," Massie blurted.

"I was talking to Kuh-laire," Alicia said. "Well—"

Massie could feel her heart racing. Just hearing his name gave her a physical reaction. She knocked a scrap of paper onto the ground, then bent over to pick it up. She casually turned to face Alicia.

"He likes you, Claire, and wants to start hanging out with you." Then Alicia looked straight at Massie. *"Alone."*

Massie slammed her hands on the table and leaned forward. Alicia must have heard wrong. . . .

"How do you know?" Claire asked, her face beaming with excitement.

"Wait, Cam likes Kuh-laire?" Massie barked.

"Yup." Alicia got up and sat on the edge of the table. She crossed her legs and leaned back.

Massie thought about shoving her onto the ground, hoping it would get rid of that cocky smile on her face. "Source?" she asked.

"Cam told me himself, Saturday after the soccer game. Didn't he, Faux-livia?"

"Yup." Olivia nodded.

The more Massie thought about it, the more Alicia's

words made sense. Claire *did* say Cam left a bag of gummy feet under her seat. But the whole time Massie assumed that they had been for *her* and that Claire had just stumbled upon them by accident. And after the game, when he came over to talk to them . . . had he *really* come to see Claire? Was it possible? Even though she showed him her roundhouse?

"So Claire, are you totally shocked and excited?" Alicia said.

"I am," Massie blurted.

Claire giggled. "I wanted to tell you, but I could never get you alone."

"That's funny," Alicia said. "Because Cam said he could never get *you* alone, Claire. He said Massie always shows up and gets in the way every time he tries to talk to you."

Massie felt like Alicia had just kicked her in the stomach with her hideous square-toed boots. She could barely choke down her own breath. Every time she tried, her mouth got drier. Her ears started ringing and the voices in the Café were starting to sound tinny and hollow. Massie wanted to run away and scream, but everyone was looking at her, waiting for her reaction.

"Look." Claire reached into her backpack and pulled out a folded piece of paper. She handed it to Alicia. "It's the first note Cam ever wrote to me. He gave it to me after we lost the uniform design contest. I take it everywhere."

Massie took a sip of Diet Coke while she watched Alicia unfold the note. She took another sip while Alicia read it aloud.

"Dear Claire, you must have really hated the CD I made

you, cuz you never got back to me about the movie. Anyway, I thought your uniform was awesome and I think you should have won. —Cam. P.S., the Keds were a cool touch." Alicia pressed the open note against her chest and shook her head slowly. "He is so sweet. But remind me to kill him for saying you should have won the contest." She forced a playful smile.

"He is a door and a ball," Kristen said.

"What?" Dylan hissed.

"A-door-a-ball." Kristen grinned.

"I love *that*," Dylan said.

Massie reached for the pug charm on her bracelet and held it tight, wishing the real Bean were there with her.

"So did you ever go to the movie with him?" Olivia asked.

"No, not yet." Claire lifted the hood of her fuchsia Gap sweater over her head. "But he keeps asking me."

Massie watched Claire squirm and fidget and wondered how Cam could possibly find her more attractive. It wasn't that Claire wasn't cute; she *was*. Massie just always thought of herself as cuter. But maybe she wasn't. . . .

"Uh, excuse me," Massie said, snapping her fingers in the air. "Attention, please. I hate to say this, because Cam is a nice guy, but he's a major EW."

Claire took her note back from Alicia and stuffed it in her bag.

"I mean, he's such an eternal Harris wannabe." Massie leaned forward in her chair and glared at Dylan.

"You're right," Dylan said. "He is like a total highlight/copy/paste of his older brother: the leather jacket, the Strokes obsession, and his green eye are all one hundred percent Harris."

"And there's nothing more pathetic than a *wannabe*," Massie said, turning to Alicia.

"But he's so sweet," Claire said.

"So is Equal, but it's not the real thing," Massie said. "You deserve someone special. Not a cheap knockoff."

Claire brought her thumb to her mouth and started chewing on her nail. Massie felt a little guilty about hurting Claire, but she was determined to wipe the smug look off Alicia's face.

"Claire, there are tons of cute boys at Briarwood, with personalities of their own," Massie said. "I'll totally introduce you."

"Puh-lease, Cam totally has his own personality," Alicia said, pulling up the low neck of her sweater. "Harris never played soccer."

"I know. Harris played lacrosse," Massie said. "Cam tried out for lacrosse but never made the team." She sat on her hands so no one would see that her fingers were crossed.

"You're just jealous," Alicia said to Massie. "I saw you flirting with him after the soccer game."

"I wasn't flirting with him," Massie hissed. Her heartbeat quickened.

"You showed him your roundhouse," Alicia said.

Massie gasped. "I did not!"

"Ehmagawd, you *did* show him your roundhouse," Dylan said.

"But that doesn't mean anything," Kristen said. "Does it, Massie?"

"Of course not—that mating call is so dead to me," Massie said.

"Claire, stop biting." Alicia knocked Claire's thumb out of her mouth. "This is all very simple."

Alicia slid off the edge of the table and slowly walked over to Massie. "Cam likes Claire. Claire likes Cam." She stood over Massie's chair. Her arms were folded across her chest. "And *no one* likes a sore loser. So accept it, Massie, and let Claire find a little happiness."

Massie stood up and looked into Alicia's big brown eyes. "Alicia, if I liked Cam, I would be hanging out with Cam." She tried her best to control her shaky voice. "Besides, Cam has BO." Massie dropped back down into her seat. She ripped a few scraps of wrapping paper before she looked across the table. "Kuh-laire, if you like Cam, don't let me stand in your way."

An expression of relief washed over Claire's face.

"But—" Massie looked straight into Claire's wide blue eyes. "If you do end up hanging out with him, don't bother talking to me. I don't want one of my *best friends* associated with an EW. It makes me look trashy."

Claire sighed anxiously and pulled on her bangs.

"Don't let her get to you," Alicia said to Claire. "Massie's just jealous because *she* likes Cam."

Claire placed her palm on the table and dragged a red ribbon scrap toward her. Her bottom lip stuck out while she looked down and tied it into a knot.

Alicia rolled her eyes. "Let's go, Faux."

"Massie, will you introduce *me* to some cute Briarwood boys too?" Olivia said.

"Sure," Massie said with fake enthusiasm. "Once we're *friends.*"

"Come on." Alicia grabbed Olivia by the arm and pulled her away.

Suddenly a voice bleated over the loudspeaker, saving Massie from having to answer any questions.

"What's up, OCD, this is Comma Dee letting you know that it's time for the Give Thanks on Thanksgiving gift exchange. Please take all of your prezzys to the auditorium so we can get started. . . ."

Kristen, Dylan, and Claire grabbed their gifts off the table and stood up. Massie stayed seated.

"Hey, here's one for ya. . . . What part of the turkey does Snoop Dogg love to eat? . . . Give up? . . ."

"You coming?" Claire asked Massie. She sounded tired.

"Yeah." Massie stood up. Her legs felt like lead.

"The GRIZZLE . . . Snoop loves to eat The Grizzle. Get it?"

Everyone groaned when they heard Comma Dee's corny punch line.

"That girl is such a loser," Dylan said.

I know," Kristen agreed. "She actually thinks people like her."

Massie walked a few paces behind her friends, wondering if one day people would be saying that about *her.*

Claire loved the rich woodsy smell of cedar in the Blocks' old horse barn. But she had been painting in there for over an hour and a sharp, pungent odor hovered in the air like a noxious cloud. Massie opened a window, but all that did was let in the cold.

"How's everyone doing?" Massie asked, taking a step back to survey the freshly painted wall.

"Good," Kristen said from the top of her stepladder.

Dylan nodded while she tightened the Pucci scarf around her head.

"I'm almost done," Claire said, dipping her brush in paint. She tapped it against the side of the can, then lifted it to the wall.

Claire knew what they were about to do was wrong. But she couldn't turn back now. Massie would never invite her to do anything with them again.

"Shoot," Claire said looking at her shoe. "I just dripped paint on my white Keds."

"Looks like you'll finally have to get rid of those," Massie said with a teasing smile.

"Why? Your clothes have paint all over them," Claire said, referring to Massie's blotchy turquoise outfit.

"Yeah, but they're supposed to be like this. These are my Primp Splatter Sweats; I bought them for the occasion." Massie ran her hand over the unicorn patch that had been sewed to the front. "And by the way, these stains are bleach, not paint."

"I can't believe your mom is letting us paint the walls," Kristen said, wiping her hands on her old gray soccer sweats. "My parents would never let me do this."

"It's part of her self-help homework," Massie said, reaching for her Dr. Juice. The clear plastic cup had *Power* written across it in big black letters. The protein-omega-3-banana-soy blend was her new favorite. "Everyone in her book club has to do something this week that shows they can 'let go.' So she said we could paint the walls."

"My mom said she's only letting us do this because they're putting mirrors on the walls in a couple of weeks," Claire said.

"Yeah, but until then this place is all ours," Massie said. "And I am officially declaring it GLU headquarters." She raised her juice and the girls cheered. "Ehmagawd, it's eight o'clock. Lucinda said she'd know by now if we got the modeling jobs." Massie flicked open her Motorola. Another purple rhinestone fell off and bounced along the hardwood floors. "I am so getting a new phone. This one isn't respond-ing well to my jewels."

Massie's amber eyes shifted back and forth while she listened to her messages. "Alicia called to say she's going to be here at eight-thirty," she reported. "That means we have to hurry up and finishing painting." Massie hit delete and Claire watched her eyes shift again while she listened to the next message.

"It's Lucinda," Massie shouted. The girls jumped off their stepladders and grabbed each other's hands like finalists on *America's Next Top Model.*

"IN!" Massie snapped her phone shut.

Claire had waited months to hear that word.

"We're gonna be models." Dylan was so excited she actually tackled Massie. They fell to the ground and landed on a dusty drop cloth, laughing hysterically.

"Go to hell, Gisele!" Kristen shouted as she dove on top of them.

"Walk the planks, Tyra Banks," Claire shouted before she joined the giddy pile.

"I am so starting a raw food diet," Dylan announced as she stood up and wiped the dust off her mother's old maternity caftan.

Dylan's serious tone was an instant buzz kill. Everyone got off the floor, smoothed her hair, and got down to business.

"Did she say when it was?" Kristen asked, opening her day planner.

"December sixth," Massie said.

"Cool, I already have that weekend off," Kristen said.

"Be careful. Something might happen to your *character* if you're not wrapping presents for a few days," Massie said.

Kristen rolled her eyes and slapped her planner shut.

Everyone laughed at Massie's joke and Claire was

relieved when Kristen joined them. She was the only one who knew that Kristen's family was poor and that Kristen was extra sensitive to the comments people made about money when she was in the room.

Claire remembered the day she snuck onto Massie's computer and got Kristen to confess over IM. Of course, Kristen thought she was confiding in Massie. When she finally found out it was Claire, Kristen begged her not to tell anyone. After that Claire had promised herself she'd never do anything mean or sneaky again. But the paint on her shoe reminded Claire that she was going back on her promise. She stared at the purple stain and sighed. This would be the very last time. . . .

"Wait until the boys at Briarwood find out we're going to be models," Kristen said. "Our stock is gonna go way up."

"Now that it's official, I can't wait to tell Cam." Claire tugged on the strap of her overalls. "I can't wait to see his face when—"

Massie shot Claire a stern look and Kristen and Dylan rushed to Massie's side. Claire could feel her heart starting to pound.

"So you're choosing Cam over us?" Massie's question sounded more like a statement.

"No, not at all." Claire hated herself for mentioning Cam. She had done such a good job keeping their recent e-mails a secret and she'd just snitched on herself. "You didn't let me finish." Her armpits were starting to sweat. "I was going to say, I can't wait to tell him, but I *won't* because I don't talk to him anymore." Claire searched Massie's face to see if she believed her. "I swear. We are so done."

Massie held out her palm.

"What?" Claire said, biting her thumbnail.

"Give me the note," Massie said, wiggling her fingers.

"Why?" Claire felt her stomach lock.

"Prove that you are done with him and give me the note," Massie said.

Claire felt like the room was spinning. She wished she could think of something that would convince Massie to let her keep the note. But nothing came.

Claire grabbed her backpack off the floor and reached inside slowly. She moved her hand around the bottom of the bag like she couldn't find it.

"I think it's at home." Claire's head was throbbing.

"Let me look," Massie ordered, coming closer.

"Oh, here it is," Claire said. She was relieved Massie didn't know about the three mix CDs Cam had burned for her. "It got stuck in the mesh cell phone pocket."

"Hurry up," Massie said, snapping her fingers. "Alicia is going to be here soon and we have a lot to do."

Claire felt like she was watching herself in a dream when she placed the note in Massie's open palm. It was covered in tiny rips and smudges from being read so many times. The familiar cherry Blow Pop stain in the bottom-right corner triggered a hot feeling behind Claire's eyes that always came right before her tears. Cam had given her that Blow Pop and written, *Have a sweet day,* in tiny letters along the stick.

Massie crumpled up the note and walked toward the cans of paint. Claire quickly looked at Kristen and Dylan for help, but their heads were down.

"Say good-bye," Massie said. She held her fist above the green paint, then opened her hand. The note bobbed on the surface, refusing to sink. Everyone ran over and stood above the can with their mouths open, except Massie. She reached for the nearest paintbrush and stabbed the stubborn note until it sank.

Claire took a deep breath, hoping the rush of air would suck back her tears. She would never get to look at Cam's perfectly neat, all-caps handwriting again.

"There," Massie said with a warm smile. "That should help." She tossed the paintbrush on the floor. "When I dump a guy, I like to destroy everything he ever gave me. I find it really cleansing."

". . . ks," Claire said. She tried to say, "Thanks," but it wouldn't come out.

All Claire could think about while they finished painting in silence was how to keep herself from sobbing. She told herself that Cam was a lame wannabe and that Massie was only looking out for her, but that didn't get rid of the feeling in the pit of her stomach or the stinging behind her eyes. And it especially didn't erase the mental image she had of Cam's note, sitting all alone at the bottom of the can, covered in green paint.

A knock on the door startled them all. It was the first sound they had heard since Massie's Maroon 5 CD ended.

"It's showtime," Massie whispered to her friends. "We'll be right there!" she shouted.

The girls scurried around the barn, straightening and tidying. They knew Massie wanted this to be perfect. Once everything was in its place, Massie yanked opened the door.

"Oh," she said when she saw who was on the other side. "I was expecting someone else."

"Who could possibly be better than me?" Todd said.

"What do you want, Todd?" Claire asked her brother. She prayed he wouldn't do anything to embarrass her.

"I just thought you ladies would be hurting for a little male companionship."

"This is GLU headquarters," Dylan said.

"What does that mean?" Todd said, poking his head inside to have a look around.

"It means Girls Like Us," Massie said, closing the door. "No boys allowed!"

But Todd stopped the door with his foot. "Whoa, what did you do to the walls?"

"Get out," Massie said, smacking his foot away. Todd lost his balance and fell on the grass. Massie slammed the door shut and leaned against it to make sure he couldn't force his way back in.

His incessant banging filled Claire with sadness. Todd was just lonely. Her friends in Florida didn't mind having him around and he was obviously missing that. Claire missed it too. But she didn't dare ask Massie to make an exception to her "girls only" rule. Claire didn't want to give

Massie any reason to kick her out, especially when she had to work so hard to get in.

"Leave us alone," Massie shouted.

The knocking continued.

"Go away," Kristen and Dylan shouted.

"It's me," a voice said. "Alicia."

"Oh," Massie mouthed.

The girls smoothed their hair and got into position. Massie looked at them to make sure they were ready. When she decided they were, Massie threw open the door.

Showtime!

"If this is a bad time, I can leave," Alicia said.

"Why would you say that?" Massie had one of her infamous I'm-about-to-take-great-pleasure-in-destroying-you smiles on her face. Her lips were shut, the corners of her mouth were curled up, and her eyes sparkled with a devious glint.

Alicia recognized the look on Massie's face and wanted to turn around and chase Dean and the limo down the street. But she'd watched him back out of the Blocks' driveway. He'd be long gone by now.

"Welcome to GLU headquarters," Massie said, giving Alicia a once-over. Alicia stuffed her sweaty palms in the back pockets of her pants.

"Don't you look faaan-cy," Massie added.

Alicia was wearing a blue satin cap-sleeve blouse, gray velvet pants, and square-toed boots, her Dixon stretched across her shoulders like a shrug. She felt ridiculously over dressed compared to Massie, who was in Splatter Sweats and sheepskin slippers. When did she buy those anyway? It felt weird seeing Massie in something new. They usually shopped for everything together.

"Uh, I was just out for dinner with my parents," Alicia said, avoiding Massie's suspicious glare.

It smelled like paint inside the horse barn and Alicia stuck her head in to see what was going on. But Massie shifted her body and blocked Alicia's view.

"We're glad you decided to come."

We? Alicia had assumed it would just be the two of them. But she should have known. Massie was never by herself.

"Well, you e-mailed me saying you made a tribute to our friendship. How could I not come for *that?*" Alicia rolled her shoulders back, showing off her perfect jazz posture.

Massie smiled sweetly. "Thanks."

"I'm glad you're ready to apologize," Alicia said. "I totally miss—"

"Who said anything about apologizing?" Massie stepped back to reveal Kristen, Dylan, and Claire.

"Oh, hey." Alicia waved at Kristen and Dylan. It felt weird not hugging them. "Claire, hi, I wasn't expecting to see you here."

Claire smiled uncomfortably and looked down at her cuticles.

"We had some extra room this week," Massie said, practically spitting the word *extra* at Alicia.

"Yeah, I guess," Alicia said, unsure of what to say next. She had left her coat in the limo and was starting to feel a chill. "Can I at least come in?"

Massie stepped aside.

The place was a mess. The floors were covered in newspaper, and paint cans and dirty brushes were lined up against the wall. Four Dr. Juice cups had been stacked on the rungs of a gray stepladder, and CDs and empty jewel cases were scattered everywhere. "Has your mother seen this place?" Alicia asked. She remembered the time Massie got grounded and couldn't go to Six Flags because she didn't pick Bean's chew toys off the floor of her bedroom.

"Yup, she's fine with it," Massie said.

Alicia felt like a stranger. So much had changed in the few days. It was like she didn't know Massie at all anymore.

"Don't you want to know what this tribute is?" Dylan asked, ripping open a bag of baked Doritos.

"Given." Alicia tried to steady her voice.

Massie snapped her fingers and Claire shut out the lights. The room was completely black and Alicia's heart started racing. She wanted to scream but kept telling herself they were only trying to scare her.

Someone had flicked on a floor lamp. "Thank you," Alicia heard herself say. Long shadows were cast against the walls and Alicia could hear the wind howling through the open window. Suddenly a cold hand brushed against her face.

Alicia jumped and whipped her head around. "Who's that?"

Kristen giggled.

"Ehmagawd, Kristen, you scared me." Alicia slapped her hand over her heart.

But Kristen didn't say a word. She just stood there twirling a purple satin blindfold around her index finger. The front said DIVA AT REST in white rhinestones.

Kristen pulled back the thin black elastic and slipped

the blindfold over Alicia's eyes. Everything went dark again.

"You guys, this is so stupid." Alicia heard the panic in her voice. They probably did too.

"We want this to be a surprise," Kristen said.

Everyone started whispering.

"What's happening?" Alicia stomped her foot. "What is this?"

She felt Kristen's clammy hand on her arm. "Just follow me," Kristen said. She started pulling Alicia across the barn.

Alicia's mouth went dry and she was desperate for a fresh coat of gloss. She tried to stay calm by imagining herself telling this story to Harris Fisher while they were at the Strokes concert. But that only made her more anxious. She still had no idea what shoes to wear.

What would the other girls do if they were in her place? Would they go along with it like she was? Would they resist? Dylan would probably burp or do something disgusting to make them all laugh. Or she'd threaten them, saying her famous mother would expose them on her morning talk show. Kristen would come up with some fact about how blindfolding people could lead to an untimely death and they would apologize immediately. Claire would keep her cool, never letting on that they were scaring her. Massie would outsmart them all and escape.

The smell of paint fumes was making her nauseous. "Okay, enough," Alicia said. "What is this?"

"The writing is on the wall," Dylan said.

"Huh?" Alicia said.

"The *writing* is on the *wall*," Dylan repeated.

"See?" Kristen yanked the blindfold off Alicia's head.

"Ouch, watch the elastic." Alicia rubbed the back of her head.

"Sorry."

Alicia looked at her boots while her eyes adjusted to the light. Finally she looked up. She felt like she had on her fifth-grade field trip to the Museum of Modern Art, trying to make sense of the abstract shapes and colors painted on the wall in front of her.

"This mural represents our friendship over the past few weeks." Massie sounded like a museum tour guide.

Alicia's mouth hung open.

Massie grabbed Kristen's lacrosse stick and pointed to the drawing of a catwalk. "Over here on the far left, we have the OCD Fashion Week Uniform Contest."

Alicia looked at a painting of two girls. One had dark hair and enormous boobs; the other had wavy blonde hair and a bandage across her nose. Alicia knew they were meant to be her and Olivia. They each had bubbles over their heads like in comic books. Olivia's said, *We're losers beyond repair. How R we going 2 win?* Alicia's said, *Cheat.*

"That's crazy," Alicia said. "You can't prove that!" She lifted her chin and tried to look cool. But her mind was screaming with panic. They knew! When did they find out? How long had they secretly hated her?

"What's that?" She pointed to a massive purple blob.

"*That's* our proof," Massie said.

"What?" Alicia screeched.

"Remember how we voted by putting a thimble in the box of the team we thought should win?"

Alicia nodded slowly, her eyes fixed on the wall. Where could this possibly be going?

Massie continued. "I painted mine purple for good luck."

"So?" Alicia hissed, getting impatient. This next part had nothing to do with her.

"So *your* box had a purple thimble in it." Massie's face turned dark red.

"You voted for me?" Alicia shook her head in disbelief. "Why?"

Massie put her hands on her hips and shouted, "You're starting to sound as dumb as Olivia."

Alicia heard Kristen's phlegmy laugh and couldn't control herself any longer. "What's so funny?" she screamed.

"I DIDN'T VOTE FOR YOU," Massie shouted. "YOU SWITCHED OUR BOXES."

Alicia quickly searched the room with her eyes. Two of the windows were too high to reach and the other two were too narrow to fit through. She could probably beat Massie, Claire, and definitely Dylan to the door, but Kristen would catch her. She was trapped.

Alicia looked straight into Claire's big blue eyes, silently begging to be rescued. If anyone knew what it felt like to be on Massie's bad side, it was Claire. But all Claire did was look at Massie, then at her cuticles.

"Ready for more?" Massie asked, redirecting everyone's attention to a big white circle on the wall. A real Ralph

Lauren blazer and a pair of jeans were tacked inside the circle, just under the words OCD UNIFORM. A big red X sliced through the whole thing. Alicia knew the hanging outfit represented her winning uniform idea, which every girl at OCD would have to wear in the new year.

"As you can see from the X," Dylan said. "There will no longer be an OCD uniform."

Alicia raised her eyebrows.

"That's right," Dylan said. "We had a meeting with Principal Burns the day after the contest and explained how you cheated. My mother came with us and made it very clear that if they went forward with your idea, she would expose the entire scandal on *The Daily Grind.*" Dylan pulled the Pucci scarf off her head and shook out her thick red hair before continuing. "And you know Burns has been terrified of my mother's talk show ever since her story 'Hidden Carbs in the Café.'"

"So there's no more uniform?" Alicia's voice quivered.

"It's done." Massie snapped her fingers.

"Done," Dylan said.

"And done," Kristen said.

"This next painting is the future, Alicia." Massie tapped the wall with the lacrosse stick. "As you can see, you're sitting *alone* on a sleeping bag, which is what you get for trying to start your own sleepover."

Alicia was finished. She knew she couldn't show up to school tomorrow . . . or any other day. She would have to move to Spain and live with her cousins.

"And now for the last part of our tribute," Massie said. "I think it speaks for itself."

There was more?

And there it was in big black bubble letters, Massie's famous State of the Union. Everyone knew she made in/out lists, but no one had ever read them.

CURRENT STATE OF THE UNION	
IN	OUT
CLAIRE	ALICIA

Claire stuffed her hands in the pockets of her overalls and rocked back and forth on her heels while the girls clapped.

"Don't be shy, Claire," Dylan said. "Take a bow."

"No, it's okay," Claire said, looking at Alicia.

"No, really," Massie urged. "Take a bow."

"Come on," said Kristen.

Claire rolled her eyes and snickered. She bowed quickly and immediately straightened up.

Tears began rolling down Alicia's face. There was nothing she could do to stop them.

"And that's the end of our tribute," Massie said, her voice cracking a little.

Alicia sniffled and wiped her nose with the back of her hand. She wanted to drop to her knees and apologize. But it was too late for that.

"Thank you so much for being such a loyal friend, Alicia.

As soon as you figure out what we did to deserve your back-stabbing, let us know."

Alicia thought she saw Massie's eyes starting to water, but everything looked so blurry and wet through her own tears, she couldn't be sure. At least they didn't know about the *Teen People* shoot!

In a flash Alicia abandoned her usual slow saunter in favor of a full-on run and darted across the barn. She slipped and slid on sheets of newspaper, but she kept on running. When Alicia finally got close to the door, the square toe of her boot got caught in the flare of her velvet pants and she fell.

Alicia heard Massie, Dylan, and Kristen crack up. She didn't hear Claire but assumed she was probably laughing too.

"Maybe now you'll stop wearing those stupid boots," Massie said.

Alicia looked up. "They're from *Spain,*" she wailed.

"*Puh-lease.* Those are about as Spanish as your father," Massie said. "They're more like Ugg boots, 'cause they're ugg-LY!"

This time Alicia heard Claire's laugh. She stood up quickly, but her knees were stinging from the fall and pain made the tears come even harder.

"I can't believe you were ever my friends," Alicia cried. Her body shook uncontrollably. She reached for the door and tugged on the heavy latch; the cold iron stung her scraped hands.

When Alicia finally made it outside, a brisk gust of wind slapped her in the face. Her head was pounding in perfect time with her heart. And her whole body felt sore. Of all the horrible things she'd seen, "Claire is the new Alicia" hurt the most.

Alicia reached into her back pocket and pulled out her cell phone.

"Dean!" she shouted into the tiny speaker.

"I'm sorry; I do not recognize that name. Please try again," said the recording.

"Dean," she shouted three more times. But the phone didn't know what she wanted because she was crying so hard.

Alicia's thumb shook as she dialed Dean's number and she kept hitting the wrong numbers. Finally she got it right and Dean's phone started ringing.

"Pick up, pick up, pick—"

Suddenly Alicia felt someone grab her shoulder. She was about to scream when a gloved hand quickly covered her mouth and silenced her.

"Shhh," said a kind voice.

Alicia whipped her head around and saw a skinny boy dressed in all black. A dark ski hat and big women's sunglasses covered his face.

"Todd?"

"You know my name?" He beamed.

"Given," Alicia said, pulling a piece of black glove fuzz off her lip.

"This is my best friend, Nathan."

Alicia lowered her eyes one more time. Nathan was petite and fragile. His disguise was the same as Todd's, except he wore a shower cap and a blue gel eye mask.

Alicia wanted to laugh, but more tears came instead.

"Why the crying, angel?" Todd asked. He held out his sleeve and Alicia wiped her nose on it.

When she lifted her head, a shiny streak of snot glistened on his black fleece Patagonia.

"Sorry 'bout that," she sniffed.

"No prob," Todd said, smiling at the stain. "I'll sell it to Nathan."

Tiny Nathan giggled, then punched Todd's leg.

"Ew, why?" Alicia said.

Todd rolled his eyes. "You're like the hottest girl at OCD."

"Shut up," Alicia said, hoping he'd continue. She was desperate for a compliment, even if it was coming from Claire's younger brother. "If I'm so hot, why does everyone worship Massie so much? What makes *her* so great?"

Tiny Nathan squeaked, "Afraid," then buried his head in his hands.

"He's right," Todd said, throwing a protective arm around his little buddy. "Massie always used to make my sister cry. And what she did to you tonight was way worse than anything she ever did to Claire."

"I know, but—wait," Alicia said. "How do you know what they said?"

"I have an eavesdropping problem," Todd said, taking off his big J.Lo sunglasses and stuffing them in the side pocket of his black jeans. "But I'm working on it."

Tiny Nathan giggled.

"You're way cooler than Massie, if you ask me," Todd said, shifting his weight from one leg to the other.

Alicia smiled.

"I thought you were in looove with Massie," Tiny Nathan said.

"That was before." Todd grabbed Alicia's hand and kissed it gently.

Alicia rolled her eyes and giggled before pulling her hand away.

"You're the future of the Pretty Committee—Massie is over," Todd said. "Like, if she's Coke, you're C2."

Alicia was about to ask how he knew they called themselves the Pretty Committee but quickly remembered his "eavesdropping problem."

Todd unzipped his fleece and handed it to Alicia. She hadn't realized she'd been shivering. "Where's your jacket?" he asked.

"In the limo." Alicia draped Todd's coat over her shoulders like a shawl, steering clear of the snot streak.

"So you're rich too? Hmmm." Todd smoothed imaginary chin hairs and nodded. "You should start your own group. Call it the Unbelievably Pretty Committee."

Nathan giggled.

"I've been thinking about it." Alicia could feel her confidence coming back. "I have a lot to offer. For starters, I won't be mean. I'll take my girls shopping every day, I'll introduce them to Briarwood boys, and I'll let them eat candy."

"Will you let us hang out with you?" Todd asked.

Alicia slapped Todd on the back. "Given!" She leaned down and patted Tiny Nathan on top of his shower cap.

When she looked up, a set of high beams shone directly into her eyes. Alicia covered her face immediately. If Todd saw how puffy and red her face was, he might think twice about calling her the prettiest girl at OCD.

Dean pulled the limo into the Blocks' circular driveway. He must have seen her call even though they'd never spoken.

He honked twice.

"Bye," Alicia shouted as she sprinted for the limo. She turned quickly and blew the boys a couple of air kisses.

"Great boobs, by the way," Todd shouted.

Alicia scowled and folded her arms across her chest. She started crying again. How could she have been stupid enough to trust them? All this time they were probably working for Massie.

"I love the square toe," Todd said. "It's cool."

Alicia turned around and smiled at the misunderstanding. "Ohhh." She unfolded her arms and stuck out her foot. "Thanks. They're from Spain."

For most of the ride home Alicia was in a daze. Her eyes felt swollen and her body felt weak from exhaustion. She curled up on the backseat and buried her head under Todd's fleece.

"How much time do we have, Phil?" Alicia whispered so Dean wouldn't hear.

"You're live in three . . . two . . ." said imaginary Phil. He gave Alicia the signal to begin her newscast.

"Good evening, Westchester." Alicia sniffled. "This just in: After a long night of severe torture and humiliation, Alicia Rivera has announced that she is leaving the Pretty Committee and starting her own. As of tomorrow she will be looking for new best friends. She has already assigned Olivia Ryan the role of beta, but there is still plenty of room for others. So if you want to be part of the *Unbelievably* Pretty Committee and you want to conquer Massie Block, go to OCD tomorrow and wear something cute. Alicia will be scouting all day. This has been Alicia Rivera. Thanks and good night."

Alicia reached under the fleece and wiped away her last tear. Finally it would be Massie's turn to cry.

Isaac stopped the Blocks' Range Rover in front of the big plastic nurse in the Dr. Juice parking lot. He rolled down his window and pushed the red heart in the middle of her white hat. She opened her synthetic blue eyes.

"Welcome to Dr. Juice. I'm Nurse Feelfine. What can Dr. Juice get for you today?" Her voice was soothing and kind.

"One extra-large Slim," Dylan shouted into the nurse's mouth.

"Medium Focus," Kristen yelled.

"Medium Comfort," Claire said. "Please."

"One large Strength and Power blend," Massie said. "Sugar-free."

But if guilt-free had been an option, she would have ordered that.

Massie spent all night wondering if she had been too harsh on Alicia. In the three years they had been BFFs, Alicia only cried that hard once—when she had broken her ankle snowboarding on a field trip to Stowe, Vermont. But Massie kept reminding herself that Alicia started all of this. And there was no telling where she would take it now that she'd been so humiliated. Could she ever top the mural?

Isaac pulled up to the front window and paid for the juices.

"Here you go," he said, handing the cups to the girls in the backseat.

"Thanks, Isaac," they cooed.

Massie took a long sip of Strength & Power. The cold, fruity mixture tasted like summer. It was perfect on such a dreary winter morning. "Yum," she said after she swallowed. She lifted the straw to her mouth and was enjoying another long sip until a sudden blow to her arm knocked the cup away. Pink mush shot all over her chin.

"Orange Uggs, no punch backs," Claire yelled after she whacked Massie on the arm. "Look." She tapped the window and pointed to a high school girl with her jeans tucked into her orange Ugg boots. She was swinging a key chain around her finger while she walked across the Dr. Juice parking lot.

Massie's mouth hung open while drops of Strength & Power dripped down the front of her fluffy white coat.

Kristen and Dylan busted out laughing. And soon everyone was cracking up.

"We only punch when we see Burberry," Massie said, wiping her chin on Claire's backpack. "Not Uggs."

"Then I just made up a new game," Claire said, talking a long sip of Comfort.

"I like it." Massie searched the parking lot for more Uggs.

Kristen banged on her window. "Black Uggs, no punch backs," she said, whacking Dylan.

"Wrong." Dylan punched Kristen. "Those are FUggs. Fake Uggs."

Everyone laughed again.

"Carpool's been fun lately," Massie said. She was about to say, "now that Alicia's gone," but didn't want to mention Alicia's name because they were having such a good time without her. "Claire, is this more fun than riding with Layne?"

"It's definitely different." Claire smiled and took another sip of juice.

Massie leaned back in her seat and grinned. She was proud of Claire for making up a game. "Speaking of Uggs, who wants to go holiday shopping Saturday?"

"It's only Tuesday," Claire said.

"So?" Massie shrugged. She liked to firm up her plans for the weekend as early as possible; even the thought of too much time alone made her nervous.

"I can't," Dylan said. She opened the mini-fridge in the back of the Range Rover and pulled out a small box of Rice Krispies. She tore the package open with her teeth. "My mom is taking me and my sisters to St. Bart's for a three-day Caribbean getaway." She stuck her tongue in the box. When she lifted it out, it was covered in the tiny rice puffs.

Massie turned away in disgust. "What about you, Kristen?"

"I'll be at the mall; I just won't be shopping. But if you buy any gifts, I'll be happy to wrap them for you."

"Yuck," Massie said. "How much character do you have to build before your parents let you have your life back?"

Kristen shrugged and turned to face the window.

"What about *you?*" Massie said to Claire. She couldn't imagine shopping alone with Claire and immediately regretted asking her. She knew Claire couldn't afford to shop in the good stores and even if she did, her taste was so fifth grade. But then again, maybe it was time to embrace Claire completely, not just as an Alicia substitute.

"I would love to go with you, Massie," Claire said. "But every Saturday, I go to the movies with Layne."

She couldn't even get a commitment from Kuh-laire! Claire was supposed to worship her. Everyone was. Alicia might have cheated, lied, and deceived her, but she would have never said no to a shopping trip. Massie took a long sip of Strength & Power.

"Unless," Claire said, leaning forward in her leather seat. "Unless we invite Layne to come with us."

Massie wanted to shout, "I adopted you, NOT that Salvation Army-loving fashion don't!" But she didn't. She needed Claire now that Alicia was gone. If Claire left her, people would definitely think she was losing her grip on the Pretty Committee. And that would be way worse than being seen at the mall with Claire and Layne.

"Has Layne ever shopped at a mall before?" Massie asked. "Does she know that everything they sell is *new?*" She couldn't resist.

Kristen and Dylan laughed.

"Forget it," Claire said to her thumbnail. "Maybe Layne and I should just stick to our regular plan."

"Oh, come on, I was kidding," Massie said. She couldn't believe she was begging to go shopping with Claire and Layne. This was all Alicia's fault. She tried to take another sip from her Dr. Juice cup, but it was all gone.

"Let's just do it another time," Claire said.

"That's probably better," Massie said. "I've been meaning to get my highlights retouched."

Isaac turned into the OCD parking lot and stopped the Range Rover right behind the Riveras' limo. Massie watched from the corner of her eye as Alicia and Olivia stepped out. They both had the exact same super-straight hairdos and Massie wondered if they'd gotten Japanese perms over the weekend. That was something Alicia always said she wanted to do with *Massie.* But that was then. . . .

┌─────────────────────────────────────┐
│   │
│   OCTAVIAN COUNTRY DAY SCHOOL   │
│   SYNCHRONIZED SWIM CLASS   │
│   1:55 PM   │
│   November 18th   │
│   │
└─────────────────────────────────────┘

The humid air clung to Alicia's skin like a cashmere sweater. Every time she stepped out of the chilly locker room and into OCD's indoor pool area, she'd close her eyes and pretend she was walking along one of the beaches in Spain. Unfortunately the Ajax-y smell of chlorine was a cruel reminder that she was about to spend the next forty-five minutes in an Olympic-sized toilet learning how to swim in a circle and wave.

Normally Alicia cursed this class because Massie, Kristen, and Dylan scored pottery as their elective and she got stuck learning synchronized swimming with Claire Lyons. But nothing was normal about this day.

A greasy film of leave-in conditioner trailed behind Alicia as she swam closer to Claire.

"Stay in formation, Alicia," Miss Kuznick said, her pinched voice echoing off the white tile walls.

Alicia swung her legs back into the center of the circle, trying her hardest to avoid touching the water-wrinkled toes of her classmates.

"Look to the right," Miss Kuznick barked.

This put Alicia in direct contact with Faux-livia's left ear.

"Did you find anyone?" she whispered.

Miss Kuznick clapped. "And to the left."

"Coral McAdams kind of reminds me of Dylan," Faux-livia whispered into Alicia's right ear. "She could work."

Alicia strained her eyes so she could sneak a peak at the big-boned girl without moving her head. "You mean *Strawberry?*"

Faux-livia blinked once instead of nodding to avoid falling out of sync.

"Hmmm." Alicia tried to imagine hanging out with Coral after she had made fun of her all semester for having over-hennaed hair. It was a bright, syrupy shade of red.

"Only problem is I hear she has a temper," Faux-livia said out of the corner of her mouth. "Her face turns pink when she gets mad and that's why they call her—"

Miss Kuznick glared at Faux-livia and clapped twice.

Once she looked away, Alicia swam right up to Faux's ear. "I always called her that because I thought she shopped at Strawberry," she said. "Where else would she get those belly chains and magnetic nose rings?"

"Duck dives," Miss Kuznick instructed.

"True," Olivia said before she went underwater.

The more Alicia thought about it, the more she liked the idea. Coral was actually kind of pretty if you could get past the neon hair. She never needed braces, because her perfect teeth looked like rows of white Chiclets, and her eyes were mint green. She had a decent amount of friends and was always talking back to teachers, which gave her major hall cred. If Alicia recruited her, she would win the respect of the fashion rebels. And there were more of them in the seventh grade than Alicia cared to count.

"Good call," Alicia said to Faux-livia when they popped back up for air.

Miss Kuznick shouted, "Switch," and everyone swam toward the ladder. They climbed out of the water and padded toward the metal bench on the side of the pool. The girls who had been sitting stood up and made stride jump entries into the water. Alicia noticed that Claire and Layne were sitting on the other side of Faux.

"I want to see good strong strokes," Miss Kuznick called out to her new group, and Alicia immediately thought of Harris Fisher and his Strokes tickets. Her father promised he would have them tonight.

The idea of placing the yellow windowed envelope in Harris's rugged hands made Alicia's stomach tingle with nervous anticipation. She couldn't wait to tell her new recruits that she'd be going to a concert with a junior; it was so alpha.

Alicia reached under the bench and pulled a Ziploc out from behind one of the metal legs that had been bolted into the ground. She held the bag behind her back and ran her thumb along the seal to open it. Miss Kuznick had caught her using a cell phone one other time while she was on the bench and threatened to throw it in the pool if she used it again. But Alicia decided to chance it. She would die if she missed a call from Harris. And she could always get another phone.

She wiped her wet hands on her burgundy-and-blue OCD towel before checking for messages.

"Did he call?" Faux-livia asked. She kept her eyes focused on the swimmers so as not to attract attention.

Alicia shook her head.

"Call *him*," Faux said.

"I don't have his number," Alicia said.

"Call Cam," Faux demanded.

Alicia was *loving* Faux today. She was turning out to be the perfect beta.

"Done," Alicia said as she hit 11 on her speed dial.

Alicia lowered her head behind the bench, pretending to search for a lost contact lens while she waited for Cam to pick up. Faux-livia lowered her head too so she could listen, but Alicia pushed it away.

"Hello, is Alicia there, please?" Cam said when he answered.

"Very funny," Alicia whispered. Her heart was pounding. "Can you talk?"

"I'm kinda in the middle of dissecting a mouse," he said. "But I guess he's not going anywhere, so yeah. Is this about Claire? Did you talk to her for me?"

"Uh, kind of," Alicia said. "I'm still working on it."

"Oh."

Alicia could hear the disappointment in his voice but didn't have time to reassure him. She pressed her mouth right up against the phone. "I need your brother's number."

"Sure, it's 914-555-04 . . ."

Alicia was punching the number into her phone, trying not to let it slip out of her hands and into the puddle under the bench. "Yeah, what's the rest?"

"You wish," Cam said. "You'll get the last two numbers when you get Claire to hang out with me."

"That's so not f—" Alicia started to say before she was cut off.

"Gotta go," he said. And the line went dead.

"Well?" Faux-livia asked. She was sitting on her hands and bouncing up and down. There were deep purple rings around her eyes because her goggles had been on too tight.

Alicia busted out laughing. She aimed her phone at Faux-livia's face and snapped her picture. Her next instinct was to click over to her address book and e-mail the funny shot to all of her friends. But she stopped herself. Who would she send it to?

"Switch seats with me," Alicia said. "I have to talk to Claire for a minute." "'Kay," Faux said as they quickly traded places.

"Keep looking for a 'Kristen,'" Alicia whispered.

When Alicia sat down, Claire turned and faced Layne.

"Claire, I need to talk to you," Alicia said. Her voice was quiet and soothing. So quiet, in fact, Claire didn't hear her. "Claire, listen—"

"Loser," Layne sneezed.

Claire giggled.

"You're calling *me* a loser?" Alicia hissed. "Funny, Layne, since you're the one wearing a see-through bathing suit and goggles with monster-eye holograms on them!" Alicia leaned past Claire and looked straight at Layne. "FYI, the see-through suit is scary enough; you don't need the goggles."

Layne stood up and walked toward the locker room, her

arms folded across her chest. "Nice split ends," she growled when she passed Alicia.

"Banana boobs," Alicia said back.

Claire looked at Alicia. Her eyes were so red from the chlorine, it looked like she had been crying. "Why are you so mean?"

"I was gonna ask you the same question, Kuh-laire," Alicia said.

Claire lifted her thumbnail to her mouth and started biting.

"Don't worry, I forgive you," Alicia said. "I know how hard it is to say no to Massie Block. You were forced to be mean to me, just like I had to be mean to you when you moved here."

Claire looked down at her pruned fingers. She sat on her hands. "I was mean because you cheated me, Alicia. Not 'cause Massie *made* me."

"I know and I'm sorry for that." Alicia rested her hand on Claire's wet back. "FYI, I'm considering therapy."

Alicia paused to read Claire's face. Was she buying it?

"Claire, look at me," Alicia insisted. "There's no way that mural was *your* idea."

Claire didn't respond. She just kicked her legs and started at the blue and white tiles on the floor.

Alicia sighed. "Sometimes I felt like I had no choice too."

Claire lowered her head and Alicia knew she finally said something right.

"I'm sorry," Claire mouthed. She raised her shoulder and wiped a tear away from her eye. "I felt so bad doing that to you, but you really hurt us. We worked so hard on that uniform design and—"

"I know," Alicia said. "And I'm so sorry." She lifted a wet strand of hair to her eye and squeezed a drop of water off the end when Claire wasn't looking. "Please, please forgive me."

Claire looked up just as a "tear" slid down Alicia's cheek.

"Here, take this," Claire said, handing Alicia the white hoodie she had stuffed behind the bench.

"Thanks." Alicia dabbed her eyes. "I can see why Cam likes you so much."

"Does he really?" Claire said, shifting slightly to face Alicia.

"He e-mails you every day; why do you sound so surprised?"

Claire shrugged. "I dunno—I guess I keep expecting him to change his mind and go for someone prettier."

Alicia watched Claire lower her eyes and turn bright red.

"The only one prettier than you is me and I'm into older guys," Alicia said with a naughty wink. "His brother, Harris, and I have kinda been hanging out lately."

Claire raised her eyebrows.

"It's true," Alicia said. "Hey, how cool would it be if we went over there one day after school? It could be like a double date."

"Incredibly cool," Claire said, clapping the soles of her feet together. "But I dunno." Her legs suddenly stopped moving and her voice trailed off. "I'm kinda having second thoughts about him lately."

"It's just nerves. Don't worry, I'll go with you," Alicia said. "What are you doing after dinner Friday night?"

Now that Friday night sleepovers were no longer on Alicia's calendar, she wanted to fill the time.

"Uh," Claire said. "*This* Friday?"

"Yes, *this* Friday." Alicia paused. "Oh, you're probably going to Massie's, right?"

"No, I was just there last night because—"

"I know, I know," Alicia cut her off, not wanting to be reminded. "You know you're not officially IN if you haven't been invited to be a regular at the sleepover. And if you're not officially IN, Massie has no right to tell you who you can hang out with."

Claire's eyes shifted back and forth while she considered Alicia's point.

"Don't worry, I won't tell a *soul.*" Alicia held out her pinky and Claire grabbed it with hers. They shook.

"Friday night is our secret," Alicia said. "I promise."

"'Kay," Claire said with a guilty smile.

Alicia jumped up and switched back to her old seat on the other side of Faux-livia. She was so pleased with herself, she could hardly sit still. "Did you find us a Kristen?" she whispered.

Faux-livia stuffed some loose strands of blond hair into her bathing cap. "What about Kori Gedman?" she said into Alicia's ear. "If you can look past the bad posture, she's actually kinda cool."

Alicia leaned forward and took a peek.

She thought Kori looked like a parenthesis because she was arched over all the time. "Explain," Alicia whispered.

"Well, she's like the second-best athlete in our grade, for starters," Faux said, "Kristen being the first. . . ."

"Yeah, yeah, no need to mention *her* name," Alicia said, waving Kristen's name out of the air.

"Sorry," Faux said. "But you have to admit she even kinda looks like *her.* You know, the thin blonde hair, the braids; she even has a psycho laugh. It would almost be like getting another Kris . . . another one."

"Yeah, without the annoying parents," Alicia said, warming up to the idea. "I like it. Good work."

"Switch," Miss Kuznick announced.

"Thanks," Faux said, feeling the top of her head for her goggles.

Alicia leaned back on the bench and touched the outside of the Ziploc. It was important that the bag was sealed and tucked safely out of harm's way before she jumped back in the pool. Now that she could deliver Claire to Cam, Alicia could get the last two digits of Harris's phone number. And she wasn't about to let the dripping wet girls in group two soak her battery.

When the bell rang, Alicia raced out of the pool and speed-walked to the locker room. She had twenty minutes to change and call Cam before French. As she was towel-drying her hair and checking for split ends, Faux burst through the locker room doors with the sealed cell phone.

"Thanks." Alicia grabbed the bag out of her hand. "If I wasn't in such a hurry, I would have grabbed it myself."

"No problem." Faux shrugged it off like it had been nothing. She seemed happy to be of service, much like Alicia had been with Massie all those years.

Alicia flipped open her phone, hit 11, and tapped her nails against a metal locker while she waited for Cam to answer.

"Hey," he said when he picked up. "Did you talk to her?"

"Yeah, we'll be over Friday night," Alicia said.

"Nice."

Alicia could tell he was trying not to sound excited. "Now give me the rest of Harris's phone number. I have exactly eight minutes."

Within seconds Alicia was dressed and dialing Harris Fisher's cell phone number. She walked over to the mirror and quickly put on a bit of mascara.

"It's ringing," she said to Faux. But spoke loud enough for Strawberry and Kori to hear too. "Shoot, I got HARRIS FISHER'S ANSWERING MACHINE. I guess I'll LEAVE HIM A MESSAGE."

Kori and Strawberry peered around their open lockers. Alicia pretended not to notice anything except an imaginary piece of hair on the sleeve of her blazer. She pulled it off casually, knowing full well that she was playing to a captive audience.

"Yo, this is Harris and if you don't know what to do by now, hang up," his voice message said.

After the beep Alicia started pacing. She loved his smooth confident voice and was determined to sound just as alluring.

"Uh, h-hey there, Harris, it's me. Alicia. You know, uh, Rivera." Alicia looked up and noticed that at least five more girls had gathered round to listen. Alicia knew she finally had something Massie Block didn't have—experience with boys.

She casually placed her foot on the changing bench and

rested her arm against the top of her leg before continuing. She wanted her pose to scream confidence.

"Anyway, just wanted you to know I'll be over Friday night around dinnertime . . ." Then she changed her tone to a soft purr. "To drop off a little something I *know* you want." She threw in a naughty giggle for effect and then ended with a "ciao."

Alicia snapped her phone shut and nonchalantly twisted her damp, tangled hair into a ponytail as though phone calls like this were part of her daily routine.

Six girls stood motionless and stared at Alicia with their mouths open. It looked like she had hit pause on a scene in a movie. It was perfect.

"That was incredible," Faux-livia said to Alicia as they pushed past the dumbfounded girls.

"Which part?" Alicia said with a Massie-esque half smile.

"All of it. I love how you started it with 'hey' instead of 'hi.' That was so cool."

"Thanks," Alicia said, bursting out of the locker room and into the busy halls. She walked with perfect jazz posture.

"Uh, maybe we should go the other way," Faux-livia said when she saw Kristen and Dylan at the Starbucks kiosk drinking Dr. Juices.

"No, it's okay," Alicia said, heading straight for them. "I knew they'd be here."

"Huh?" Faux-livia said.

"We won't have to find a knockoff Kristen and Dylan if we can have the real ones, right?" Alicia said, never taking her brown eyes off her targets.

"Brilliant," Faux said.

Alicia took a deep breath. "Wait here—I'll be right back."

"Good luck," Faux whispered as Alicia marched on.

"Hey," Alicia said when she stopped in front of Kristen and Dylan. She spoke as if nothing had happened. "Why aren't you drinking chai lattes?"

Dylan popped a yogurt-covered soy nut in her mouth and stared off into the distance.

"Well?" Alicia said with a playful smile.

Kristen lowered her head and searched her LeSportsac.

"I'm sorry for cheating, okay?" Alicia said. "I didn't mean to hurt you. I was just so over Massie bossing me around—"

"We get it," Kristen whispered, looking around to see if Massie was coming. "Massie made us do the mural thing. We actually felt pretty bad about it. But you shouldn't have cheated us."

"I know," Alicia said. "Believe me, I wish I could take it all back. I miss you guys."

"Yeah, it sucks," Dylan said, dropping a handful of soy nuts into her open mouth. "But we can't be friends *now.*"

"Why? You don't *have* to stay friends with Massie." Alicia spoke quickly. "I'm doing so much better on my own. I have plans with Harris Fisher Friday after school, and a few of the girls from synchro want to start hanging out." She paused for dramatic effect. "I feel free."

"Pause. Rewind," Kristen said, punching imaginary buttons in the air. "You're hanging out with Harris?"

"Yup." Alicia raised her palm in the air.

"Think you could introduce me to some of his friends?" Dylan asked.

"Given," Alicia said with pride. "I am also setting up weekly shopping trips into the city. Massie still only does those once a month, right?" Alicia didn't give them time to answer. "Oh, and my loco cousin Nina is visiting soon from Spain. She's the one who taught me how to make out."

"Really?" Kristen whispered.

"Yup."

"Back away from the EW; move quickly or risk contamination," a familiar voice said.

Alicia felt a chill run down her spine. She turned and came face-to-face with Massie, who was sipping from a big plastic cup that said Sugar-Free Strength on the side.

"Let's go," Massie said.

Alicia looked at Kristen and Dylan, urging them with her eyes to tell Massie off. "Coming," Kristen and Dylan said at the exact same time.

Alicia waited for them to whisper something to her like, "We'll call you later," but they simply walked away without saying another word.

"Bean, stay away from the Godivas. They're for the guests."
Massie pulled the gold foil out of her dog's mouth and put the
chocolate back in the center of Kristen's goose down pillow.
She smoothed the sleeping bags with her hands and pulled
the bottoms to make sure there were no creases in the nylon.

"It's easier setting up for three, isn't it, Bean?" Massie said.

Bean barked twice.

At first Massie set up a fourth place out of habit but
immediately stuffed the bedding back in the closet when
she remembered that Alicia wouldn't be joining them.

Massie checked her cell phone. Kristen and Dylan were
sixteen minutes late. She added a few more BBQ soy nuts
into the white china bowl on the juice bar and restacked the
chocolate-covered Rice Krispie squares so they made a perfect pyramid. The Sub-Zero fridge was stocked with Perrier,
Red Bull, and Inez's virgin piña coladas, and the chilled
pasta salad was the perfect temperature. Red licorice and
big swirled lollipops jetted out of crystal Tiffany vases
on the window ledges, and the thirty vanilla candles that
had been placed around the room were already giving off
a warm, sweet smell. Even the six-CD player was loaded
with the perfect mix of pop and rap. Everything was in its

151

proper place. Her guests were the only things missing.

Massie quickly looked up when she heard the sliding glass door open.

"It's about time," she said.

"What, sweetie?" Kendra said. Bean ran over to her side and started nipping at the bottoms of her black satin pajamas.

"Mom, what are you doing here?"

"I brought a few extra cashmeres just in case you get cold." She pulled three cream-colored blankets out of an orange Hermès shopping bag.

"Thanks," Massie said, looking at her naked wrist. She had taken off her red leather Coach watch while she was helping Inez ice the Rice Krispie squares and forgotten to put it back on. "What time is it?"

"I stopped wearing a watch three days ago," Kendra said, shaking out the blankets. "We just finished *The Power of Now* in my self-help book club and it's all about living in the present. So technically, the time is now." She smiled and looked at Massie with raised eyebrows.

Massie rolled her eyes and grabbed her cell phone out of the pocket on her green Juicy hoodie. She flipped it open and saw that it was 8:19 PM . . . almost twenty minutes late! She snapped it shut and heard another purple rhinestone land on the new light beige floors.

Kendra hung the blankets over the thigh adductor machine. "It's going to be great having a home gym, isn't it?" She walked toward Massie, her kitten heel slippers clacking against the floors with every step she took. She put her thin, bony arm around Massie's shoulders and pulled her close. "Isn't it?"

"I guess," Massie said, looking around the barn that used to belong to her horse, Brownie.

When the horse was little, Massie had covered the walls with posters of young fillies that she thought Brownie would find sexy. She drew pictures of big grassy fields and rainbows for her horse and tacked them into the soft wood around his stall. She even buried her old shirts in the haystacks so Brownie would always know that Massie was close by. But now the white stallion lived at the upscale stable Galwaugh Farms. And the only thing left from Massie's past was the mural she had painted with Kristen, Dylan, and Claire.

"I can't wait for the mirrors to go up," Massie said, turning her back to the wall.

"It's a shame we have to cover up your painting," Kendra said, admiring her daughter's mural. "It was such a neat art class assignment. We never did anything like that when I went to OCD."

"I already handed in photos of the mural, so I don't need it anymore."

"What did Mrs. Nish think of it?" Kendra asked.

Massie walked over to the fridge, pulled a piece of ziti out of the pasta bowl, and dropped it in her mouth. She casually dropped one for Bean, hoping her mother wouldn't notice. "She said it was very effective. I think I got an A."

"That's great, sweetie," Kendra said in a relaxed tone.

Usually her mother's voice sounded strained and anxious. "What else are you doing in school these days?"

Massie watched as her mother lowered herself onto an exercise bench. She crossed her legs and leaned forward, her chin resting in the palm of her hand. It was like she was about to watch one of her favorite Lifetime movies.

"We're learning all about J. C.'s campaigns and how he did everything because he wanted to be popular and famous," Massie said.

Kendra jumped to her feet. Her inner-peace moment was over.

"They're teaching you that Jesus Christ did everything to be *popular?*" She sounded ready to sue.

"No." Massie crinkled her nose and looked at her mother like she had gone mad. "Julius Caesar."

"Ohhh," Kendra said, sitting back down again. She closed her eyes and exhaled slowly. "Go on."

"He wanted to be known for being a great leader," Massie said. "He even wrote about all of his campaigns in a journal and sent his books to Rome so people would know his name throughout history."

"Sort of like you when you were younger," Kendra said, a soft smile forming on her tight face. "You used to keep those in-and-out lists. They were *so* cute."

"Ehmagawd, I still do that," Massie said in a burst of uninhibited excitement. "Me and J. C. are so the same."

"And don't you love Caesar salads?"

Massie rolled her eyes and looked at the door. "Thanks

for the blankets, Mom. You probably want to get back to the house before the rain, right?"

"Rain?"

Massie looked at her Steve Madden sheepskin slippers and nodded. With any luck, Kristen and Dylan would be arriving any minute. And she didn't want them to know her mother had been in GLU headquarters, even though technically Kendra was the owner.

Kendra hurried over to her daughter and kissed her on the forehead. "Have fun, my little Caesar. You too, Bean." She shook the dog's paw.

After her mother had left, Massie lifted Bean onto her lap. "Bean, if I'm going to conquer Alicia, I have to create loyalty among my troops. It's the only way to keep them from leaving me and joining her army. Julius probably did the same thing."

Bean barked three times.

"What? What's wrong? I'm not hurting anybody this time. It's a *nice* plan," Massie pleaded.

"Who are you talking to?" Kristen said as she pulled open the sliding glass door.

"No one." Massie's face turned red.

"Heyyy." Dylan and Kristen scurried over to hug Massie.

"Did we come to the right place?" Dylan said, looking around. "The barn looks totally different."

"How much did this whole thing cost?" Kristen looked at the free weights, exercise machines, balls, ropes, and mats strategically placed around the room. She slowly moved toward the row of plasma TVs that hung above each of the four cardio machines as if she were in awe of their beauty. "Seriously, how much?"

"I dunno, like a million dollars or something; who cares?" Massie said, waiting for them to apologize for keeping her waiting.

"Dylan told me to ask," Kristen said.

"I did not," Dylan snapped.

Kristen laughed her phlegmy laugh, then Massie joined in. She forgot all about how late they were. Nothing made her happier than laughing with her friends and she didn't want to waste another minute of their sleepover being mad.

Massie noticed Dylan staring at the mural. "Why were you talking to her in the halls the other day? It's like you miss her or something."

"Please." Dylan sat down on her sleeping bag and unwrapped the chocolate on her pillow. She popped it in her mouth and continued speaking. "I miss my retainer more than I miss *her.*"

Kristen lay beside her. She pulled open her A&F overnight bag and took out a book of crossword puzzles, a Bic pen, and a mini-flashlight. She placed them on the floor beside her. "Yeah, and I miss the T. J. Maxx cardigan my mother makes me wear to school more than I miss her."

"So what were you talking about?" Massie crouched down and stuck her thumbnail into her chocolate.

"We told you a billion times," Kristen said. "She was bragging about some date she had with Harris Fisher, like that was supposed to impress us."

"Yeah, try going out with a guy in *our* grade," Dylan said, peeling the silver wrapper off a Hershey's Kiss. "Now, *that* would impress me."

"Puh-lease. She's not really hanging out with Harris," Massie said, passing around a vase of licorice. "Is she?"

"She's going over there tonight," Dylan said. "Or at least that's what she said. We all know what a liar she is."

"Besides, if Harris *is* hanging out with Alicia, it's probably because he knows he can't get *you*," Kristen said.

"Too true." Massie slapped her thigh with a Twizzler. "I'm over those Fisher boys, especially Cam."

"Whaddaya mean?" Kristen said, sitting up on her knees.

"Well, it's a secret." Massie tore her licorice into tiny pieces.

"About who?" Dylan reached for the chocolate on Kristen's pillow. She unwrapped it without taking her eyes off Massie.

"Me." Massie lowered her eyes. So far, her plan was working perfectly.

"Ooohhh, tell us." Dylan's green eyes widened and her cheeks turned the color of her hair. Massie thought her friend looked pretty and almost felt guilty for manipulating her. But she was in the middle of a war.

"I can't," Massie said. "It's personal."

"Seven-letter word for *you're full of it*, please." Kristen pounded her fist on the floor. "I thought we told each other everything."

"Yeah, well, this is different."

"Why don't you trust us?" Dylan asked.

"Ever since Alicia betrayed me, I don't trust anyone,"

Massie said. "And now that I know you're talking to her, I really can't trust you."

"We're not talking to her," Kristen insisted.

Massie ignored her and continued. "Alicia is a gossip master. If anyone could get you to talk, it would be her. And if she knew my secret, I'd be so over." Massie shook her head. "No. No way, I can't."

"Oh, please, we'll do anything," Dylan said.

"Hmmm." Massie scratched her head. "Well, I guess if you told me your deepest, darkest secrets, I could trust you."

"Okay," Dylan said without even thinking about it. "Tell us everything—don't leave one thing out." She lay facedown on her sleeping bag and propped herself up on her elbows.

Kristen did the same.

"No way," said Massie. "You first."

"I dunno, mine is *really* top secret," Kristen said, twirling one of her blond braids around her finger. "What if you tell?"

"You have my word that as long as we are friends, I will never tell." Massie held out her pinky.

"But what if we stop being friends?" Dylan chimed in. "Are you going to tell then?"

"I guess this means we'll have to stay best friends forever," Massie said.

"Done," Kristen said.

"Yeah, done," Dylan agreed.

"Okay," Massie said, holding out her pinky. "I, Massie Block, swear that as long as we are friends, I will never repeat what I am about to hear to any soul, living or dead. Not even for gossip points."

Kristen and Dylan repeated the pledge and the three girls locked pinkies. Massie breathed a sign of relief. Now her friends would never leave her for Alicia or anyone else. Never.

Massie leaned over and grabbed Kristen's pen and book of crossword puzzles. She tore a page out of the book and pulled off the blue pen cap with her teeth.

"Hey," Kristen snapped. "What are you doing?"

"We'll draw names to see who goes first," Massie said. She wrote Kristen's name twice and Dylan's once. Massie was willing to share her secret; she just didn't want to go first. She crumpled up the three pieces of paper and put them in her palm. She held it out for Kristen. "You pick."

Kristen reached out her fingers, plucked up a ball of paper, and quickly opened it. "Ugh, I got me!"

Massie closed her fist and rolled onto her stomach. "Go ahead."

Kristen sat up and crossed her legs. "I don't really have anything."

"Forget it, then," Massie said.

"Okay, wait, now that I think about it, there's this one thing. . . ."

Kristen's aqua eyes searched their faces. "You swear you're not going to tell?"

"Swear," Massie and Dylan said at the same time.

She sighed heavily, then began. "'Kay, well, you know how you pick me up every morning at the Montador for carpool?"

"Yeah," Massie said. Her heart started to pick up speed.

"Well. I. Kinda. Don't. Really. Live. There." Kristen spoke slowly, checking their faces after each word.

"Huh?" Dylan said.

"I live next door in the Brickview Apartments."

"Ew, why?"

"We're poor."

Bean buried her face in her paws.

Massie didn't know what to say next and wished she had turned on the stereo before they started. Was Kristen making this up? She looked at Dylan to see her reaction.

"I shouldn't have told you," Kristen said, rolling onto her stomach. She pulled her pillow over her face and kicked her legs.

"Yes, you should have," Massie said as she processed the news. Everything suddenly started to make sense: the after-school job, the obsession with money, the lack of designer clothes. . . . "Wait, I thought your dad was a famous art dealer."

"He *was*," Kristen said into the pillow. "Heostllfhismoney-aewyearsoverore."

"What?" Dylan ripped the pillow away from Kristen's face.

"I said . . ." Kristen wiped her eyes. "He lost all of his money a few years ago. That's why I've never invited you guys over before."

"I always wondered about that," Massie said. "I just thought your parents were too uptight."

"Well, they are." Kristen looked at her fingers. "But that's not why I never had you over."

"How can you afford OCD?" Massie asked.

"Scholarship," Kristen said. "Why do you think I'm always studying?"

"I just thought you were a geek," Massie said.

Kristen let out a small phlegmy chuckle. "You know the OCD benefit at your house every year?"

Massie nodded, afraid of what she might hear next.

"Last year the money went to me," Kristen said.

"No way, that's so cool," Massie said.

"I can't believe no one knows this but us," Dylan said.

"Actually, Claire knows," said Kristen.

"Kuh-laire?" Now Massie was *really* shocked. "She knows one of your secrets before I do?" Massie felt dizzy. She stood up and walked to the fridge to get some Perrier.

Kristen stood up and followed her. "I *thought* I was telling you one night when we were IM'ing, but it was the time Claire got on your computer, so—"

"And she never told anyone?" Massie said, yanking open the fridge door.

"Nope," Kristen said. "Not a soul."

"What an idiot—you know how many gossip points she could have scored?" Dylan said, walking toward them.

Kristen put her hands on her hips and glared at Dylan.

"Kidding." Dylan pushed past Massie and grabbed a virgin piña colada out of the fridge.

"Claire was really cool about it," Kristen added.

"Impressive," Massie said with a distant smile. She turned back to Kristen and held out her arms for a hug. "Great secret, Kristen; you have our trust."

Kristen hugged Massie back.

"My clothes are your clothes."

Dylan put down her frothy drink and joined them. "Yeah, and I'll totally give you half of my allowance."

"I'm not third world." Kristen cackled, then wiped her eyes. "But thanks." She pulled out of the group hug. "Okay, who's next?"

"I'll pick the next name," Massie said. She made a show of mixing the remaining two pieces of paper by shaking them around in her hand like a pair of dice. Finally she stopped and read one. "Dylan."

"'Kay." Dylan sat down on one of the white leather stools at the juice bar. She tapped her nails on the marble countertop a few times before she spoke.

"Come on," Kristen urged.

"I'm thinking!" Dylan said. She took in a deep breath, then let it out slowly before she finally spoke. "Okay, so you know how I told you my mother is taking me and my sisters to St. Bart's tomorrow?"

"Yeah," Kristen said.

Massie was too excited to speak.

"Well, she's really sending me to St. Barf's." Dylan pulled the cherry out of her piña colada and bit off the stem.

"That fat camp in upstate New York?" Massie asked.

"Yup," Dylan admitted. "I forget the real name; it's something like St. Bartholomew's. But whatever it's called, it's supposed to be good. Half of the guests on my mom's show have been there."

"Why are you going?" Kristen said.

"My mom doesn't think I have the self-control to stick to my diet."

"I didn't know you were on a new diet," Massie said.

Dylan rubbed the cherry stem between her thumb and index finger. "I guess that's her point."

"Well, you look *beautiful* to us," Massie said, drawing Dylan into another group hug. "Dieting is hard. You think I have an easy time staying away from sugar? I swear I don't know how Claire stays so thin."

"I bet her poop is shaped like a gummy bear," Kristen said, then cackled at her own joke. Massie and Dylan laughed too.

"We love you, no matter how fat you are," Massie said before their next group hug.

"Thanks, you guys." Dylan wiped her runny nose on Massie's shoulder. "I guess the cool part is my mom told me if I lose ten pounds, she'll get me a nose job."

Massie looked at Dylan's tiny button nose. "You want a nose job?"

"Nah," Dylan said. "She's just trying to be nice."

"Cool." Massie clapped. "Now who wants some Rice Krispie Treats? I iced them myself."

"Wait, what about *your* secret?" Kristen narrowed her eyes.

"Oops, I totally forgot." Massie knew she'd never get away with it but loved herself for trying. "Thanks for reminding me." She paused. "This goes to the grave, right?"

"YES!" Dylan and Kristen shouted.

Massie picked her nails, trying to look nervous. "My secret is that Alicia was right. I had a crush on Cam Fisher." She raised her eyes and looked at their faces. They looked anxious to hear more.

"Yeah," Dylan said. "And?"

"And it started at my boy-girl Halloween party and kept going past the OCD fashion show. We e-mailed for a while and I thought he was sweet, but when I found out Claire liked him, I gave up."

"What? Why?" Dylan said.

"Uh, because I knew I could find someone else and Claire probably couldn't."

"That is sooo sweet of you," Kristen said, and then paused. "Wait, why did you tell her that he was an EW and that she should break up with him? Is it because you realized you were hopelessly infatuated with him and you couldn't bear to see him love another?"

Massie forgot they had witnessed that and had to think fast.

"NO, I told her that because I realized he was a total Harris wannabe and I was trying to protect her. By that time I was totally over him anyway."

"Oh," Kristen said.

Massie hoped to God that answer satisfied her. "Group hug?"

"You may have a broken heart, but it's made of gold," Dylan exclaimed as she wrapped her arms around Massie.

"You're the best friend anyone could ever have," Kristen said as she joined them.

Suddenly Massie heard someone walking in the dried leaves outside the barn.

"What was that?" Dylan hissed.

"Is someone listening?" said Kristen. "I'll die if anyone heard I'm poor."

"I bet it's Claire," Dylan said. "I mean, can we completely trust her?"

"Yes," Kristen and Massie said at the same time.

"Well, you never know," Dylan said.

"It was probably just Bean," Massie said, looking at the doggie door.

"Wearing boots?"

Massie felt her insides freeze when she thought of their secrets falling into the wrong hands.

"I'm positive," Massie said, trying to stay strong for the others. Unsure of what to do next, she walked over to her sleeping bag and sat down. She felt a little dizzy and slightly nauseous.

"Ehmagawd," Massie gasped. *Bean was sound asleep on her pillow.*

"What is it?" Kristen shouted.

"Nothing, stay there, it's okay," she said, covering Bean with a cashmere blanket. "I thought I saw a mouse, but it was just my cell phone."

Massie hung her head between her knees and prayed for the sick feeling in her stomach to pass.

The tires on Claire's green bike crunched over the gravel as she rolled it down the Blocks' driveway. She stopped every few steps, held her breath, and listened, just to make sure Massie, Kristen, and Dylan didn't hear her. She didn't want them to know she was sneaking off to Cam's with Alicia. They'd call her a FEW (Friend of Eternal Wannabes) and that would be the end of their friendship, which had only just begun.

When she made it safely to the street, Claire threw her leg over the middle bar and plopped down on the black padded seat. The jeans Alicia lent her were too tight and Claire could feel the button digging into her stomach. She'd called Alicia to tell her they were too small, but Alicia insisted she wear them anyway.

"Guys love tight jeans," she told Claire. "Trust me."

But these days Claire had no idea who to trust. . . .

Was Massie really looking out for Claire by telling her to stay away from Cam? Or was Alicia right? Was Massie just jealous? Claire shook the questions from her head and hoped the answers would come soon. She was about to face Cam and still had no idea what to tell him.

Claire flicked on her bike light and pedaled as fast as she could, trying to ignore the cold winter wind that bit her ears and stung her hands. She'd thought about bringing a hat but didn't want her bangs to be pressed against her forehead when she saw Cam.

At the corner of Holly and Rutherford, Claire slammed on her brakes and waited for Alicia under the streetlight. They'd promised to meet a block away from the Fishers' house so they could show up together.

The wind whistled as it snaked around the naked tree branches above her, and the chimes on the front porch of 50 Holly started clanging like they did in horror movies, right before someone got stabbed. Claire bit her nails and searched the street for Alicia. . . .

Suddenly Claire heard a "pssst." Or at least she thought she did. She didn't want to turn around suddenly, afraid of what she might see.

"Claire," the voice whispered again. "Sorry I'm late."

Alicia appeared under the yellow light on a brand-new vintage-looking Schwinn. The red-and-silver bike looked thick and heavy, like something kids from the 1950s rode on paper routes. But because Alicia was on it, it looked cool.

"Why are you whispering?" Claire asked, not realizing she was whispering too.

"I have no idea." Alicia laughed.

Claire giggled nervously.

"Where's your hat?" Alicia pulled the white cashmere cap off her head and stuffed it in her bag. It had looked beautiful against her dark complexion, but Claire knew exactly why it had to go.

"I didn't want it to mess up my hair." Claire rolled her eyes, fully aware of how girly and silly she sounded.

"That's why I brought these." Alicia pulled out a wood brush and a black-and-white art deco compact. She brushed her hair and the sweet smell of green apple conditioner filled the air. It mixed with her Angel perfume and completely canceled out Claire's new kiwi oil from the Body Shop.

"You want?" Alicia held out the brush and mirror.

Claire took them and brushed her bangs. The metal bristles scratched against her forehead, but she ignored the pain.

"Remember," Alicia said, dabbing frosty pink gloss on her plump lips, "don't act dorky and squirmy when you're there. Try to be confident. Boys are like dogs—they can sense fear."

Claire pulled a thin tube of vanilla-flavored Softlips SPF 30 out of her front pocket and rubbed it across her mouth. "How do you know all of this?"

"I have a lot of *experience*," Alicia said.

"Aren't you even a little bit nervous to see Harris?" Claire asked.

"Puh-lease. Do I *look* nervous?"

"No."

"How *do* I look?" Alicia asked. "Rate me."

"Huh?" Claire said.

"Out of ten," Alicia said. "Ten being the best."

"Nine point three," Claire said knowing it was an understatement. Alicia looked beautiful. Her dark eyes were lined with black pencil and her lids were dusted with a touch of sparkly gold shadow. Her cheeks were rosy and her hair was thick and smooth. Claire couldn't see Alicia's outfit under her gray fitted coat but knew it had to be incredible.

"Why not higher?" Alicia asked.

"You can only get higher if you're really dressed up," Claire said, making up her own last minute rule.

"Good." Alicia sounded satisfied. "I like that."

"What about me?" Claire asked shyly.

"Eight point seven," Alicia said. "Love the tight jeans and the lavender sweater, but you lose points on the paint-stained Keds." Alicia shrugged. "Sorry, but you know how I feel about sneakers." She took one last look at Claire and then held out her hand.

"What?"

"Give me that lip stuff," Alicia said. "I can't stand to see you put that back in your pocket. It puts a lumpy line in the jeans."

Claire slapped the tube down in Alicia's glove like she was giving her five. "Is there anything you *don't* know?"

"Yeah, I *don't know* how Massie is going to get by without me." Alicia shook her head and sighed. "Oh, well. Let's go."

Alicia dropped the tube of Softlips SPF 30 in her bag, then pushed off on the pavement with the bottoms of her red leather boots. Claire followed.

"Alicia?" Claire shouted above the wind. "I'm really sorry about what we did to you."

"I know. Thanks," Alicia said. "I'm sorry too."

"Do you think you and Massie will ever be friends again?" Claire reached down and quickly unbuttoned her jeans because she couldn't bike, talk, and breathe at the same time.

"Doubt it." Alicia kept her eyes fixed on the road ahead. "I like having my Friday nights free. And I can hang out with whoever I want, especially boys. Massie never hangs out with guys. It's so boring."

Claire felt a wave of regret and sadness. She would never know what it had been like to hang out with the Pretty Committee in the golden days, when they were all friends. Claire was a part of the new generation and had a sinking feeling it wouldn't be as much fun.

"Alicia, do you really think Cam is a Harris wannabe?"

"No," Alicia said. "For starters, Harris doesn't write notes like that. That's all Cam." Alicia stopped her bike and held out her hand. "Let me read it again."

Claire stopped too. She felt a sudden rush of cold prickly sweat in her armpits. "Uh, I don't have it anymore. I lost it."

"What do you mean?" Alicia held out her hand again.

"Well, Massie kind of got rid of it for me." Claire regretted telling the truth as soon as she saw Alicia's mouth fall open. "It was for my own good."

"Did you ask her to?"

"No, but—"

"I'm sorry, but a good friend wouldn't do that." Alicia started pedaling.

Claire knew she was right but couldn't imagine being on Massie's bad side again. Nothing was worse than that . . . not even heartache.

When they arrived at the Fishers' house, Claire smiled to herself. It was number 277, the same number her house was in Florida . . . a good sign. They even had the same American flag tacked above the doorway.

Cam's house wasn't like the ones in Massie's neighborhood. The driveway wasn't circular or a mile long. It seemed barely big enough for their black Mustang.

"Where do they put their other cars?" Alicia whispered. "Do you think there's a big garage in the back or something?"

Claire shrugged. "Maybe they only have one car."

"Impossible."

They dropped their bikes on the front lawn in front of the modest white house. The gray porch that led to the door was cluttered with rakes, skateboards, and Timberland boots. Claire felt instantly comforted by the mess.

A flash of light appeared near the Mustang. Claire and Alicia jumped.

"Hello?" Alicia said, reaching for her bike.

"Yo," said a deep voice. "Over here."

As the girls got closer to the hood of the car, Claire thought she smelled a fire. Then she saw another flash of light. It was Harris. He was sitting on top of his car, lighting matches and tossing them on the asphalt.

"Another fun Friday night in suburbia," he said when he saw them. "Hi, I'm Harris. You must be Claire."

The instant she looked into his emerald green eyes, Claire felt the backs of her knees tingle. He had a model's features and a movie star's charm.

"Uh, yeah." She shook his hand. It felt strong and a little calloused, like he had been lifting weights. "How did you know?"

"Cam described you perfectly."

Claire was desperate to ask what he meant. Did Cam say she was pretty and Harris agreed and that's how he knew who she was? Or did he say she had blond stringy bangs that sometimes split down the middle and looked like an upside-down *V*?

Claire remembered Alicia's advice and tried to act "confident."

"Thanks."

The squeak of the screen door distracted them from the awkward moment. Cam appeared wearing a red Volcom T-shirt, torn jeans, and white socks. He ran out onto the front porch, rubbing his bare arms and hopping up and down.

"Come inside—it's freezing out," he said, waving them in.

Claire walked toward him, secretly buttoning her jeans under her coat. It wasn't until she stepped up onto the wooden porch that she realized Alicia and Harris weren't behind her. They were still on the hood of his car.

"Forget about them," Cam said. "They obviously enjoy freezing to death."

But Claire couldn't just "forget about them." They were supposed to be her buffers. Now Claire was alone with Cam.

"So," Cam said, waving his arm through the air. "This is my house."

Claire stood in the dimly lit hallway and smiled gently at the pea green carpet that lined the short flight of stairs to the second floor. It felt nice to be in a home that didn't look like a museum.

"I love it."

"Can I take your coat?" Cam asked Claire. His smile was soft and his voice was kind.

She slipped out of her blue puffy jacket and handed it to him. Claire felt her fingers brush up against his wrist by accident. Her stomach dropped like it did when she rode the Scream! at Six Flags.

"Smells like kiwi," he said when he took the jacket. He placed it over the banister, then pressed his hand on it, just to make sure it wouldn't fall.

Claire giggled and shrugged. She looked at her Keds. This was the longest she and Cam had ever been alone together. Where was Alicia?

"Come meet my parents." His green and blue eyes flickered. "They're in the kitchen."

Claire followed the lasagna smell into a quaint country-style kitchen. Oatmeal-colored lace curtains had been draped over the window above the sink and all of the cabinets were painted red and white. The round wood table was full of sauce-stained dishes, but Mr. and Mrs. Fisher didn't seem to mind. They looked happy, sitting together drinking coffee.

"Mom, Dad, this is Claire," Cam said.

"Nice to meet you, Claire; we've heard a lot about you," Mrs. Fisher said, pushing up the sleeves of her pink Old Navy sweatshirt. She was the first mother Claire had seen in Westchester who actually looked like she had kids.

"Nice to meet you too." Claire could feel her face turning red.

"I understand you're from Florida." Mr. Fisher wiped his mustache with a white paper napkin. "We used to take the kids to Disney World all the time, but I got sick of standing on line for eleven hours with sweat dripping down my back, you know?" He laughed, then started coughing.

Claire smiled and tugged her bangs.

"Wanna go downstairs?" Cam asked. "I was just playing Underground 2. I have two control panels."

"Cool." Claire wondered if she should have told him she thought video games were boring. "Nice meeting you both." She waved, and Cam's parents smiled.

Claire followed Cam down the stairs to the basement. The walls were covered in the same brown carpet that lined the stairs and Claire let her fingers brush across it as she followed him. It was the first time she had ever seen carpet used as wallpaper.

A big mushy mustard-colored L-shaped couch was in the center of the room and the glass coffee table had been pushed aside. A can of Coke and a bag of pretzels were on the floor along with a jumble of black wires and two Xbox control panels. Cam sat on the floor beside the soda and leaned back against the couch. Claire quickly unbuttoned her tight jeans, then did the same, thankful for her bulky lavender sweater.

"Your parents seem nice," Claire said, wondering what Alicia and Harris were talking about.

"Yeah, they're pretty cool." Cam handed Claire a control panel.

There was an awkward silence while Cam rebooted the game. Did he think she was dull? Did he regret inviting her over? Could he hear her breathing?

"It's cool that we're finally hanging out," he said to the TV screen. "I wasn't sure you were gonna show up."

Claire wanted to tell Cam that she liked him way more than as a friend. That she was so excited to be hanging out with him . . . that she didn't mean to avoid him, but Massie made her . . . that she only listened to Massie because she was finally IN and couldn't stand being OUT again . . . But she didn't. He wouldn't understand.

"Of course I showed up." Claire bit her thumbnail. She pretended to cross her legs so she could lean into his armpit to take a whiff. She wanted to know if Massie was right about his BO problem. Claire inhaled deeply. All she could smell was his Drakkar Noir. He smelled great.

Cam bobbed his head. "How killer is the sound track on this game?"

"Awesome," Claire said about some grating hip-hop song she had never heard before.

"I'll burn a CD for you." Cam shook his floppy bangs out of his eyes. But the sudden jerky movement sent his red car into a metal garbage can. "Nooo," he shouted when it burst into flames.

"Bummer," Claire lied. "I guess the game's over."

"Huh?" Cam's gaze was still fixated on his burning car.

"So what's going on with your brother and Alicia?" Claire asked. "Are they, you know, *together?*"

Cam finally shut off the TV and looked at Claire. "What?

No, they're not *together.* He's like four years older than she is."

"So why are they hanging out?"

"They're not. She's just dropping off Strokes tickets," Cam said, reaching for a pretzel. "How gross would that be if he started dating Alicia? Can't he go to jail for that?"

Claire shrugged and helped herself to a pretzel even though she didn't have an appetite. She hoped the chewing would keep her mind off the one question that had been racing through her mind like the red car in the video game. . . . What if Massie found out she was with Cam?

Cam stuck the control panel under Claire's nose and waved it around like a hot pastry. "Wanna play?" he asked. "I bet you'll beat my score."

"Uh, normally I would, but I should get going." She snapped a pretzel in half but didn't eat it.

"You just got here," he said, lifting his soda can and taking a small sip. "Do I smell or something?"

Claire immediately thought of Massie.

"No, it's not that." Claire giggled. "I actually like the way you smell. It's just that, well, I—I have a boyfriend back at home, in Florida, and it's his birthday and I forgot to call him." She had no idea where that excuse came from, but it was a lot better than saying, "I think you're the coolest guy I've ever met, but Massie won't like me if I hang out with you because she thinks you're a Harris wannabe."

Cam's face turn red. The burst of color made his blue eye look greener than usual. "A boyfriend?" His expression hardened. "What?"

Claire wrapped the laces on her Keds around her index finger until it turned purple and throbbed.

"If you don't like me, just say so," Cam said softly. Then his voice cracked. "You don't have to lie."

"I like you," Claire said too quickly. "I mean, I'm not lying."

"Then why didn't you tell me sooner? Why didn't your brother ever mention it?" Cam crushed the Coke can in his fist and the popping sounds of the aluminum sounded like gun shots.

"I—I didn't think you liked me that way." Claire knew Cam would never buy that excuse, but the words came out of her mouth before she had a chance to stop them.

"How could you not know?" he asked. "I wrote you letters, burned CDs for you, and always asked you to hang out."

"I thought you were being friendly," Claire said. "You know, 'cause I'm new here." She felt her throat lock.

Cam couldn't bring himself to look at her. He was too busy digging his thumb into the carpet.

"If I didn't have a boyfriend, I'd definitely like you." Claire knew that sounded stupid and was desperate to tell him the truth. But it was too late.

Cam jumped to his feet and ran his hands through his dark wavy hair.

"You should probably leave." Cam pointed to the stairs. "I'm sure your *boyfriend* is wondering where you are."

Claire wanted to hug him and smell his Drakkar Noir one last time. She wanted to tell him that she'd memorized his note because she had read it more than one hundred times. She wanted him to know that she'd learned every word to every Strokes song on the CD he made for her and that she thought his leather jacket looked cool all beat up, even though Massie insisted he'd look cuter in a new one.

"Sorry," Claire said as she stood up. It was the only thing she'd said all night that she actually meant.

"Whatever," Cam said to the brown carpet.

Claire ran up the stairs two at a time. She raced past the kitchen and bolted out the front door. Her coat was still on the banister, but she was too upset to go back in and grab it. All Claire wanted to do was go home, take off Alicia's tight jeans, and cry in peace.

The Fishers' porch light was off and the driveway was empty. There was no sign of the black Mustang or Alicia's Schwinn. Were they actually out on a date? Whatever they were doing, Claire knew Alicia was having a much better time than she was. The backs of Claire's eyes suddenly felt hot. The tears came.

Claire was about to get on her bike when the rustling leaves of the neighbor's shrub caught her attention.

"Alicia? Harris?" she whispered. "You back there?"

There was no answer, just more rustling. Claire was about to call again when she thought maybe they didn't want to be disturbed.

"Pssst," Claire heard from behind the bushes. "Over 'ere."

"Alicia, what are you doing?" Claire searched the darkness and wiped her eyes. She could feel the cold air penetrating her sweater but didn't care. All she could think about was the sadness behind Cam's eyes and how she was responsible for it.

"Pssst," she heard again. Someone poked a red, white, and blue Firecracker Popsicle out of the bushes and waved it around in the air. Claire started crying again. This time they were happy tears.

"Layne!" Claire said, running toward the Popsicle. "You're the best!" Layne's orthodontist had recently banned her from popcorn and mustard, which she'd been munching for the last month, because he thought the kernels might crack one of the brackets on her teeth. So she switched and made Popsicles her latest food obsession.

Layne tossed her Popsicle on the neighbor's lawn. She crawled out of the bushes on her hands and knees. Once she was on her feet, the girls hugged and rocked back and forth.

"What are you doing here?" Claire asked when they broke apart.

"I got your message," Layne said. Her lips were stained blue and her teeth were chattering.

"Huh?"

"You told me you were breaking up with Cam and you wanted to know if I would go with you," Layne shouted. "Am I too late?"

"Shhh." Claire put her hand over Layne's mouth. She had forgotten all about the message but was happy she'd left it.

A voice from behind the bush said, "Hey, Lyons."

Claire jumped and grabbed Layne's arm. "Who's that?"

"It's Eli," Layne said. "I had to bring him. My mom wouldn't let me bike alone in the dark."

Normally Claire didn't like hanging out with Layne's

know-it-all, eyeliner-wearing, punk rock boyfriend Eli. But tonight she welcomed the friendly face.

"Can we get out of here?" Claire said.

"Gladly," Layne said, picking her bike up off the ground. It was covered in bumper stickers and had silver tassels hanging from the handlebars. Eli's plain black bike looked naked in comparison.

The three walked their bikes down Holly Road, shivering and talking in hushed tones.

"I would ask how the breakup went, but I can pretty much tell by looking at your bloodshot eyes," Layne said.

Claire wiped her face with the back of her ice-cold hand.

"Why did you dump him if you like him so much?" Eli asked, twisting his silver skull bracelet.

Layne adjusted the orange floppy pom-pom on top of her striped hat. "I'm sure it had something to do with Massie Block."

"What does Massie have to do with it?" Eli asked.

"She's a controlling witch who thinks she has a right to tell Claire who she can like."

"That's not totally true."

"Yeah, whatever," Layne said. "You're ten times cooler than those girls. Stop trying to make them like you. It's pathetic. Why aren't I good enough for you?"

"Yeah, what's wrong with Layne?" Eli said, ringing the bell on his bike for emphasis.

"Of course you're good enough. It's not that. But I practically live with her. It would be nice if we got along." Claire was so upset, she barely felt the cold wind whip her tearstained cheeks. "Besides, how many times have you asked me what Massie's bedroom looks like or what kind of grades she gets or what she wears on the weekends?" Claire said, suddenly wishing she had never left that message for Layne. "You've even asked me if they talk about you."

"Yeah, but that was before," Layne said.

"Before what?"

"Before I stopped caring."

"Yeah." Eli rang his bell again.

Claire rolled her eyes. "Right, like you don't care."

Layne stopped in front of the iron signpost. It said The Block Estate in white script. "I'll prove it. You'll see."

Claire had no idea how Layne would "prove" she didn't care what Massie thought of her. But she hoped Layne wouldn't go too far. Claire didn't want her to be Massie's next victim.

"I'll call you tomorrow," Layne said as she rode off on her bike.

"'Kay." Claire waved goodbye. "Thanks for being there."

Claire rode past GLU headquarters on her way to the guesthouse and decided to stop in and say hi to Massie, Kristen, and Dylan. If they were nice to her, she would know she did the right thing by breaking up with Cam. And if they weren't . . . She shook the thought from her head.

Claire tapped on the glass door and the three girls shrieked.

"It's just me." Claire stepped inside.

"We thought you were a murderer." Massie's hand was on her heart. Kristen and Dylan were hiding under their cashmere blankets.

"How long have you been outside?" Dylan asked.

"Yeah." Kristen elbowed Dylan. "Have you been listening to us *all night?*" She spoke slowly, like she was talking to a foreign exchange student.

"No, it's freezing out," Claire said, annoyed that they were already accusing her of something. "Anyway, I just got home."

"Why is your face all puffy?" Massie demanded. "Salt your popcorn much?"

Dylan and Kristen laughed.

Claire could feel her eyes welling up all over again. "I told Cam I didn't want to hang out with him anymore."

"Tell me what happened." Massie walked over to Claire and held her close. The smell of Chanel No. 19 filled the air and surrounded her like an invisible fortress. "Tell me everything," Massie said, rubbing her back.

"H-he l-looked so s-s-aaad," Claire wailed. She was a leaky mess of tears and snot.

"Why don't you stay with us tonight?" Massie offered. "You can have Alicia's old sleeping bag."

"Yeah," Dylan said, clearing a space.

"You can share my blanket," Kristen offered.

"Really?" Claire wiped her cheeks with the sleeve of her lavender sweater.

"Of course," Massie said. "Consider yourself the newest member of the Friday night sleepover."

A warm feeling washed through Claire's entire body. Layne and Alicia were *wrong*. Massie *was* looking out for her. She cared.

"I just have to get pajamas and tell my mom."

"Okay, hurry," Massie said.

Claire ran out of GLU headquarters. She jumped on her bike and then quickly got off. *What if it was a trap?* She crept up to the side of the barn and pressed her ear against the cold wood. She couldn't make out every word they were saying, but she did hear "poor thing" and "feel bad for her." Claire exhaled and smiled.

She did it. She was IN. She was part of OCD's infamous Pretty Committee. From now on she would know their secrets, get their inside jokes, and go to their parties. They would never make her cry again. Why would they? She was *finally* one of them.

While Claire was changing into her plaid flannel pj's, Cam's face popped into her head. What he was doing right now? Was he still playing video games or was he lying on his bed, listening to music? Was he still upset or was he over her?

Claire headed back to GLU headquarters, thrilled that she was running across the lawn to join Massie, not escape her. But as she got closer, she was overcome by an intense hollow feeling, like there was a big empty space inside her. It was loneliness. And it was worse than anything she experienced during her first few months in Westchester. Tears flooded Claire's eyes.

"What's wrong with me?" she asked the whistling wind. "Why can't I just be happy?"

But deep down inside, Claire already knew the answer. The only person she wanted to share her victory with was the one person she was forbidden to see. And for some reason that felt worse than being alone.

Alicia raced to the parking lot after school. She couldn't wait to tell her new friends about Harris. Once they heard about their Friday night date, they'd know they were being led by a true alpha.

When Strawberry and Kori arrived, Dean opened the door to the limo and the three girls piled inside.

"This car is bigger than my bedroom," Kori said, twisting one of her blond braids around her finger.

Strawberry shifted her magnetic nose ring from her right nostril to the left. "You act like you've never been in a limo before."

"You act like you *have*," Kori fired back. She unzipped her sporty red North Face ski jacket and slouched in her seat. Alicia wondered how such a good athlete could have such bad posture and made a mental note to work on it.

Strawberry twisted a mess of wavy pink hair to the top of her head, then fastened it with a banana clip. She reached into her mint green hobo sac and pulled out a bag of Baked Lays.

Alicia grinned. It was exactly like carpooling with Kristen and Dylan.

"Sorry I'm late," Faux-livia panted as she climbed into the limo. "I had trouble opening my locker."

"Really? That's so unlike you," Alicia muttered under her breath. To her surprise, everyone laughed. . . . She was a natural.

"Welcome to the inaugural trip of my carpool," Alicia announced when Dean started the limo's engine.

"Yaaaaay!" the girls cheered. They high-fived each other as Dean pulled out of the OCD parking lot.

"Okay, so who wants to play What Would You Rather?" Alicia asked once they were on the road. Massie always thought of fun games for carpool and Alicia would be no different.

"What's that?" Kori asked. She was slouching so severely, her butt was hanging off the edge of her seat.

"Yeah, how do you play?" Strawberry said.

"I'll give you a scenario and you say which one you'd rather do."

"It's fun," Faux added, clearly trying her best to be a good beta.

"I'll start," Alicia said, sitting up tall. She looked out the window for inspiration. "Okay, I have one." She whipped her head around to face her audience. "What would you rather? Count every strand of hair on your head or every breath you take?"

"Hair," Faux yelled out. "The second I think about breathing, I can't breathe anymore. And then I would die."

"What about you guys? Hair or breath?"

Kori and Strawberry stared back at Alicia, then eventually turned to look at each other. They giggled nervously before Kori finally spoke.

"Uh, I don't think either is really possible." She chuckled through her nose. "For starters, who can count that high?"

"And what if you lose count? Do you have to start over?" Strawberry pounded her fist against the limo window. "You'd have to be crazy to pick either one."

Alicia looked at Faux-livia and widened her brown eyes in a subtle cry for help.

"What?" Faux asked Alicia.

Alicia quickly looked away.

"Okay, how about we try another one." She was desperate to re-create the fun times she had in Massie's Range Rover. "Would you rather cry every time someone said something funny? Or laugh every time someone said something sad?"

Faux was the first to answer again. She shouted, "Cry when funny."

"This isn't a game show," Alicia said, expecting her new friends to laugh. But they didn't. Instead Kori sympathetically placed her unmanicured hand on Faux's shoulder.

"I was only joking," Alicia said. In all the time she spent with Massie, she never had to apologize for a comeback. Usually a good mean one would get her a high five.

"I have one," Strawberry announced.

Alicia leaned forward in anticipation.

"Would you rather be smart or pretty?"

"Ugh, that's *such* an old one," Faux said. "Bo-ring."

Alicia elbowed her beta in the ribs. Faux shouldn't criticize the new girls. It was too soon.

"Pretty," Kori said.

"Pretty," Strawberry said.

"Pretty," Faux said.

"Smart," said Alicia.

The girls gasped and looked at Alicia.

"Really? You'd pick *smart?* Why?" Faux asked.

The others leaned in.

Alicia gathered her black glossy hair and dropped it over the left side of her neck so it cascaded down to her collarbone.

"Because I'm already *pretty,*" she said with a coy wink and a shrug.

Strawberry, Kori, and Faux were silent. Alicia held her breath, waiting for their reactions, and prayed she wouldn't have to say she was "only joking" again. She smiled a little to give them a hint. Once they saw *that,* the girls cracked up.

Alicia reached into her new Marc Jacobs Liya bag and pulled out two colorful Louis Vuitton knockoff scarves. She finally had a use for them and had finally gotten Faux-livia to sell them to her for double the street price.

"Since we're going to be hanging out all the time, I want you to have these." Alicia tossed up two scarves and watched as the blasting heat made them look like they were dancing on air.

Kori and Strawberry held out their hands, anxious to catch the scarves before they landed. Alicia could tell by their wide-eyed expressions that they were moved beyond words by the gifts they were about to receive.

"Perfect," Alicia heard herself say. "Every day we have to find a new way to wear them." She lifted the bottom of her peach mohair sweater to show them that she had used her scarf as a belt. Faux showed them that she had done the same. Of course, no one would ever know that Alicia's Louis was real.

"Everyone is going to be so jealous of these," Strawberry said. She put down her bag of chips and wrapped the scarf around her bicep. It was too small to fit around her waist.

"Yeah, thanks," Kori said, sitting up straight for the first time. "I know how expensive these are."

"No problem," Alicia said, pinching Faux to remind her not to mention that they were knockoffs. "And just so you know, those scarves are like your VIP passes. They give you full limo access to and from school, a guaranteed seat at my lunch table—numero 16—and unlimited gossip."

"Are you *serious?*" Strawberry's mint green eyes almost exploded out of her head.

Faux nodded as if to say, "It's sooo great."

"All you have to do it stay loyal to me no matter how hard Massie Block may try to steal you away."

"Why would *Massie* try to steal *us?*" Kori asked. "She doesn't even know my name. She's been calling me Rebecca since fifth grade."

"It's a long story." Alicia slowly shook her head. "Just promise."

"Promise," Strawberry said.

Alicia looked at Kori.

"Promise," she said.

"Pinky swear." Alicia held out her pinky and the other girls did the same. "And swear on your pets."

"What if I don't have any?" Kori asked.

"It's okay," Alicia said.

"I had a gerbil once that I named after my grandfather," Strawberry said. "But my brother twirled it around by the tail and its body went flying out the window. I think he still has the tail. I can swear on that."

"Nah, pinkies are fine," Alicia said. Once they were sworn in, Alicia raised the glass partition between them and Dean so she could have some privacy.

"Now you're finally ready to hear about my date with Harris Fisher," she said.

"You really hung out with him?" Strawberry asked.

Alicia folded her arms across her chest and nodded. "First we sat on his car and threw lit matches onto his driveway and then—"

"He has a car?" Kori asked.

"Given," Alicia said.

"Let her finish," Faux-livia said.

"Sorry." Kori returned to her favorite slouch position. Her neck shot forward and her shoulders touched her ears. "So it was just you and Harris on his car? No one else was there?"

"Exactly."

"Tell them what he said to you," said Faux.

Alicia was grateful for the prompting; it made her look less conceited.

"He said he wished more girls looked like me when he was in the seventh grade. And then he asked me if I had his Strokes tickets."

"Did you?" Kori asked.

"Totally," Alicia said. "But I wasn't going to tell *him* that." She quickly glossed her lips. "I said I'd drop them off just before the concert."

"Why?" Strawberry asked.

"So I'd have a chance to see him again, stupid."

Strawberry's face turned red and Alicia immediately regretted calling her stupid.

"Uh, but that was a good question. I would have asked the same thing if I were you," Alicia said.

Strawberry's expression softened.

"Wait, you haven't heard the best part." Alicia leaned forward. "We drove around the block in his black Mustang so he could play me his favorite Strokes song."

"Tell them what it's called," Faux said.

Alicia leaned in farther and this time the other girls joined her. "It's called 'Barely Legal.'"

The girls squealed and stomped their feet up and down. Alicia pulled out her *Lucky* stickers and covered her own body with *yes*es. The chorus of "oh my God"s and "no way"s was so loud, Dean lowered the partition.

"Then what?" Strawberry shouted.

"Shhh." Alicia tilted her head toward the front seat.

Strawberry covered her mouth in anticipation.

Alicia lowered her voice. "Then he dropped me and my bike off at home and told me to call him as soon as I have the tickets."

"He's totally going to ask you to go with him," Kori said.

"Did he kiss you good night?" Strawberry said a little too loudly.

Alicia could see Dean's brown eyes watching them from the rearview mirror.

"Uh, no," Alicia said. She pointed her chin at Dean, indicating that there was more to the story, but it would have to wait. She could tell by their awestruck faces that she made the right decision by letting them think more might have happened. They never had to know he'd patted her lightly on the back when she walked away, pushing her bike. Besides, she was certain she'd have her first real kissing story after the concert.

No one noticed the car had stopped moving until Dean turned around and said, "Kori, is this the right address?" They were in front of Brickview Apartments, a weathered-looking building right next door to the Montador, Kristen's luxury high-rise. Alicia looked around nervously for Massie's Range Rover, hoping to avoid a surprise encounter with the rival carpool.

"I was having such a good time, I didn't realize I was home," Kori said.

"Well, you better get going." Alicia leaned across Kori and opened her door before Dean had a chance. "I'll e-mail you later. See you in the morning."

"Byeee." Kori stood on the curb and waved until they were halfway down the road.

Alicia waved back, wondering why anyone would choose to live in that hideous place when the extravagant Montador was right next door.

Alicia was relieved when they pulled into Strawberry's driveway. Hers was a medium-sized stone house with a big front lawn and a swimming pool in the back. And it was nowhere near Dylan's or Massie's house. "Nice place."

Strawberry smiled and stepped out of the limo. "Thanks for the ride. This sure beats the OCD bus."

"See you tomorrow morning around seven-thirtyish," Alicia shouted out the window as they backed out of her driveway.

"Dean, you can just drop me off at my mother's real estate office," Faux-livia said.

Once all of the girls were gone, Alicia closed her eyes and rested her head on the armrest in the middle of the seat. Carpool was hard work.

"We're home." Dean drove through the iron gates and stopped the limo in front of the wide stone steps that led up to the Riveras' Spanish-style mansion.

Alicia opened her eyes and stretched her legs. "Thanks for the ride, Dean." She yawned.

He smiled and exhaled sharply through his nose, like he always did after she thanked him. Then he got in the limo again and circled around back to their ten-car garage.

"Hooooot, hooooot," Alicia heard. It was coming from behind one of the massive clay flowerpots on the steps.

"Is it you?" Alicia asked, stopping on the bottom step.

"Hooooot," the voice answered back. Alicia ducked behind the tallest pot, even though the security cameras didn't come on until 8 PM.

"So?" Alicia hissed. "What have you got for me?"

"Not so fast. Do you have what I need?"

Alicia sighed and reached around the inside of her bag until she felt the envelope. She took it out and pushed it across the step. She peeked out from behind the plant and saw Todd's little arm reach out and pat the cement. He pinched the envelope and slid it behind his flowerpot. Alicia heard him tear it open.

"The tickets are all there," she said out loud. "Can you come out now?"

"You're no fun," he said, holding up three tickets to WWE at Nassau Coliseum. One was for Todd, one for his father, and one for Tiny Nathan. "I'll give you Nathan's ticket if you want to go. I'd much rather see the show with you, Sugar Lips."

"Puh-lease," Alicia said, folding her arms across her chest. "What's the point of a *fake* fight?" She quickly changed her tone once she realized Todd still had what she needed. "But if I did want to watch fat men act, there's no one I'd rather go with."

"Really?" Todd said, moving closer to Alicia.

"Really," Alicia said, taking a tiny step back. "Now tell me what you know"—she swallowed hard—"Sugar Lips."

Todd told her everything he heard Friday night while he was eavesdropping on GLU headquarters. He told her Kristen was poor, Dylan was going to St. Barf's, and Massie liked Cam. Alicia listened to every word, making sure not to miss a single syllable.

When he was done, she stuck a *yes* sticker on his fore-head and gave him a quick peck on the cheek. "You rule!" Alicia said.

She ran into her house and slammed the heavy oak door behind her—leaving Todd alone on her steps, where he stood motionless for the next half hour.

The next day Alicia went to school with two more scarves, one for Dylan and the other for Kristen. Now that she knew their secrets, they were as good as hers.

"Hey, guys, got a second?" Alicia called after Kristen and Dylan. It was the next morning when she cornered them on their way to art. She knew Massie was on another floor, headed for design.

"No," Dylan said before they picked up their pace.

"Hey, Dylan, maybe if you moved that quickly all the time, you wouldn't have to go to St. *Barf's.*"

Dylan stopped in her tracks and looked around to make sure none of the passing girls heard what Alicia had said.

"What are you so afraid of?" Alicia asked. "I just want to give you something to show how much I miss you." She dangled a scarf in the air.

Dylan turned around.

"I have one for you too, K." Alicia held out her other hand.

Kristen refused to budge.

"And it's *free,*" Alicia said.

Kristen whipped her head around and clenched her fists. And the three girls faced each other.

Kristen shook her head in disgust. "Six-letter word for *snitch*."

"*Massie,*" Dylan snarled.

"Congratulations," Alicia said. "It's the first time you ever answered one of those right."

Dylan rolled her eyes.

"Wear these scarves from now on and your secrets are safe with me," Alicia said, handing them each a knockoff Louis.

Kristen twirled her blond hair around her finger. "And if we don't?"

Alicia answered Kristen's question with a shrug and a mischievous grin.

Kristen and Dylan looked at each other and Alicia knew exactly what they were thinking. If they wore the scarves to school, they would face Massie's wrath. And if they didn't, their secrets would spread among the students faster than a picture of Josh Hartnett's bare butt.

Alicia waved the scarves at them one last time. "So? What's it gonna be?"

Dylan yanked a scarf out of Alicia's hand and wrapped it around her ponytail.

"I have a feeling I'm going to regret this," Kristen said as she tied hers to the belt loop on her Juicys.

"We *all* will," Dylan said to Alicia.

Alicia's arms were suddenly covered in goose bumps. What if they were right?

┌───┐
│   │
│   **THE BLOCK ESTATE**   │
│   GUESTHOUSE   │
│   │
│   4:47 PM   │
│   November 25th   │
│   │
└───┘

Claire stepped out of the Blocks' Range Rover, right behind Massie. It had been her fourth time carpooling as an official member of the Pretty Committee and so far, no one had said a single mean word to her. The hardest part had been trading in her gummy bears and sours for those healthy Dr. Juice drinks Massie was into. But it was a small price to pay.

They stood on the lawn between their two houses before parting ways for dinner.

"So you're telling me you didn't notice *anything* weird about Kristen and Dylan today?" Massie asked, shifting back and forth in her new gold ballet flats. "Nothing at all?"

"They were a little quiet," Claire said. "Maybe they're upset because we said we would do our homework together again tonight."

"But we've been saying that since last week," Massie said. "It's never bothered them before."

"Well, I dunno," Claire said, searching her mind for the right thing to say. Massie was finally confiding in her and Claire didn't want to let her down. "Maybe they don't like having me around." As soon as the words left her mouth, Claire regretted saying them. What if she was right?

"Puh-lease," Massie said. "If I like you, they like you."

"Oh," Claire said. Something about Massie's answer didn't sit right with her. It left an empty, almost hungry feeling inside her stomach.

"Anyway, I'm sure it's nothing." Massie shook her hand in the air like she was waving hello in fast motion. "Wanna work in my room tonight?"

"Sure. I'll burn a new CD."

"Perf. I'll call you after dinner." Massie's smile reappeared. "Cheers, big ears."

"Same goes, big nose." Claire giggled and the girls took off in opposite directions.

Claire burst through the door to the guesthouse and stood shivering in the hallway. Once her hands stopped shaking, she began peeling off her layers. These days she wore a long john shirt, a turtleneck sweater, a cardigan, her yellow raincoat, and two scarves to keep warm. Her winter coat was still at Cam's. He had e-mailed her at least a dozen times to let her know he had it, but Claire simply replied, *Thx* ☺, and other blasé things like that. She secretly liked that Cam had something of hers and hoped he wouldn't burn it out of spite. Besides, Massie promised to take her coat shopping on the weekend, which was only three chilly days away.

"Score!" Claire heard Todd call from the living room. The explosive sound of the cheering crowd made Claire roll her eyes. She didn't understand why boys got so excited over video games. Then she thought of Cam again. Would it ever stop?

Claire hung her second scarf on a plastic hook inside the front closet.

"You are such a gawd!" she heard another voice yell.

Claire crinkled her eyebrows in utter confusion. It was a girl. That meant an actual female was hanging out with her brother. Claire kicked off her Keds and hurried toward the living room.

A silky black ponytail hung over the back of the couch. Claire could feel her heart starting to race, as if *it* knew who the girl was before she did. As Claire crept closer, she became engulfed by a thick cloud of Angel perfume.

"Alicia?" she said. "D-did we have plans today?"

Todd sighed and hit pause on the game.

"No," Alicia said casually, as if it wasn't completely freakish for her to be hanging out with Claire's ten-year-old brother.

"So, why are—"

"She's *my* guest," Todd said, putting his hand on Alicia's knee. Claire couldn't help chuckling when Alicia picked it up like a stinky sock and dropped it back on Todd's leg.

Alicia tilted her neck back so her face was upside down when she spoke to Claire. "Harris is pretty into video games, so I thought I'd come here to get a little practice."

"Wait, who's Harris?" Todd asked, tossing his new cordless controller on the brown couch.

Alicia ignored him. "I bet Massie is practicing too."

"Huh?" Claire was tired of looking at Alicia's upside-down head and walked around to the front of the couch. "Why would Massie be practicing? She thinks video games are for boys who suck at sports."

"Because Cam loves them," Alicia said.

"So?" Claire felt a rush of prickly heat all over her body. It made her palms itch.

"So," Alicia said with a trace of "duh" in her voice. "Massie likes Cam."

"She does not!" Claire shouted a lot louder than she meant to. But the thought of being double-crossed at this point seemed beyond evil. Even for Massie.

"Then why did she make you dump him?" Alicia shouted back.

"Because he's a wannabe and she thought I could do better." Claire tried to sound convinced as she lowered herself onto the glass coffee table. She had no idea who to trust and it was making her knees feel weak.

"Alicia's right," Todd said.

"How would you know?" Claire snapped.

"He was eavesdropping on GLU headquarters when Massie told Kristen and Dylan." Alicia's tone would have been the same if she was talking about her class schedule.

Suddenly memories of Massie talking about Cam flashed in Claire's mind with sharp clarity, as if they were photographs she had taken with her digital camera. She began scrolling through them one at a time. . . .

The big smile on Massie's face when Claire said she'd ended things with Cam, Massie's offer to buy Claire a new coat so she could avoid seeing Cam, the heartless way Massie destroyed his letter, the BO rumor, and the constant "checking in" to see if Claire returned any of Cam's e-mails.

The images came faster and faster until they played like a horror movie. Claire could feel the tears starting to come.

Alicia bit her lower lip and put her hand on her heart to show how sorry she was for Claire. But that brought little comfort. Lately it seemed like everyone was pretending to care about Claire when they were really just scheming and backstabbing.

"Maybe this will help." Alicia pulled a scarf out of her pocket. "Wear it to school and no one will mess with you ever again."

Claire dabbed her eyes with the silky cloth. She wanted to know how a stupid scarf could possibly protect her, but she couldn't bring herself to ask. All she wanted to do was get to her bedroom before Todd saw her cry. He'd never let her live it down.

Claire stood up without saying another word to either of them and made a run for the stairs. When she got up to her room, she slammed the door and locked it behind her. Then she marched straight over to her window, pulled the string, and lowered the curtains so Massie couldn't see her. She ripped the phone jack out of the wall and wrote an IM away message that said, *I am sick. Please do not disturb*. Claire didn't want to hear from Massie now, after dinner, or ever again.

Two BCBG's saleswomen were fussing over Massie, Kristen, and Dylan, and they wouldn't have had it any other way. Between Christmas, Hanukkah, and New Year's, Massie had six invitations stuck to the purple magnetic board in her bedroom, not including the OCD/Briarwood Nondenominational Tree-Lighting Ceremony. And she didn't have a single new thing to wear.

Dylan burst through the door of the dressing room wearing a pink beaded V-necked tank top and silver wide-legged satin pants. She did a full 360-degree turn, then froze with her hands on her hips as if the famous fashion photographer Patrick Demarchelier were about to take her picture.

"Does this make me look *too* sexy?" she asked, laughing at her own goofy model pose.

"I dunno, but does this make me look *too* gorgeous?" Massie said. She emerged in a gold-and-green halter dress.

But no one even looked at her outfit.

"Dylan, you look like an eight-letter word for *great,*" Kristen said as if Massie weren't even there.

"Ah-mazing?" Massie shouted immediately.

"I was talking to Dylan," Kristen snapped. She was sitting on a fold-out chair outside the dressing rooms, doing a crossword puzzle.

"Are you pissed because I said I didn't want to go to Abercrombie?" Massie said to her own reflection in the three-way mirror. "'Cause you know they won't have anything party-worthy at A&F."

"I don't need any holiday clothes," Kristen said. "I have tons from last year."

"Why not drink a carton of expired milk while you're at it?" Massie said, expecting to hear Dylan laugh. But the dressing room was silent.

"Kristen, want me to buy you something?" Dylan asked Kristen.

Massie turned away from the mirror and looked at her friends. Of course! Why didn't she think of it sooner? Kristen was just upset because she couldn't afford new holiday clothes. She wasn't mad at Massie. Kristen was mad at her poverty-stricken parents.

"Yeah, we'll get you something new," Massie said.

"No thanks, I don't need your charity," Kristen said, stuffing her crossword puzzle book in her bag.

"But that's what friends are for." Massie put her arm around Kristen's shoulders.

"Yeah, some friend," Kristen murmured before pushing Massie's arm away.

"What's your problem?"

"Nothing," Dylan chimed in. "She doesn't have a problem, do you, Kristen?"

"No." Kristen crossed her legs.

"See," Dylan said. Then she turned to Kristen. "Hey, why

don't you try something on anyway? You know, just for fun."

"'Kay." Kristen shrugged. She stood up and started browsing.

Massie looked at Dylan and whispered, "What's up with the female dog?"

Dylan shrugged and went back into the dressing room.

Massie rolled her eyes and did the same.

"Can I help you find any sizes?" someone shouted.

"No thanks, I'm all done." Massie stepped out holding an armful of clothes. "Here you go," she said as she unloaded them on her salesgirl, Ava-Jade. "I'll take everything plus whatever my cranky blond friend wants."

"Great," Ava-Jade said with an elated smile that showed off her over-bleached teeth.

Massie reached into her red suede Prada push lock bag and pulled a card out of the inside zipper pocket. She placed it on top of the pile in Ava-Jade's arms. "Charge it."

Ava-Jade looked confused. "Uh, we don't accept the OCD student ID, just Visa, American Express, and MasterCard."

"Oops, sorry." Massie giggled. She sat down on the foldout chair and began searching the inside of her bag. "I know my Visa is in here somewhere."

Massie took out her cosmetics case, Chanel compact, cell phone, iPod, PalmPilot, house keys, dog treats, and silver Tiffany pen. Then she turned her Prada upside down and shook it. She looked up at Ava-Jade and bit her bottom lip. "Uh, I think I left my wallet in the Hermès."

Ava-Jade dumped the pile of clothes onto Massie's lap and walked away.

"That sucks," Dylan said when she stepped out of her changing room. She made a big show of handing a heap of clothes to Collette, her salesgirl. "I know there's a lot here; do you need some help taking it all to the register?" Dylan placed her mother's ultra-exclusive black American Express card on top of the pile.

"No, Miss Marvil, you wait here. I'll be fine."

"Great." Dylan smiled and sighed. "I hope I can carry it all home." She chuckled.

Massie rolled her eyes and looked away. "My life sucks," she muttered under her breath.

Kristen walked back into the changing area holding a navy blue T-shirt dress.

"Massie brought her OCD card," Dylan announced. "But don't worry, I'll pay for it."

"Thanks," Kristen said with a relieved smile. "You're the greatest friend in the world."

As soon as Kristen shut the dressing room door, Massie slapped Dylan's arm. "What's going on here?"

"Massie!" Dylan shouted when Massie's slap knocked her Marc by Marc Jacobs cross-body bag to the ground. Everything spilled out. "You broke my bag."

"I did not." Massie dropped to her knees. She started scooping up the various lip glosses, brushes, Luna bar wrappers, and loose soy chip crumbs. She had never felt so pathetic in her entire life.

Suddenly Massie recoiled. "What's this?" She picked the shiny white scarf off the floor and rubbed it against her cheek. Then she held it up to the light and examined it from both sides.

Dylan's face went white. "Oh, that's my mom's hankie. She used my bag last night and must have forgotten to take it out."

"Don't lie to me," Massie said as she bunched it up in the palm of her hand and whipped it back on the ground. "It's a knockoff! Your mom wouldn't even use this to wipe dog poo off her shoes."

"Yes, she would." Dylan grabbed the scarf from the floor and stuffed it back in her bag.

Massie felt her entire body starting to quiver. She stood up, gently resting her hand on her stomach, fighting the urge to puke on Dylan's new Dolce & Gabbana mules. "You got this from Alicia, didn't you? How could you?"

"How could I?" Dylan stood. "How could *you?*"

"What?" Massie felt dizzy. She leaned against the mirror. The cool glass felt good against the back of her neck.

"Whaddaya think?" Kristen bellowed as she threw open the dressing room door. She walked out modeling the navy T-shirt dress.

"Kristen, do you have any lip gloss in your bag?"

Kristen crinkled her blond eyebrows and nodded, obviously confused by Massie's reaction.

"Can I grab some?" Massie kept her eyes on Dylan, making sure she didn't throw any signals to warn Kristen. But before Kristen could answer, Massie had already locked the changing room door and was rifling through her LeSportsac.

"What do you think of this dress?" she heard Kristen ask Dylan.

"Who cares?" Massie heard Dylan say.

"What's wrong with you?" Kristen asked.

Dylan was silent.

Massie got a paper cut from brushing her hand past Kristen's crossword puzzle book but ignored the stinging pain. She was determined to find what she was looking for.

"Aha!" Massie pulled the scarf out like a birthday party magician would. She stepped out of the changing room, waving it like a victory flag. "Et tu, Brute?"

Kristen and Dylan stood beside each other with a look of utter panic in their eyes.

"What did she just say?" Dylan asked Kristen. Her eyes were still fixed on Massie and the scarf.

"It's Latin for 'you too, Brutus?'" Kristen explained. "It's what Julius Caesar said when he found out his friend Brutus was one of the people who betrayed him."

"Oh." After a brief pause Dylan spoke again. "Well, if anyone betrayed anyone, it's *you*." She pointed to Massie. "You're the Brutus."

"How am I the Brutus? You're the one who joined Alicia's army."

"We only joined because we had to," Kristen chimed in. "She threatened to tell our secrets if we didn't."

"What secrets?" Massie screeched.

"The ones we trusted you with," Kristen said. "The ones *you* told her."

"I didn't tell her anything," Massie said. "We pinky-swore!"

"That obviously doesn't mean anything to you," Dylan said.

Massie gasped. She threw her Prada bag over her shoulder and marched toward the exit.

Dylan and Kristen followed her.

"Wait, Miss Marvil." Collette scurried across the store carrying three bags of clothes and an unsigned credit card slip.

"Signature, please," Collette panted. She clicked her pen and held it in front of Dylan's face.

Dylan kept walking while she scribbled her mother's name on the slip. She placed the black plastic tray in a mannequin's hand and continued after Massie.

"Thank you, Merri-Lee," Collette shouted before she dropped Dylan's bags beside the security guard. "Happy holidays."

"How could Alicia possibly know everything we told you at the sleepover if you didn't tell her?" Dylan shouted at Massie.

Massie stopped and turned around. "I have no idea. Maybe she *guessed*."

"Well, for some reason she didn't *guess* about you liking Cam," Kristen shouted after her.

Massie stomped her foot on the ground. "Will you be *quiet?* There are people from school all over the place. What if someone hears you?"

"Now you know how we feel," Dylan said.

"I didn't tell Alicia anything," Massie insisted. "Besides, if you really thought I betrayed you, why would you go shopping with me?"

"We needed a ride." Kristen shrugged.

"Nice. Thanks a lot," Massie said. She walked straight through the metal detector and back into the mall, where she was instantly surrounded by a torrent of holiday shoppers.

Kristen ran after her. "I would rather be poor than a liar."

"Congratulations, you got your wish," Massie shouted over her shoulder.

Suddenly a piercing alarm rang in BCBG. Massie stopped and turned. She saw the customers cover their ears and crane their necks, hoping they might see something. But all anyone saw was a beefy security guard grab Kristen by the arm and yank her back into the store. She had run out in the T-shirt dress and the tags had triggered the alarm. Dylan hurried to her rescue, waving her black AmEx in the guard's face.

Massie snaked her way through the crowds, desperate to escape before anyone from school saw her crying. She wiped her eyes at least ten times, but the tears kept coming. How could they not? Her worst fears had come true: the Pretty Committee had officially fallen apart and she was stuck at the mall without a credit card.

"Finally." Massie sighed when she got to Sears. No one from school shopped there.

Massie took out her phone and speed dialed Isaac. She waited for him beside the men's ties and watches.

"Are you lost, dear?" a nice old saleslady asked when she heard Massie's heaving sobs. "Did you lose someone?"

Massie tried to smile. "Kind of," she said. "But I'll be okay."

Massie ran up the stairs two at a time and darted into her bedroom. She slammed the door behind her and went straight to her bay window to see if Claire was in her room. She was desperate to tell someone about her brutal experience at the mall. But Claire's blinds were closed, just like they had been all week.

Massie tried calling again. "Hi, Judi, is Claire home yet?" She used her most polite voice.

"No, she's still out with Layne," Judi said. "I told you I'll give her the message as soon as she gets home."

Something was definitely going on and Massie hung up, wondering if Judi was lying to her. For the last few days it seemed like Claire was never home. Her blinds were always shut and she never replied to IMs. She even flaked on their homework plans and showed no interest in coat shopping. Maybe she was still mourning Cam. Massie understood that. After all, she missed him too.

Massie checked her inbox. No messages. Same with her voice mail. She had never felt so lonely in her entire life. Even her parents were out with friends.

"Bean," Massie shouted. "Be-ean?" She felt her heart starting to race. Did Bean leave too? "BEANNNNN!"

Massie called a few more times before she heard her dog's familiar bark coming from the front hallway. She hurried down the steps. Bean whimpered and jumped into Massie's open arms.

Massie squeezed her dog and kissed the top of her tiny black head. "Ehmagawd, what are you wearing?" A red satin cape had been tied around her neck.

"Where are you, Red Riding Hood?" Massie heard a squeaky boy's voice call. Bean squirmed in Massie's arms.

"Hullo? Who's there?" she called, holding Bean close to her chest and reaching for her cell phone holster. She gripped the top of the Motorola and slowly pulled it out, ready to dial 911.

"Goldberg, is that you?" someone said. Massie recognized the voice and tucked her phone away. *"Todd?"*

"Uh, yeah, hi," he said. He walked into the front hall dressed in a pair of women's black tights. His chest was completely bare.

"What are you doing?" Massie untied Bean's cape and threw it on the ground. "And what did you do to Bean?"

"Nathan and I are wrestling," he said, as if it were obvious. "I'm Goldberg and he's Eddie Guerrero. AND IF HE DOESN'T COME OUT OF HIDING SOON, I'M GOING TO GIVE HIM THE JACKHAMMER."

"Oh yeah?" a mousy voice called from the living room. "WELL, I'M GOING BUST OUT MY LASSO FROM EL PASO AND ROPE YOUR NECK."

Just then Tiny Nathan ran out from behind the curtains,

wearing the same outfit as Todd. They chased each other around the room until Todd threw himself on top of Tiny Nathan.

"Stop it!" Massie yelled. "STOP! ENOUGH!"

Todd was squeezing Nathan's head between his kneecaps. "Say Goldberg is the world champ," he insisted. "SAY IT!"

"What is going on?" Massie insisted. She pulled Todd off Tiny Nathan. "Why are you in my house?"

"There's more room to wrestle here," Todd said. "It's like ten times bigger than the guesthouse."

"Why are you *wrestling?*" Massie was getting impatient.

"Because Alicia got us box seats for the WWE Smackdown and we're going tonight," Nathan chirped.

"Oh," Massie said sarcastically. Then all of a sudden something strange occurred to her.

"*Alicia* got you tickets?" Massie asked.

"Yeah," Todd said, puffing out his chest. "We've been spending a lot of time together lately. Way more than you and I ever did. Wayyy more."

Massie put her hands on her hips. "Is that supposed to make me jealous, Todd?"

"Yeah," Todd said. "Is it working?"

In a tiny way it was. He was another person who'd left Massie for Alicia.

"It is working, isn't it?" Todd said. "Look at you—your face is getting red. You're jealous."

Massie rolled her eyes. There had to be some kind of explanation for all of this. . . . And in a flash everything became clear. Alicia was walking around with top secret info and Todd, the infamous eavesdropper, had box seats. It all made perfect sense.

"Okay, well, have fun at the show," Massie said, turning toward the stairs. "Oh, one question," she called down to Todd. "Do you know the name of the fat camp in upstate New York? I have a friend who's interested and I spaced on the name."

"St. Barf's," Todd called back.

"Thanks." Massie smiled to herself. Case closed.

She ran back down the stairs and pushed Todd into the living room. "Take that, Goldberg," she said as she slammed him against the leopard print wallpaper. "You better start talking or I'm going to show you *my* version of the Smackdown. And there won't be anything fake about it."

Alicia whispered into her phone, "You're not going to believe this, but I'm standing in Harris Fisher's bedroom."

"No way," Faux-livia said.

"Swear," Alicia barked. "Four-way Strawberry and Kori and I'll tell you what I see. Hurry, he'll be back from the bathroom any minute."

"No problem," Faux-livia said. "How do I do it?"

"Ugh, are you serious?" Alicia hung up. "Useless," she grumbled.

The musky smell of boy's deodorant mixed with laundry detergent and sweaty socks was everywhere. Alicia wasn't sure if she actually liked the odor but decided she'd better get used to it.

She lifted her cell phone and took a picture of his chocolate brown walls. They were covered in posters of Al Pacino, Marlon Brando, and a bunch of rock bands Alicia couldn't care less about.

"Cute." Alicia sighed when she saw his twin beds and their matching blue comforter covers. She took a picture of his color-coordinated throw pillows.

Alicia got shots of his white digital clock radio, the

stack of *Car and Driver* magazines by his bed, and a glass of moldy orange juice.

A *Sports Illustrated* swimsuit calendar was tacked above his computer and Alicia leaned in to see what he had planned for the holidays. Were they going to any of the same parties? *THE STROKES* was written in big red letters beside the dates of their New York tours. Just below that, in blue he'd written, *ASK "A" TO GO*.

Alicia's palms started to sweat uncontrollably and she fought the urge to scream. "Ehmagawd," she whispered to herself.

Alicia took four pictures of the calendar and then quickly stuffed her phone in her pocket when she heard Harris's footsteps.

"Sorry 'bout that," he said as he strolled back into the room. He pulled a black tube of ChapStick out of his Levi's pocket and smeared the peach-colored wax all over his naturally red lips.

"It's okay." Alicia giggled. She shifted from one foot to the other before leaning back and resting her butt on the edge of his dark wood desk. . . . Now what?

When Harris had driven her home, the music in his Mustang was blasting, so they didn't have to talk. But it was silent in his bedroom and he was staring straight at her.

"Cool shirt," Alicia said, pointing to his baggy white tee. "Who makes that?"

Harris turned his neck and pulled the label out of the back. "Hanes."

"Love them," Alicia said. She turned her head slightly to

the side and raised her eyebrows, forcing herself to look into his green eyes. She had seen that move drive a man wild on *The Young and the Restless*. But Harris didn't seem to notice. He sat on his bed and grabbed his iPod off the night table. He started clicking through his playlists. Once he found the right song, he pushed a button and a loud, thrashing guitar solo blasted through his speakers and filled the room with the sound of angst.

"How awesome is this?" he said, playing air guitar.

Alicia loved watching his long dark bangs flop around his face. Their kids would definitely have perfect hair.

"So, uh, what are you doing this weekend?" she asked, hoping he would finally ask her to the concert. The anticipation was maddening.

"You know, the usual." He was still strumming.

"Cool," Alicia shouted over the music. And then, in a final attempt to do something sexy, she winked.

"No way," Harris said. "My chemistry teacher has the exact same eye twitch as you. I think it's kind of cute. But then again, anything's cute on a hottie." He flashed Alicia a mischievous smile. She could feel herself blush.

"I don't have an eye twitch," she said with a playful lilt in her voice. "But I sooo love that you think I'm a hottie."

Harris threw his head back and laughed.

"Actually it's my chemistry teacher who's the hottie. You should see her. She looks like Halle Berry, you know, but with a twitch." Harris held his gaze on Alicia for a second too long. She scratched her forehead, hoping her hand would cover her pout.

Harris turned down the music, moved closer to Alicia, and put his arm around her. "You'll be even hotter than her, though, when you get older," he said.

Alicia smiled. "Whatevs," she said softly.

Harris backed away from Alicia and sat on the edge of his bed. "So, do you have the Strokes tickets?" He rubbed his hands together as if he were trying to stay warm.

"Given," Alicia said. She opened her green Coach vintage hobo bag and pulled out a small yellow envelope. "Here."

Harris grabbed it and fell backward onto his bed. He pulled the tickets out and examined them. "Box seats! You rule!"

Alicia said nothing. She was still trying to adjust to the fact that he would choose his twitchy chemistry teacher over her.

Harris leaned over the side of his bed and pulled out an old tin film canister. He pried it open with his thumb and pulled out a thin stack of twenties. He counted out $180 and handed it to Alicia.

"No, that's okay," she said, waving her hand at the cash. "Consider it an early holiday present."

Harris's face lit up like a Christmas tree, even though he said the required, "Naw, I couldn't. I'd feel terrible."

"Well, maybe I could go with you, then." She was tired of waiting for him to ask her. "And then you won't feel so bad."

"That would be great," he said.

"Really?"

"Yeah." Harris nodded.

"Cool, I can pick you up in my limo, or you can drive the Mustang if you want; it's your call—"

"But I already promised my friend Angela."

"Oh." Alicia felt her throat dry up.

Harris held out his arm, offering the money again. Alicia shook her head and pretended to pull a piece of hair off her low-cut sweater. She thought of how excited she had been when she saw his calendar and punched herself in the thigh for being so stupid.

"What was that for?" Harris asked, walking toward her.

"Leg cramp."

Harris grabbed Alicia by the shoulders and pulled her to her feet. Then he took her in his arms and squeezed her tight. But she knew this was nothing more than a pity hug.

Alicia pulled back, anxious to get away from his musty armpit. Then she lifted her dark eyes and looked up at him.

"Can I call you in a few days?" he asked with a warm smile.

"Given." Alicia could feel herself blush. Maybe there was hope. Maybe Angela was just a friend. Maybe . . .

"The White Stripes are about to announce their tour dates and I'd *kill* for box seats to their show."

The "game over" sound effect from Todd's video games played in Alicia's head. "'Kay, well, I have to go."

"Thanks again," Harris said, flashing every white tooth in his beautiful mouth.

"Yup." Alicia picked her leather bag off the floor and stormed out of his room, slamming the door behind her. She considered running back in and blaming her dramatic exit on a sudden gust of wind. But why bother? If he wanted to think she was upset, let him. Maybe next time he would think twice about using her.

The tears started to come and Alicia raced down the stairs, hoping to get away before she ran into Cam. She had been humiliated enough for one day . . . or so she thought.

When Alicia opened the front door, she gasped.

"Massie?" Alicia said. She hadn't spoken to her ex-friend in days and her name sounded strange coming out of Alicia's mouth.

Massie looked away. "Is Cam here?"

"Hi, Alicia." Cam appeared from the kitchen with a smile. "Come on in, Massie."

"Thanks." Massie pushed past Alicia.

"Is Harris still upstairs?" Cam asked.

"Oh yyyeah." Alicia tried to look sexy and devious when she answered him. She wanted Massie to think they had spent the afternoon kissing. "I had to tear myself away because I have to meet a bunch of friends. It wasn't easy."

"Uh, okay." Cam looked confused.

"Cam, let's go to your room." Massie smacked him playfully on the butt and he took off up the stairs. She chased after him.

"Bye, Alicia!" Cam yelled.

But Alicia was too choked up to answer. She let herself out and ran toward her silver-and-red Schwinn that she had dumped on the lawn.

Once she was halfway down Holly, Alicia cried openly. She

hated that Harris chose Angela over her. But most of Alicia's tears were for Massie. They were complete strangers.

If they hadn't been fighting, Alicia would have been on the phone with Massie right now, making plans to meet at Starbucks. Once they got there, they would have sat beside each other on the purple velvet couch by the window, blowing on their fattening chai lattes and resting their feet on the coffee table in front of them. Alicia would have made Massie pinky-swear that she would not repeat the truth about Harris. And Massie would explain why she was going behind Claire's back to be with Cam. By the time the sugar and caffeine kicked in, they would be doubled over laughing.

But now that Alicia and Massie were enemies, there would be no meeting at Starbucks.

The tears were coming even harder now and Alicia wiped her eyes with the Louis Vuitton scarf that was tied around her wrist. The Block estate was only five minutes away and if she pedaled fast enough, she could be there in three. She was desperate to tell Claire what really happened at the Fishers' house. Of course she would skip the part about Harris and Angela and go straight to the story about Massie and Cam.

Massie stared at the same math problem in her textbook until the numbers looked blurry. Claire usually helped Massie plot her x and y intercepts. But for the last week Claire insisted on doing her homework alone. A knock on the bedroom door brought Massie's attention back to reality.

"Come in." She sighed. But her mother had already stepped into the room.

"When you have a minute, would you please get your CDs and sleeping bags out of the horse barn? The workmen will be putting up the mirrors tomorrow and they need room to move around in there."

"'Kay, I'll do it in a bit."

Kendra formed a tight O with her mouth and exhaled slowly. "Thank you." Her rigid expression softened. "Now, that wasn't so hard, was it?"

Massie shrugged and turned around to face her flat-screen Mac computer. Moments later she felt her mother's thin hands on her shoulders and a tender kiss on the top of her head. The gesture reminded Massie of the way her mother treated her when she was a little girl. Massie couldn't help wondering if her mother could sense how

221

upset she had been lately or if her self-help book club was actually starting to relax her.

"Mom, can I ask you something?" Massie pushed her chair away from her desk and walked over to her bed. She leaned down, scooped up Bean, and crossed her legs.

"You can ask me anything you want." Kendra sat on the edge of the bed to avoid messing up the sheets.

"Do you and Dad ever fight?"

"Of course we do." Kendra's posture stiffened. "Why? Did you hear our argument about the new paintings in the living room? Because if you did, you don't have to worry. I don't really think he's passive-aggressive."

"No, this isn't about paintings," Massie said. "I was just wondering what you say to Dad when you know he's mad at you."

Kendra lifted her chin and smoothed her dark brown bob. "Thanks to that workshop on surrendering control, I have learned to apologize."

"What if you didn't do anything wrong?"

"Honey," Kendra said, "it's never my fault, but I still say I'm sorry."

"Why?"

"Because if I waited around for *him* to say it, I'd be a very hostile woman," Kendra said. "Besides, it takes strength to apologize. It's a power move."

Massie rubbed the backs of Bean's ears.

"Why? Is something going on at school?" Kendra asked.

"Maybe." Massie hung her head and bit her lower lip.

Then she lifted her eyes and looked straight at her mother for the first time. "But I didn't do anything." She squeezed the gold crown charm on her bracelet so hard the tiny spikes dug into her palm.

"Stay here—I'll be right back." Kendra hopped to her feet and left Massie's bedroom and returned with a stack of paperback books.

"Read these." She dumped them on Massie's bed and smiled with great satisfaction. "When's the last time you ever saw me mess up a bed like that?"

"Never," Massie said.

"I know, isn't it great?" Kendra clapped. "These books have really helped me let go."

Massie looked at the pile of schoolbooks on her desk and sighed.

"Don't worry, I highlighted them," Kendra said. "It won't take you long. But if you only have time for one, I suggest *How to Win Friends and Influence People,* by Dale Carnegie. It's a lifesaver." She handed the purple-and-green book to her daughter.

"'Kay." Massie flipped through the coffee-stained pages. "Thanks."

"Don't thank me." Kendra turned to leave. "Thank Dale." She winked and gently closed the door behind her.

Massie sat on her bed for the next hour reading about Dale's twelve principles on "how to win people to your way of thinking." Numbers 3, 4, and 8 appealed to her the most.

```
┌─────────────────────────────────────────────┐
│              CURRENT STATE OF THE UNION        │
│        IN                      OUT             │
│                 Principle #3                   │
│   If you are wrong, admit it.    Blaming others, │
│                           especially when you are guilty. │
│                 Principle #4                   │
│   Begin in a friendly way.   Making hate murals to show │
│                              how hurt you are. │
│                 Principle # 8                  │
│   Try to see things from the    All of my friends │
│   other person's point of view.   are backstabbers! │
│                                                │
│   Advice from Dale Carnegie.    Advice from Bean. │
└─────────────────────────────────────────────┘
```

When she was done, she opened her e-mail and began drafting her apology letters.

DEAR K & D,

HI. THOUGHT I'D DROP YOU A "FRIENDLY"
E-MAIL. I'M SORRY I WALKED AWAY WHEN
KRISTEN GOT STOPPED FOR SHOPLIFTING FROM BCBG.
(BTW—ARRESTED? HOPE NOT ☺.) I WAS JUST UPSET
THAT YOU THOUGHT I TOLD ALICIA YOUR SECRETS.
BUT IF I HAVE TO SEE THINGS FROM YOUR POINT OF
VIEW, I UNDERSTAND WHY YOU THOUGHT THAT. I
WOULD HAVE TOO. ANYWAY, I KNOW WHO TOLD HER.
CALL ME IF YOU WANT TO FIND OUT.
                                    XOXO

Massie hit save, then wrote another one.

DEAR CLAIRE,

HI. THOUGHT I'D DROP YOU A "FRIENDLY"
E-MAIL. IF YOU ARE STILL SICK, I HOPE YOU
FEEL BETTER. IF YOU ARE UPSET ABOUT CAM
OR MAD AT ME FOR SOME REASON, PLEASE CALL
ME. I WOULD LIKE TO SEE THINGS FROM YOUR
POINT OF VIEW SO I CAN ADMIT I'M SORRY.
PLUS I'M GOING TO FAIL GEOMETRY IF YOU
KEEP THIS UP ☺.

XOXO

Massie hit save again, then wrote one last e-mail.

DEAR ALICIA,

HI. THOUGHT I'D DROP YOU A "FRIENDLY"
E-MAIL. ALICIA, I ADMIT WE'RE EVEN, OKAY?
LET'S END THIS WAR BEFORE SOMEONE (YOU)
GETS HURT.

XOXO

When Massie was done, she dragged her e-mails into her drafts folder. She wanted to give her friends a little more time to apologize first.

Massie grabbed her cell phone and ran at top speed out to the horse barn. "I must be filled with apology power," she said to Bean, who was trying her hardest to keep up. The dog's tongue was hanging out of her mouth and she was starting to wheeze.

"Sorry," Massie panted. "I'll slow down." Right as Massie stopped, Bean took off. "Hey, that's not fair, you cheater!"

But Massie became concerned when Bean started barking. "Chill out," Massie called after her.

Bean ran around the side of the barn to the sliding door. From a distance Massie could see the dog jump up on her hind legs and scratch the glass. Maybe some workmen were inside?

"Quiet, Bean." Massie picked up her pace. "No one's in there."

But when Massie got to the glass door, she saw that she was wrong.

All of her ex-friends were sitting on the floor, surrounded by bowls of snacks, CDs, and scattered Polaroid pictures. Even Claire was there, sucking on a lollipop and laughing. She didn't look the least bit sick or depressed.

Massie felt her heart leap. Were they throwing her a surprise party? Was her mom sent to lure her there? No wonder everyone had been acting so weird. But the happy feeling disappeared as quickly as it came. Her birthday wasn't until July.

Massie yanked the handle on the glass door and slid it open. Beyoncé was blasting from the stereo. No one heard her come in.

"What's going on?" Massie asked. She turned down the

music and asked again. "What's up?" She felt like a stranger in her own home.

Claire, Kristen, Dylan, Olivia, and two girls who looked like Kristen and Dylan were sitting on *her* yoga mats surrounded by makeup and hair accessories. They wore Alicia's knockoff scarves around their wrists.

"What are *you* doing here?" Alicia said. "No one invited you."

"I LIVE HERE!" Massie shouted.

"So does *Claire*. And *she* invited us."

Massie looked at Claire, expecting her to look scared and ashamed. But she didn't fidget or bite a single fingernail. Instead Claire met Massie's eyes and stared straight into them. It was Massie who finally had to look away. She searched her mind for some of Dale's words of wisdom, but the only thing that came to mind was, "Kuh-laire invited you?"

"We're practicing our poses for the *Teen People* shoot." Alicia peeled off a *maybe* sticker and stuck it on a Polaroid picture of herself.

Massie glared at Kristen and Dylan, then raised her eyebrows, wondering why they sabotaged the revenge plan. Alicia wasn't supposed to *know* they were booked for the photo shoot. They were going to shock her by just showing up. It was all about stealing her spotlight, just like she had done to them. . . . And now all of that was ruined.

Kristen and Dylan looked away, not offering a single word of explanation.

Alicia opened her new phone and turned her back to

Massie. "Now, if you don't mind, we have a phone call to make."

Everyone surrounded Alicia while she placed the call, using the speakerphone.

Massie stood at the back of the barn and watched. She reached into the pocket of her black Juicy hoodie and ran her fingers along her Motorola, feeling the empty spaces from the missing rhinestones.

"Hey, Lu," Alicia said into the phone.

Massie rolled her eyes when she heard the nickname Alicia gave to Lucinda. She knew this would have been a good time to leave, but she was so curious, she couldn't pull herself away.

"Hey, Alicia." Lucinda's voice came through the speaker.

"Do you have the info for us?" Alicia glared at Massie.

They could hear the sound of Lucinda shuffling papers in the background. "Ch-ch-ch-ch-chhhhh . . . The itinerary is here somewhere. . . . Got it!" she shouted. "Ohhh-kaaay, dinner at Sushi Samba Friday night, say eight-ish. Dress downtown chic; you know, West Side bohemian with money. Don't wear anything by J. C. Penney, J. Crew, or J.Lo, and absolutely nothing that even looks like dirty Lower East Side indie-music lover. You'll stay at the Soho Grand Hotel with *moi* as your chaperone. Then Saturday morning you'll shop for holiday clothes, and we'll shoot you with Santa in the afternoon."

The girls cheered silently and exchanged a round of soft high fives. "Will the magazine cover the shopping expenses?" Kristen asked.

"Who just asked me that?"

"No one," Alicia said, punching Kristen on the thigh.

"So who's up for spending the weekend in the big city?" Lucinda asked, shaking off Kristen's insult.

"YEAH!" The girls screamed and cheered.

Massie watched everyone hug each other. She felt like a ghost looking in on a life she had left behind.

"Great." Lucinda laughed. "Will you need a car to pick you up on Friday?"

"No," Alicia said. "We'll take my limo."

"Heart you," Lucinda said.

"Heart you too," Alicia said. But Lucinda had already hung up.

Massie took a deep breath and marched over to Alicia. She stood over her and put her hands on her hips, looking straight down into her big brown eyes. Principle #4 was calling to her, reminding her to "begin in a friendly way. . . ."

"Will you *please* get out of my house, you wannabe, or the only thing you'll wanna be from now on is DEAD!"

Everyone looked at Alicia, wondering how seriously they should be taking Massie's threat.

"NOW!"

"Let's go to my house." Alicia gathered up her Polaroids and dropped them in her green Prada bag. "At least *my* gym is *decorated*." She turned on the heel of her brown velvet ballet flats and headed for the glass door. Everyone scooped up their bags and followed her.

Massie and Bean stood in the horse barn surrounded

by snack crumbs, yoga mats, crushed makeup, and CDs.

Massie raced to her bedroom, deleted her apology e-mail messages, and threw her mother's self-help books down the laundry chute.

"Dale Carnegie may know how to win friends and influence people," Massie said to Bean as she walked back out to the barn with a big green garbage bag. "But he doesn't know the first thing about Westchester."

```
┌─────────────────────────────────────────────┐
│                                               │
│     OCTAVIAN COUNTRY DAY SCHOOL               │
│                                               │
│                                               │
│                2:10 PM                         │
│              December 5th                      │
│                                               │
└─────────────────────────────────────────────┘
```

Claire stood in front of her open locker, barely taking the time to appreciate the twenty strands of Nerds Rope candy Layne had hung for her. Usually she loved Layne's surprise locker gifts, but today Claire had more important things on her mind.

Suddenly Comma Dee's low voice came through the loudspeaker and broke Claire's concentration.

"Hey, OCD, this is Comma Dee, yeah, you know me . . ." she rapped. *"I just want to give a shout out to the six glamour girls who are city-bound to model for the* Teen Peep *holiday issue. Hey, Alicia, if you're still here, I have a joke for you. Tell this one to your new fashion friends. . . . What do you call Seven jeans for fat chicks?"*

Claire heard a chorus of moans and groans echo through the halls. The only things the students loathed more than Comma Dee were her jokes.

"Give up? I'll tell ya. . . . The new Seven jeans for fat chicks are called Eights. Get it? EIGHTS? That's all for now. Have fun and don't forget Comma Dee when you're famous."

Claire checked her watch and slammed her locker shut. She heard a few of the Nerds come crashing down inside but decided to deal with them on Monday, along with her neglected history assignment.

She tossed her backpack over her shoulders and sprinted down the hall. Alicia's limo was waiting in the school parking lot and she didn't want to be the last one to arrive. What if they left without her?

"Slow down." Claire heard a familiar voice behind her. "Did you see your locker present?"

Claire stopped and turned around. "Oh my God," she gasped when she saw Layne's face. "Who *did* that to you?" Claire covered her mouth with her palm and shook her head in utter disbelief. "Was it Massie?"

Layne held her head high as she walked past a huddle of snickering girls. If she wasn't blind to their finger-pointing and deaf to their name-calling, she sure was acting like it. She caught up to Claire and smiled with pride.

"Walk with me." Claire grabbed Layne's arm and tugged her down the hall. "I'm late. And besides, you need to get out of here."

"Why?" Layne asked as she got pulled through the halls by Claire. "Are you embarrassed to be seen with me?"

"Do you know what you *look* like right now?"

Claire was referring to the headgear that was fastened around the back of Layne's neck and hooked into her upper molars. The metal wire around her face was covered with refrigerator magnets and dangling key chains; some flashed pink and green lights. It looked like a decorated Christmas tree branch was in orbit around her jaw.

"Tanya Fuchs said I look like I crashed into Spencer Gifts. But I think I look festive," Layne said, holding her

Hello Kitty magnet in place as Claire pushed her toward the back door. "Why are we going out here? Aren't you getting picked up in front of the school?"

"Yeah, but I don't want anyone else to see you like this," Claire said, noticing the white-and-blue World's Best Mom pin that Layne had fastened between Homer Simpson and a goggle-eyed frog.

"Why?" Layne giggled.

"Because I *like* you," Claire snapped.

"Awwwww." Layne smirked. "You're tho thweet," she teased.

"It's not funny, Layne." Claire looked straight into Layne's narrow green eyes. "Everyone is laughing at you."

Layne stopped walking. Claire stopped too and turned around to face her.

"What?" Claire stomped her foot and held out her pink Baby G-Shock watch. "I'm late."

"Claire, did I shove you out some back door when you showed up on the first day of school wearing white Keds and overalls?" Layne asked.

"That's totally different." Claire started walking again. She could hear Layne inching up behind her. "People thought I was out of style, not out of my *mind.*"

"True." Layne chuckled. "Well, anyway, now will you believe I don't care what people think of me?" She swung her canvas Sunshine Tours bag back and forth like a giddy little girl.

"Oh yeah." Claire suddenly felt a rush of admiration for her quirky friend. She waited for Layne to catch up to her before continuing on to the parking lot. They walked in comfortable silence until Claire felt a drop of moisture land on her face.

"Did you feel that?" She looked up at the sky, hoping it wasn't about to rain. This was her first big trip into Manhattan and she didn't want anything to block her view of the skyscrapers.

"Oh, sorry," Layne said, wiping a pink droplet off Claire's cheek. She immediately stopped swinging her bag. "I have a Popsicle in here." She patted the stained canvas. "It must have melted."

Claire giggled. "You reaaally *don't* care what people think, do you?" They both burst out laughing at Layne's sticky bag.

They were still laughing when they rounded the side of the school and stepped onto the paved parking lot. Claire spotted Dean and Alicia immediately. They were both standing with their arms crossed in front of the open car door.

"Hurry," Alicia screamed.

"Coming from the girl who moves slower than detention," Layne murmured.

Claire giggled, then started to run. Layne was following close behind.

"What are you doing?" Claire huffed and puffed. "Don't you have class?"

"I want to give you a proper send-off."

Claire could feel herself getting annoyed all over again. "You don't have to."

"Kuh-laire," Alicia shouted. "Everyone's waiting."

"Ugh," Claire said in total frustration. She started running again, too frazzled to care if Layne was behind her or not.

"Ehmagawd," Alicia squealed when she saw Layne. "It looks like you barfed up a waiter's suspenders from TGI Friday's."

Kristen, Dylan, Faux-livia, Strawberry, and Kori stuck their heads out the window of the limo. They burst out laughing when they saw Layne's headgear.

Claire looked at Layne out of the corner of her eye. Layne was smiling.

"That's a pretty good one," Layne said. "For you."

"Help," Claire mouthed to Alicia when Layne wasn't looking.

Alicia winked at Claire and held up her index finger to let her know she'd be a minute. She disappeared inside the limo and came out dragging her lime green snakeskin Prada bag. She opened the side zipper and pulled out one of her signature knockoff Louis Vuitton scarves.

"Layne," Alicia said. She sounded like a kindergarten teacher about to discipline a bad student. "I'll make you a deal."

"Yeah," Layne said. She looked bright and cheery, like she had no idea she was embarrassing herself.

"If you take that antenna off, *right now,* and promise never to wear it to school again," Alicia said, waving the scarf in front of her eyes, "I'll give you my very last Louis."

Layne tapped her index finger against the bar of her headgear as if she were carefully mulling over the offer.

"It's totally worth it," Alicia said, sounding like a desperate salesgirl working on commission. "It allows you to hang out with us whenever you want."

Claire knew Layne was wondering how she could be friends with such a conceited girl and felt slightly embarrassed for having bought into Alicia's rap.

"Whenever I want?" Layne cracked her knuckles.

"When-*ever*," Alicia said, anxious to close the sale.

"Fine." Layne took off her headgear and clipped it around the handle of her Sunshine Tours bag. Alicia placed the scarf in Layne's open palm.

"Thanks, I totally needed this." Layne stuffed the scarf into her bag. It was covered in gooey pink liquid when she lifted it out.

Alicia gasped.

"Oops, my Popsicle melted and I ran out of tissue," Layne said. She tossed the sopping wet Louis at Alicia. "Have fun on your shoot, Claire," she called over her shoulder as she walked away. "Call me when you get back."

"I will," Claire promised with a huge grin on her face.

Claire avoided Alicia's eyes when she slipped into the limo.

"How can you be friends with her?" Alicia asked when she sat down.

"How could I not?" Claire giggled.

"Let's go, Dean," Alicia called into the front seat. "We want to get there before dark."

Claire sighed, relieved that Alicia had changed the subject.

"Aren't we waiting for Massie?" Dean asked into the rearview mirror.

"She's not coming." Alicia raised the glass divider between them.

Claire was tempted to ask how Massie was going to get there but decided not to. Why should she care? They were no longer friends.

Alicia clapped once they started moving and bounced up and down in her seat. "We're off!"

"Yippeee!" Strawberry, Kori, and Faux-livia bounced and cheered. Kristen and Dylan said nothing. They didn't even bother looking up from the pages of *US Weekly* to see what all the excitement was about.

Eventually the yelling got to them. Dylan turned to Alicia. "Why are *they* here?"

"Yeah, they're not even modeling," Kristen added.

"Uh, we can hear you." Strawberry clenched her fist.

"Good, so maybe *you* can tell me why you're coming to New York," Kristen said.

"Because they are my *friends*," Alicia said firmly.

"Whatevs," Dylan said, returning to her *US Weekly*.

Claire watched Strawberry and Kori examine the contents of the fridge, play with the stereo, and fiddle with the sunroof. She felt like she was watching herself three months ago.

"Where are your scarves?" Alicia asked the girls. They looked up at her with the startled expression of someone who just realized she left her homework assignment on the school bus. "I thought you were going to wear them around your necks."

"I did." Faux-livia beamed, pulling her turtleneck sweater to one side.

"I have mine around my ankle," Strawberry said, lifting up her winter white cords. "How cute is it there?"

"Mine is around my wrist," Kori said. "I thought it looked good with my beaded bracelet." She slouched down and shook her wrist so the beads knocked up against the scarf.

"And *yours?*" Alicia turned to Kristen and Dylan.

They both tapped their bags and grinned, making it very clear to Alicia that they refused to play by her rules.

"Fine," she said, immediately turning her attention to Claire.

"I forgot about the neck thing." Claire pulled the scarf out of her back pocket and began to tie it. "Sorry." She felt a little stupid following an order from Alicia but knew she wasn't on the same level as Kristen and Dylan. She was still relatively new and had to play along.

"That's better," Alicia said with a satisfied smile. "Now, who has gossip?"

No one said a word.

Dylan and Strawberry took turns digging into a big bag of Utz pretzels while Kori and Kristen twirled their blond braids around their fingers. Claire couldn't believe how much Dylan and Strawberry were alike. They both had the same bright hair and loved eating, while Kori and Kristen had identical hairstyles and were both great athletes. For a split second Claire wondered if Alicia had tried to re-create Massie's Pretty Committee by finding Dylan and Kristen look-alikes but decided that would be way too psychotic, even for Alicia.

"No one has *any* scoop?" Alicia said. "I'll give ten gossip points to the first good piece."

"Yeah, who has some juice?" Faux-livia echoed.

"What are gossip points?" Kori asked.

"You get points for good gossip," Kristen explained, sounding over it. "The better the gossip, the higher the points."

"What do you get with the points?" Strawberry asked. "Stereos and stuff?"

"This isn't the American Express Membership Rewards program," Dylan snapped. "At the end of the week the person with the most points wins."

"There's no reason to yell," Strawberry said.

"There is if you're going to ask stupid questions." Dylan opened her mouth and showed Strawberry her pretzel-covered tongue.

Claire and Kristen laughed.

"Gross," Strawberry said, whipping the pretzel bag at Dylan's face.

"Stop it!" Alicia snapped.

Everyone was quiet until Kori broke the silence. "So what *do* we win?"

"Five-letter word for *satisfaction*," Kristen said. "Can also be a pack of lions."

"Huh?" Faux-livia asked.

"Pride," Claire said with a degree of modesty in her voice. She was tired of all the fighting.

"But wait." Alicia shot her index finger in the air.

"Maybe I *should* start giving out prizes. You know, change it up a little."

"Love it!" Faux-livia shouted.

"That's stupid," said Dylan. "Do you really want to buy a new gift every single week? And what if you win? Do you buy yourself a gift? Then what?"

"Yeah, it worked perfectly the old way," Kristen said.

"Just like everything else," Dylan said under her breath.

"So how many gossip points did Todd Lyons get?" Faux-livia asked.

Alicia kicked Faux-livia in the shin.

"OUCH!"

"Sorry," Alicia said, her eyes wide and pleading.

"It's okay." Faux flashed a forgiving smile.

"Todd *who?*" Claire asked.

"Your brother, stupid." Faux obviously didn't clue in to Alicia's warning.

"What did Todd do?" Kristen asked.

"Oh, is Todd that kid who eavesdropped on Massie's sleepover and then told—" Kori stopped talking after Strawberry's fist jabbed her ribs.

"Ehmagawd, you got our secrets from *Todd?*" Dylan said.

"Not Massie?" Kristen asked.

All Alicia could do was shrug.

"He's so dead," Claire said, just to make sure she wouldn't get blamed for her brother's crime.

"We thought *Massie* told you," Dylan said.

"It may have been Massie," Alicia said. "I can't remember. That was so last week."

Dylan and Kristen stared out the window in silence for the next ten minutes. Dylan scraped salt chunks off the pretzels with her thumbnail while Kristen re-braided her hair. Claire could tell they were thinking about all the terrible things they had said about Massie. She would have felt guilty too, but she wasn't mad at Massie for spilling her secrets, she was mad at her for stealing Cam. And that was never going to change.

"Wait, I have some gossip," Faux announced.

Claire couldn't believe anyone could be so oblivious to tension.

"What?" Alicia asked, obviously over it.

"Shay Goldhar peed in her pants after lunch yesterday," Faux said. "She had a big wet spot on the back of her jeans."

"That wasn't pee," Strawberry said. "She fell in a puddle during lunch. There were at least ten witnesses."

"Well, I heard it was pee."

"I heard that too," said Kori.

"Sorry, no points," Alicia said.

Faux crossed her arms over her chest and pretended to sulk.

While they were arguing, Claire saw Kristen and Dylan text messaging. She knew exactly who they were speaking to and what they were saying.

"I can't believe we left without her," Claire heard Kristen whisper to Dylan.

Dylan squeezed her eyes shut and shook her head. She felt terrible about it.

Their thumbs moved at high speeds as they sent messages to Massie. Claire watched them bite their nails and exchange worried glances while they waited to see if Massie could ever forgive them. Suddenly they both smiled and sighed. They were back IN.

"Yes!" Dylan said softly. She reached for the bag of pretzels and dug in. "She's on her way into the city."

Claire mouthed, "How?"

"Harris," Dylan mouthed back.

"Who else?" Claire asked.

Dylan shrugged.

Claire felt her stomach drop. Was Cam there too?

Kristen and Dylan looked relieved when they slipped their cell phones back into their bags. They sat up in their seats and touched up their lip gloss. They finally seemed excited for the weekend to get started. And Claire couldn't wait for it to end.

Massie felt her frozen cheeks begin to thaw the minute she stepped into the crowded restaurant. She had cursed the broken heater in Harris's Mustang almost as many times as she'd cursed his earsplitting boy music. But from what Kristen and Dylan said, it was still better than being in Alicia's limo, although Massie wasn't entirely convinced.

"Are you sure it's okay if we crash your big models-only dinner?" Derrington was bouncing up and down, trying to get the circulation back in his bare legs. They were waiting for one of Sushi Samba's lanky hostesses to show them to their table.

"I told you." Massie dragged a tube of light pink gloss across her lips. "Lucinda said it was okay because Harris drove me here."

"But what about us tagalongs?" Cam put his arm around Derrington.

"I took care of it, okay?" Massie dabbed her mouth on a book of matches she grabbed off the tall oak hostess stand and put them back in the stack.

"Very sexy." Derrington giggled. Massie laughed too.

A beautiful Asian woman with a blond afro held a stack of menus under her arm like a Fendi clutch. "May I help you?" she asked Derrington's purple knees.

Massie stepped forward, blocking Derrington and his baggy blue shorts from the hostess's view. "Yes, I'm here to meet Lucinda Hill. She's a fashion editor for *Teen People*." Massie watched to see if the hostess's face lit up when she heard that a real fashion editor was there. But it didn't. She still looked bored and hungry.

"Ms. Hill has been seated on the roof," the exotic hostess said.

"Of course she has," Harris said, mocking her snobby tone.

Massie swung her black Barneys shopping bag into his knee.

"Ouch," Harris said playfully. "What's in there?"

"Don't worry about it." Massie hit him again.

"Don't hit my brother." Cam slapped Massie's butt.

Massie laughed, then made a fist. She was winding up for a punch when the hostess grabbed her arm.

"You KIDS can follow me," she said.

Massie, Cam, Harris, and Derrington giggled as she led them through a thick crowd of glamorous people drinking colorful cocktails at the bar and shouting over the loud samba music. Massie thought everyone looked like models, even the men. And she hoped they could tell that she was a model too.

"I think I'm overdressed," Derrington said.

Cam, Harris, and Massie busted out laughing.

Waitresses dressed in silver microminis, white-fur-trimmed wife beaters, and Santa hats scurried from table to table balancing wood trays of elaborately decorated sushi rolls on their frail palms. Derrington pushed Cam into a blond, big-chested waitress, but Cam managed to catch his balance before he went slamming into her chest.

The two boys burst into a fit of hysteria.

The hostess rolled her eyes and pointed to a spiral staircase that had been sprinkled with small metallic snowflakes. Red and green tinsel hung off the banister and made Massie think of fake eyelashes.

"Your party is up there. I'm sure you'll find them," the hostess said.

Then in a flash she was gone.

The closer Massie got to the top, the quicker she moved. She couldn't wait to see Kristen, Dylan, and Claire now that they were friends again.

When she stepped onto the roof, Massie gasped. It was covered by a puffy white canvas dome that reminded her of the indoor tennis courts at her country club. Flickering light from the candles on the tables reflected off the tented ceiling and made the whole place look like it was surrounded by flames. A Jamaican steel drum band playing a reggae version of "Winter Wonderland" gave Massie the urge to jump up on the nearest table and start dancing. If she hadn't been wearing her two-inch turquoise platform clogs and a satin navy minidress, she might have.

"This place is awesome," Harris said when he got to the top.

Massie made a mental note to consider Sushi Samba for her sweet sixteen party.

"Heeeyyy," shouted two familiar voices. "Over here." Kristen and Dylan were waving frantically.

"Heyyy," Massie called. She zigzagged her way through the maze of chairs and tables until she got to the long rectangular booth in the back of the room.

A tall girl wearing a skintight denim pantsuit and a tangle of gold chain belts and necklaces jumped up from her seat and held out her arms. "You must be Massie," she said, pulling her into a hug. Her big blue eyes added a welcome splash of color to her porcelain white skin. "I heart that I'm finally meeting you." She looked down at Alicia, who was in the seat beside her and smiled proudly.

"Don't you just heart that I say heart now?" she asked Alicia.

"I totally heart it," Alicia said, avoiding Massie's eyes.

"You must be Lucinda," Massie said, putting the woman's attention back on her.

"In the flesh." She ran her long red fingernails through her short black hair and turned to the tall thin man standing beside her. "This is Paolo, our photographer," Lucinda said, lifting her arm and resting it on his shoulder. Massie noticed he had an August tan in December and assumed he had just returned from some exotic beach location. His shark tooth necklaces and the unruly stubble on his face were dead giveaways. Massie lifted her hand and tilted her head slightly to the right so he could see her best side.

"'Allo, Mahzzie," he said, sounding French or Italian or something.

"Hey," Massie said. Then she quickly turned her attention to the table, afraid she was about to get stuck with a bad seat. Cam and Harris sat on the loser side of the table, near Alicia and the EWs, and Derrington had taken the empty seat beside Kristen. There was only one left—between him and Claire. Massie sighed as she sat down, wishing she were closer to Kristen and Dylan. She kicked her big Barneys bag under the table and put the brown cloth napkin on her lap. A waiter immediately swooped in and placed four bowls of edamame on the table. Paolo snapped a picture of everyone reaching for them at once.

"Finish your story about the secret celebrity couple," Alicia urged Lucinda.

"Right," Lucinda said, sliding the peas into her mouth, then tossing the empty green pod in a bowl. Massie noticed that the pod was covered in her red lipstick and reached behind her chair, hoping to tap Kristen on the shoulder and show her.

"Massie, I never knew," Derrington said when he felt her arm on the back of his chair.

"Puh-lease," Massie said, feeling herself blush.

"So my sources tell me"—Lucinda leaned in to the table and said in a hushed tone—"this actress is only dating him to help her brother get a part in his next movie."

"Oh my God, that's worth like a thousand gossip points," Strawberry said.

"More like a million," Kori said, clapping.

"It's not worth *anything*," Dylan announced. "That rumor is not true."

"'Scuse me?" Lucinda's mouth hung open and her eyes bulged.

Massie leaned forward in her chair and tapped her chopsticks on the table. She loved that Dylan knew everything about celebrity gossip.

"*You're* challenging *me?*" Lucinda said.

"I'm not challenging you; I'm correcting you," Dylan said. Kristen let out a phlegmy laugh. Lucinda flared her nostrils.

Dylan turned to face the camera to let Paolo know he should get a shot of her. He clicked away.

"She isn't dating him so her brother can get a part in his movie. They've been married for two years. In fact, they're about to have a baby. They just don't like the press, so they keep their personal lives a secret." Dylan cocked her head and took a sip of her virgin cosmopolitan. "But there's no way you could have ever known that, so don't be too hard on yourself."

"And how would *you* know?" Lucinda squinted suspiciously.

"My mom told me."

"And who's your—"

"Merri-Lee Marvil," everyone said at once.

"Ah." Lucinda looked down and opened her menu.

"Don't worry, Luce," Alicia said, touching Lucinda's shoulder. "It's probably a fake item."

Massie felt her pulse quicken. She widened her amber eyes and placed both of her palms on the table. "You should know!" She didn't care if the entire restaurant heard her.

"What's that supposed to mean?" Alicia yelled from the other end of the table.

Paolo swiveled his head back and forth, snapping pictures as though he were shooting a tennis match at Wimbledon.

"It means it takes a fake to know a fake," Massie hissed. "Those wannabe Louis scarves you've been giving out should be illegal. I wouldn't be surprised if you all have rashes around your necks when you take those things off tonight. And what about those two?" She pointed to Kori and Strawberry. "They're total knockoff versions of K & D."

Kristen and Dylan smiled with deep satisfaction and sat up a little taller in their seats.

"Now that I think of it, you do look like Dylan and Kristen," Harris said to the wannabes.

"Totally," Cam agreed.

"Thanks," Kori said sweetly.

"Yeah, thanks." Strawberry beamed.

Paolo quickly changed his roll of film. Lucinda was scribbling notes on her cloth napkin and saying things like, "Oh this is good," to herself.

"Why are you taking their pictures?" Massie asked Paolo. She was pointing at Strawberry and Kori. "They aren't even modeling tomorrow."

"Whoops," Paolo said, screwing on his lens cap.

Massie looked at Claire, hoping to find her laughing at the chaotic scene. But Claire seemed oblivious as she slapped her bowl of rice with a piece of edamame.

"What's wrong?" Massie asked.

"Headache," Claire said without looking up.

"Oh." Massie wanted desperately to ask Claire why

she'd been ignoring her lately but decided to wait until her headache was gone.

Massie was forced to turn her attention to Derrington.

"So what's with the shorts?" she asked the second he popped a spicy tuna roll in his mouth. "It's the middle of winter."

Derrington held up his hand to let her know he'd answer her when he was done chewing. He made a big show of swallowing and then opened his mouth. "All gone." He laughed.

"Gross." Massie giggled. She couldn't help it. He had a boyish look in his brown eyes that actually made him look cute.

"You're showing just as much leg as I am," Derrington said.

"Yeah, but I'm wearing tights," Massie said, though she was somewhat impressed by the grain of truth in his argument.

"Well, then, honey, next time you're at the mall, you just mussst pick up a pair for me," Derrington said in a flamboyant voice. Massie threw her head back and cackled. Alicia watched her, probably wondering what Derrington had said to make Massie laugh so hard.

Alicia hooked a piece of hair behind her ear and turned to Lucinda, pretending to be interested in the story she was telling about a rained-out Hilary Duff shoot in Maui.

"Hey." Derrington spun in his seat and faced Massie head-on. "What would you rather wear?"

Massie clapped, excited that he liked to play her favorite game. "Shorts all winter long or cashmere sweats all summer?"

"You can buy cashmere sweats?" Massie asked. "Why didn't I know about that?"

"You can't, I don't think," Derrington said. "I just made that up."

"Phew." Massie wiped pretend sweat off her forehead. "I thought I was missing out."

"So?" Derrington said. "What would you rather?"

"Cashmere sweats," Massie said, popping a piece of ginger in her mouth.

"Ugh, why?"

"Because I'd be the first one to have them," Massie said with a smug smile.

This time Derrington threw his head back and laughed. When he straightened up, he batted a messy blond curl away from his eyes and said, "You're awesome."

Massie felt a rush of tingly, prickly heat on the bottoms of her feet and immediately wanted to ask if he was joking. No other guy had ever complimented Massie like that except her dad, and he didn't count. She looked around to see if anyone else heard him say that, but they were still caught up in Lucinda's Hilary Duff story.

"What would *you* rather?" Massie asked, desperate to move past the awkward moment. "Shorts or cashmere?"

"Uh, isn't it obvious?" Derrington said, pointing to his shorts.

"Oh yeah, sorry." She giggled.

Massie could feel her face turning red. She lowered her head under the table and pulled out her Barneys shopping bag.

"I almost forgot," she said, handing it to Claire. "This is

for you."

"What is it?" Claire asked. She looked annoyed that Massie was interrupting her conversation with Paolo.

"Open it," Massie said. "Maybe it will get you out of this *mood* you've been in lately."

"It's not a 'mood.'" Claire moved a piece of avocado around on her plate with a chopstick, then stabbed it.

Massie clenched her fists and tried to keep her breathing slow and steady. "Kuh-laire, did you join the circus?"

"No, why?" Claire sounded bored.

"Because you've been acting like a TOTAL FREAK." Massie heard Derrington laugh and bit her bottom lip to keep herself from smiling. "Now, are you going to take this or what?" She stuck her hand inside the Barneys bag and pulled out Claire's winter coat. The one she'd left at Cam's.

"Look," Massie said, rubbing the puffy down jacket against Claire's hand. "You can stop wearing all of those ridiculous layers now."

Claire grabbed the coat and buried her own head in it. "There? Is that better?"

"What are you doing?" Massie screeched.

"Rubbing my face in it." Claire's voice was muffled. "Just like you wanted."

Massie laughed out loud, impressed by Claire's clever comeback.

But Claire was breathing heavily and her entire face was scrunched up like she had just sucked on a lemon.

"What's your problem?" Massie pleaded. "You're acting

like a ten-year-old."

And then, as soon as the words had left her mouth, Massie figured it out. *Todd!* He must have told Claire he heard Massie saying she liked Cam. Or maybe Alicia told her about the time she saw Massie at the Fishers'. . . .

"You're not my friend," Claire whispered. She pushed her chair back from the table and ran to the bathroom.

Massie sat frozen in her chair.

"Can someone please go make sure she's okay?" Lucinda said. "We have a long day tomorrow and I don't need her sulking and bringing everyone down."

"I'll go," Alicia and Massie said simultaneously. They paused and looked at each other. At the exact same moment they both jumped out of their seats and raced through the restaurant to the single restroom by the upstairs bar.

Alicia knocked wildly. "Claire, it's Leesh—let me help you."

Massie shoved her out of the way. "Claire, it's Massie. Let me in—we have to talk."

"Leave me alone," Claire sobbed. It sounded like she was choking.

"I'm not leaving until you let me in," Massie said to the door.

"Go flirt with your *boyfriend*," Claire shouted.

"Derrington is not my boyfriend," Massie shouted back.

Alicia gasped and put her hand on her mouth.

"I'm talking about *Cam*." Claire sounded frustrated. "I'm not an idiot."

"I never said you were an id—"

"Massie, I'm so over you!" Claire wailed. "I don't care if you throw things at me in the halls or if you spread rumors about me or . . . anything! I'd rather be a complete loser than have you as a friend . . . you . . . you *boyfriend* stealer." She started crying even harder.

Alicia's jaw dropped. She had obviously never heard anyone talk to Massie like that before, and the cocky smirk on her face showed that she loved every minute of it.

"Kuh-laire." Massie pressed her lips right up to the door. "I would never steal your boyfriend. How *As the World Turns* do you think I am?"

"Alicia told me everything, okay?" Claire said. "She even saw you at his house, so don't try to lie."

A line was starting to form outside the bathroom, but Massie did her best to ignore it. "Kuh-laire, I went there to get your coat."

"Yeah, right!"

Massie took a deep breath and exhaled slowly before she continued. "And to tell him that I put you up to the dump," she said softly.

"Liar," Claire said flatly.

"I swear on Bean," Massie said, holding her palm up to the closed door.

"Really?" Claire opened the door slowly. At first she revealed the tip of her nose, then a tear-soaked cheek, and eventually the side of her mouth. "Did you tell him *you* liked him and that's why you did it?"

Massie leaned closer to the crack. "Yeah, right!" She rolled her eyes. "I told him that I heard he liked to look up girls' skirts and that I was looking out for you."

Massie heard Claire blow her nose and laugh. "And he believed you?"

"Of course," Massie said.

"Puh-lease, Claire," Alicia said, pushing up the sleeves of her navy velvet blazer. "Do you really buy that?"

"I believe her," said an older woman with a neat gray bob and thick black glasses. "Now settle the rest of this on *Ricki Lake* and let me pee."

Massie ignored the woman. "Look, if I wanted to steal Cam, I would. Simple as that."

Claire finally opened the door. She was met with a round of applause from a group of strangers leaning against the wall with their legs crossed tightly. She stepped out of the bathroom and was instantly pushed aside by the woman with the gray bob.

"So does he still like me?" Claire asked Massie.

"Why do you think he's here?" Massie asked. "I saw him waving to you all night, but you kept looking away."

"I thought he was waving at you." Claire sighed. Then her face broke into a slow smile as she processed the news. She giggled with relief.

Massie leaned over the bar and grabbed a stack of cocktail napkins. She handed them to Claire. "Blow."

Then she held out her arms, hoping for a hug. "Hello? Are you gonna make me stand here like a loser forever?"

Claire sniffled and wiped her eyes. "Maybe."

"I would," Alicia said.

But Claire ignored her and hugged Massie.

Alicia made a retching sound and stormed back to the table, trying to look like everything had turned out exactly the way she had wanted it to.

Massie and Claire returned with their arms around each other.

"Where are Cam, Harris, and Derrington?" Claire asked once they sat down.

"Mr. Fisher came to pick them up," Dylan said. "They're spending the weekend at his apartment in SoHo."

"Isn't our hotel in SoHo?" Claire asked.

"Yes, it is," Lucinda said while she signed the check. "But there will be no boys tonight. I need my models looking fresh in the morning. Save your flirting for the playground."

Claire quickly hopped out of her seat. "Look," she said to Massie, her face glowing. Cam had left a CD on her chair called *The Claire Doesn't Have a Boyfriend in Florida Mix*. "How cute is he?"

Claire pinched Massie's elbow and smiled excitedly. And Massie giggled and pinched back. Only it was the idea of seeing Derrington on Monday that made *her* happy. That and the fact that she could pinch Claire's elbow again.

Alicia tightened the white cashmere scarf around her neck, wishing she had chosen a different outfit. Her black draw-string satin karate pants and gray cowl neck were keeping her warm; it wasn't that. She just didn't look half as "West Side bohemian with money" as Massie did and was suffer-ing from an extreme case of ensemble envy. Alicia would have given anything to trade her boring Calvin Klein sepa-rates for Massie's wispy knee-length paisley dress and faded boot-cut Juicy jeans. The only thing she had going for her was the Dixon that wrapped around her thigh.

"What is that on your leg?" Lucinda asked. They were standing on the corner of a gritty cobblestone street called Gansevoort in the Meat Packing District, New York City's latest IT shopping mecca.

"What do you mean?" Alicia said, looking confused. "It's the Dixon you gave me. The thing Avril was wearing on her cover shoot."

"Why is it on your leg?"

"You said there were fifty-eight ways to wear it," Alicia said. "I assume this is one of them." She looked at Faux-livia for backup.

"Yeah, the leg is number thirty-seven," Faux said.

"Well, I made a bit of a mistake," Lucinda said. "That thing you're wearing was part of the packing materials. It's a scrap. My brain-dead assistant pulled the wrong thing. The Dixon is really a soft wire accessory that can be bent into fifty-eight different shapes."

"Oh." Alicia and Faux-livia quickly rolled the mesh scraps off their legs and tossed them in a trash can. Luckily Massie had been whispering something to Kristen, Claire, and Dylan and missed the whole thing.

"All right, ladies." Lucinda adjusted her oversized black fleece cowboy hat. "You have until two o'clock to buy the looks you want to wear on the shoot this afternoon."

"It took me longer to buy a winter coat for my *dog*," Massie whined. The girls giggled, so she continued with her gripe. "How are we supposed to find something ah-mazing to wear in *two hours?* It's not like we shop in the Meat Packing District every day."

Alicia had been thinking the same thing and was mad she hadn't spoken up sooner. "Do you have a floor plan or something?"

Everyone laughed at Alicia's question.

"I'm only kidding." She giggled, trying to hide her embarrassment. Alicia was still trying to get over the humiliation she felt after losing Claire to Massie at Sushi Samba. Any more mess-ups and Strawberry, Kori, and Faux-livia would lose all faith in her as an alpha.

"You'll be fine," Lucinda said, trying to reassure them. "This area is more concentrated than Paul Mitchell's Hair Repair."

She smiled to herself. "Scoop, Jeffrey, Stella McCartney, and Alexander McQueen are all right here. If I only shopped in these four stores for the rest of my life, I'd be set." She tossed her gold-coin-covered scarf over her shoulder. "Let's move."

Lucinda led the way. A pigeon lay dead with its guts spilled out in the middle of the road and a group of women in high-heeled boots stepped in it as though it were a glistening drop of spring water. Big green bags of trash were stacked on the curb outside every restaurant they passed, and the smell of chicken feathers hung in the unseasonably still air. Alicia swallowed twice, trying her hardest not to barf up the bagel and cream cheese she had for breakfast.

"Isn't this neighborhood the coolest?" Lucinda turned around and asked the girls. "You'd never know that just a few years ago, these stores were animal slaughterhouses."

"Uh, I would," Massie shouted. She was trailing behind the rest of the group with Kristen, Dylan, and Claire. "It's disgusting."

Everyone laughed at Massie's honest reaction, even Lucinda. And Alicia cursed herself again for not beating Massie to the punch.

"Let's cross here," Lucinda said. She stood on the curb in front of the Little Pie Company, waiting for the Pretty Committee to catch up. She reminded Alicia of a parent chaperone on an OCD field trip. "These jagged cobblestone streets will take you down if you're wearing heels, girls, so walk on your tiptoes."

Paolo jogged backward, snapping shots of all eight girls

walking toward their first store. "Girls, will you *please* get closer together? My lens is only so wide, you know."

Alicia, Faux, Kori, and Strawberry stopped walking to let Massie, Kristen, Alicia, and Claire catch up. But every time Lucinda slowed down, they did too.

"Ugh," Paolo said, showing his frustration. "You girls are killing me."

Lucinda tapped her green leather cowboy boot while she waited for everyone to cross. "Now remember," she said once they were all together again, "don't buy anything with horizontal stripes—they make you look wide—no black because it's dowdy, and *nothing* with a logo or label on the front. You're models, not billboards."

"No *labels?*" Alicia snapped, pleased with herself for speaking up before Massie.

"Of course no labels," Massie said. "Do you know how much money the magazine makes on advertising? Why give it away for free when they can get paid for it?"

"She's absolutely right, Alicia," Lucinda said to Massie. She was clueless to the growing tensions among the girls. "Wow, I'm impressed."

Alicia stuck her tongue out at Massie, and Massie responded with one of her cocky half smiles. Paolo managed to capture the entire exchange.

"You girls should have your own reality show," he said, still walking backward. "This is pure money."

"You should be on *ER*," Massie said to Paolo.

"Why?"

"Because you're about to fa—" Massie shrieked.

Paolo backed right into a heap of stuffed garbage bags. His long skinny legs shot straight up into the air and disappeared over his head. Three containers of film rolled into the middle of Washington Street.

"Ehmagawd," the girls shouted.

Alicia looked up at the bloated silver sky, trying her hardest not to laugh. She caught Massie's eye for a spilt second and thought it looked like she was about to lose it too. Alicia knew that if they were still friends, they'd be doubled over in hysterics.

"I'm okay." Paolo rolled onto his side, pushed himself off the trash heap, and stood up. He scooped up his camera gear and began blowing on his lens. "Watch out, little girl," he said to Massie. "I know your bad side."

"To know it is to love it," Massie said, throwing her arms around Dylan and Kristen.

"To know it is to love it," Paolo mimicked, doing his best bratty Massie impersonation.

Everyone laughed, even Alicia, who suddenly found herself missing her old best friends. She longed for the old beta days, when she would spread gossip, not instigate it, and regretted ever thinking she could be a better alpha than Massie. But it was too late to turn back now. She had Fauxlivia, Strawberry, and Kori now. And they needed her.

"You each get three hundred dollars," Lucinda said, doling out the cash while Paolo documented the transaction. "Except you two," she said to Strawberry and Kori. "Sorry."

The two girls shuffled to the outside of Lucinda's tight circle of models.

Alicia ignored Strawberry and Kori's pathetic expressions and reached inside her gold hobo sac. She touched her pink leather wallet to make sure she had her credit cards. Three hundred dollars would barely cover the cost of the chandelier earrings that were dripping off the mannequin in the window of the ultra-trendy Scoop.

Paolo went in first so he could snap the girls walking into the store. He took a few establishing shots of the fake Christmas tree in the middle of the store and the pierced and tattooed salespeople refolding messy piles of turtlenecks.

"Can we go in now?" Faux-livia asked.

Lucinda tapped on the window to make sure Paolo was ready for them. He gave her a thumbs-up. "Go ahead."

"I feel like I'm in heaven," Alicia said to Faux-livia, Strawberry, and Kori when they entered the all-white store and saw the incredible jeans selection on the back wall.

"Look at those shiny bags," Faux said, pointing to festive glittery clutches along the glass countertop by the register.

"And those cool lace dresses," Strawberry said. "I'm gonna go take a look."

"I wanna check out their boots," Kori announced before taking off and slamming into Massie, who had been carrying an armload of miniskirts that were now all over the ground. Kori and a salesguy raced to pick everything up while Massie stood above them with her hands on her hips.

"I can't stand to watch this anymore," Alicia said to

Faux-livia. "I have to get those chandelier earrings before anyone else grabs them."

On her way to the jewelry display, Alicia passed Dylan. She was looking at the lace dresses and stuffing her face with the free sugar cookies that had been hanging on the tree branches in wax envelopes.

Strawberry wandered up beside her and started looking at the same dresses.

"Why are you breathing down my neck?" Dylan asked Strawberry. "Do you want something?"

"'Kay," Strawberry said, putting her clammy fingers all over the two cookies Dylan had in her hands.

"Uch, just take them," Dylan said.

"Thanks," Strawberry said with a grateful smile. "So what are you gonna buy?"

Alicia wanted to shop for earrings but couldn't help listening in on their conversation, in case she had to jump in and save Strawberry.

"I don't know what I'm gonna buy yet," Dylan snapped.

"Let me help you—you know, since we kind of look alike and all," Strawberry said.

"Puh-lease," Dylan shouted. She wiped her crumby hands on a pair of pin-striped pants. "Your hair color comes from a packet of Kool-Aid and by the look of those thighs your nickname should be Pear, not Strawberry."

"I was only trying to help," Strawberry screeched. Her face turned bright red.

Alicia put the earring back on the velvet display board

and ran to Strawberry's side in case she started crying. "You okay?" she asked. But Strawberry ignored Alicia.

She grunted twice and whipped her half-eaten cookie on the shiny white floor. "You moose!" she shouted from a place deep within her and pushed Dylan into the metal rack of lace dresses.

Paolo snapped as many shots as he could before the security guard grabbed Strawberry by the back of her pink ponytail and dragged her outside.

Alicia buttoned her gray wool coat and ran after her. She followed Strawberry out of the store and chased her across 14th Street. She could hear Lucinda calling their names but ignored her.

Alicia finally caught up to Strawberry inside the Little Pie Company.

"You okay?" Alicia asked again, trying to catch her breath. She felt cold and sweaty at the same time and hoped *Teen People* would be doing her hair and makeup before the shoot.

"She's lucky I didn't take one of those leather belts to her," Strawberry said, without a trace of humor. "Blueberry tart, please!" she called to a man behind the counter who was in the middle of serving another customer.

Alicia felt her phone vibrating and reached into her bag to answer. She was grateful for the distraction.

"Hullo?"

"Hey, it's Lucinda; we're going to Jeffrey." She hung up before Alicia could ask how Dylan was.

"You're getting that tart to go," Alicia told Strawberry.

When they got to Jeffrey, they were greeted by a doorman in a tuxedo. "You'll find everything you need right up those stairs," he said. They walked up three marble steps and straight into the cosmetics department. "Enjoy your beauty."

The store looked more like Bloomie's than a boutique. Beyond the makeup and perfume was an endless selection of clothes and shoes that seemed to stretch on for miles.

"I love it already," Alicia said to Strawberry, who was sucking blueberry off her thumb. "Remember, stay away from Dylan. You're better than her. Besides, you don't want her to sue you. Her mother knows a million Hollywood lawyers."

"Isn't your dad a lawyer?" Strawberry said, wiping her hands on her coat.

"Yeah, her mother's," Alicia said.

"Whatever," Strawberry said. "She started it."

Alicia saw Massie and Dylan weaving in and out of the shoe display that cut through the middle of the entire store. Dylan's ponytail was a little messy, but other than that, she looked fine.

"I have to shop," Alicia said, trying to make up the time she lost chasing Strawberry.

"Fine, I'm going to hang in the front of the store by the cosmetics," Strawberry said. "I need some new gloss."

"Cool, see you in a bit." Alicia sprinted toward the designer clothes in the back.

She knew exactly what she wanted. She had seen a fashion spread in *Teen Vogue* called Grecian Yearn, and Alicia wanted to make it her look for the holiday season. She needed a pair of pencil-straight jeans, preferably in a dark wash, and an ultra-feminine Greek-goddess-type minidress to wear over it. High heels, hopefully in a bold metallic color, would complete the look. Just then Alicia spotted the perfect pair.

"Do you have these bronze snakeskin mules in a size five?" Alicia asked the tidy, thin salesman in the shoe department. His black turtleneck was tucked into his black pleated pants and fastened with a thin black belt. He reminded Alicia of her mascara brush.

He plucked the shoe out of Alicia's hand and turned it over to look at the price. "Is your mother a size five?" His free hand was bent behind his back.

"These are for *me*," Alicia said.

"Honey, maybe you read the tag wrong," he snipped. "These are six-hundred and forty-nine dollars, not sixty-four dollars and ninety cents," he said, replacing the shoe on the big white display cube in the center of the floor.

"Maybe *you* read *me* wrong," Alicia said, picking the shoe up and placing it back in his hand, making sure the heel dug into his palm. "I know how much they cost, *honey.*"

He grabbed the shoe and disappeared into a back room. Alicia sat on the couch and waited, wishing Massie had been there to hear her tell him off. Alicia had one hour left to find her dream outfit and was starting to feel the pressure. Everyone was at the back of the store sorting through racks of dresses and Paolo was taking their pictures. Alicia was desperate to get to the action.

She shuffled to the back of the store in her socks to get

Kori. Maybe she wouldn't mind waiting for the shoes while Alicia shopped and got in a few of Paolo's pictures.

Alicia found Kori in the middle of a conversation with Kristen and decided not to interrupt. If they hit it off, maybe Kristen would join forces with them once again.

"If I were you, I'd pocket the three hundred dollars and wear *that*," Kori whispered to Kristen.

"I can't wear a Juicy sweat suit on the photo shoot. Besides, they're so two years ago," Kristen said. "I'm just wearing it now because it's easy to get in and out of while I'm trying things on."

"Yeah, but don't you, like, *need* the money?" Kori asked.

"What?" Kristen's aqua eyes looked a little glassy. Alicia knew where this was going.

"Hey, Kori, sorry to intrude, but—"

"There's nothing wrong with being poor, Kristen," Kori said, ignoring Alicia. "Don't forget, I live in the Brickview too."

"Probably because your mother spent her entire savings on those face-lifts that made her look like Michael Jackson," Kristen said, loud enough for the two older ladies at the next rack to hear.

"She needed them for her sinuses." Kori stomped her foot. "She had a deviated septum."

"So they removed her entire nose?" Kristen shouted.

"At least my mother could afford surgery," Kori screeched before she took off running.

"Well, maybe she can *afford* to get you soccer lessons, 'cause you suck on defense this year."

"Thanks a lot, Kristen." Alicia sighed. She ran through the store in her socks, chasing after Kori. On her way out, Alicia passed the exact same Greek goddess dress she had seen in *Teen Vogue*. She grabbed it off the rack and tossed it in the arms of the first salesgirl she saw.

"Can you please hold this for me? I'll be right back."

"Of course, madame," the rail-thin blonde said.

Alicia got outside just as the first flake of snow fell to the ground. "Great," she said to her new yellow cashmere socks.

Kori was squatting on the ground with her back against the outside wall of Jeffrey, crying.

"Kori." Alicia crouched down and rubbed her friend's kneecap. "Why are you so upset? You know your mother doesn't look like Michael Jackson."

"She always had a narrow nose," Kori cried. "Even before the operation."

"I know." Alicia tried her hardest to keep a straight face, but inside she felt a pang of regret. After all, it was Alicia herself who had spread the story about Kori's mother's surgery, months ago. She even taped pictures of Michael Jackson to Kori's locker every day for a week. Alicia, Massie, Kristen, and Dylan would hide and wait for her to tear them off. Once she did, they would laugh until they had tears rolling down their cheeks. Kori never figured out who put those pictures there or why they did it.

"Let's go back in." Alicia checked her silver Gucci watch. "It's starting to snow."

"I'm gonna stay here," Kori said.

Alicia reached into her pocket and pulled out the three hundred dollars from Lucinda. "Share it with Strawberry," she said, stuffing the crisp twenties into Kori's cold hand.

"What are *you* going to use?" Kori said, wiping her tears.

"The same thing I always use." Alicia held up Len Rivera's Platinum Visa.

Kori threw her arms around Alicia and hurried inside to grab Strawberry.

Alicia ran in behind her, bolting up the front steps inside Jeffrey's two at a time. She couldn't wait to try on her dream dress. If it fit, she would run across the street to Dernier Cri and buy the super-straight-legged jeans she saw in their window.

"Excuse me, miss, would you mind showing me where you put that turquoise dress?" Alicia asked the blonde salesgirl.

"Oh, you're beck," she said, turning to the shoe guy who had helped Alicia earlier. "Luis, ze petit girl is beck."

"I thought you left." His hands were clasped behind his back and he rocked back and forth on his heels.

"I just ran outside for a second," Alicia said, putting on her boots. "Sorry about that. So where is the dress?"

The girl searched the store with her eyes and stopped on Massie, who was standing at the cash register. "She is buying it right now."

"You're kidding, right?"

The woman stared blankly into Alicia's eyes and it was clear she had no idea what "kidding" even meant.

"But that was *my* dress," Alicia said, not aware that she was whining to a complete stranger. She felt two hands grab the back of her shoulders.

"Let's go, gorgeous," Lucinda said to Alicia. "The limo is waiting. We have to be camera ready by four or else we lose our Santa."

Alicia felt her mouth go dry. She felt like she was going to pass out.

"But I didn't get to buy one thing," she said.

"What were you doing for the last two hours?" Lucinda asked her BlackBerry.

"I was *trying* to be a good friend." Alicia watched her ex-friends file out of the store, swinging their bags and comparing purchases. Paolo was right behind them, capturing it all.

"So does this mean you still have the three hundred dollars?" Lucinda held out her palm.

Alicia froze. "Uhhh—"

"Just kidding." Lucinda cackled. "Keep it. It's not my money. I'll give you something from The Closet. So what if it's all from the spring collections; at least you'll stand out."

"Thanks," Alicia said, trying to hide her intense disappointment. It wasn't easy. Even Kori and Strawberry had two new belts to show off.

The radio was blasting a JoJo song and Kristen, Dylan, Massie, Claire, and even Faux-livia were giving each other ideas on how they should wear their hair.

"What did you get?" Faux-livia asked Alicia.

"Lucinda said I could wear something from The Closet," Alicia piped up, like it was a special privilege.

"You're so lucky," Faux said, bouncing up and down on her hands.

"I know, I can't wait," Alicia said, eyeing Massie's shopping bags.

"Well, I can't wait to wear this baby." Massie pulled out the Greek goddess dress. A sheet of white tissue paper landed by Alicia's feet. "I loved it the minute I saw it in *Teen Vogue.*"

Alicia crossed her legs, then uncrossed them. She shifted her weight from one butt cheek to the other. No matter how much she squirmed, she couldn't squash the urge that was building inside her. She even tried biting her tongue to keep herself from saying anything, but that just *hurt.*

"Admit you saw me pull it off the rack first," Alicia said.

Massie laughed through her nose and shook her head. "You're the wannabe, not me."

Kristen and Dylan broke into a round of high fives. Claire fidgeted with the automatic door lock button. Strawberry and Kori looked at Alicia to see how she would react. But it was Faux-livia who spoke first.

"Massie, I know you bought the dress to bother Alicia," she said. "I heard you talking about it with Dylan." Faux looked at Dylan and smirked.

"How can you hear anything with all of that dry hair covering your ears?" Dylan said.

"Well, at least her hair isn't the same color as Ronald McDonald's," Alicia said.

"Heyyy," Strawberry said. "I take offense to that."

"Heyyy is for horses," Kristen said.

"Yeah, like Dylan," said Kori.

"And sails are for boats," Alicia said. "Unless you're Kristen."

"At least I have a job," Kristen said. "What are you going to do when old man *Rivers* dries up?"

"His last name is RIVERA!"

"Are you related to Joan and Melissa?" Strawberry asked.

"Shut up," Alicia snapped. "Why can't you be cool for one second? Gawd, how hard is it?"

Strawberry's mouth opened wide and she crossed her arms in front of her chest.

"Sorry," Alicia said, protecting her face with her hands. "Remember, my father's a lawyer."

Strawberry stuffed her fists in her coat pockets.

The middle partition rolled down and Lucinda popped her head into the backseat.

"We're here," she sang.

"Now that we've stopped, lemme get one fun shot in the limo," Paolo said. "Say 'Merry Christmas.'"

"Merry Christmas," Claire said flatly, just before the flash went off. No one else uttered a single word.

The girls entered the gray cement building in silence, but once they stepped inside the photo studio, they gasped. The spacious room looked like the inside of a snow globe. Big fluffy chunks of fake snow fell lightly to the ground and gathered in heaps like mountains made of Sweet'N Low. A big red velvet throne surrounded by brightly wrapped presents was in the center of the room and cute little boys dressed as elves ran around playing tag. A jolly-looking Santa, holding his white glue-on beard, paced the floor, rubbing his fat belly like a pregnant woman. Camera assistants dressed in black T-shirts and jeans were adding the final decorations to the tall blue Christmas tree beside Santa's throne.

Alicia breathed in deeply, inhaling the sweet smell of pine.

"Is that real?" she asked, wondering how a fake blue tree could give off such a strong smell.

"Yeah, we dyed the needles," Lucinda said.

"Does that bother you?" Massie asked.

"Huh?" Alicia said.

Massie turned to Lucinda and said, "Alicia likes everything to be fake."

Alicia wanted to shout, "I hate fake things. The knockoff

scarves were an act of desperation. So were Kori and Strawberry and the cheating and everything else I did."

But she didn't.

Instead she felt everything she'd gone through the past few days boiling up inside her. Then she took a big step back and charged Massie, knocking her into one of the elves. They both caught their balance before either one of them fell.

"Excuse me, there's no hitting in fashion," Lucinda said.

"There is now!" Massie said as she ran full speed into Alicia. This time they both landed in the "snow." Alicia could feel Massie's bony butt on top of her back as Massie bit at her hair. Alicia turned around and tried to lick Massie's cheek, hoping it would make her get up. But every time she stuck out her tongue, Massie would grab it and pinch it.

"Et off eeee," Alicia screamed. It was the closest she could get to, "Get off me," without the use of her tongue. She wrapped her fingers around Massie's charm bracelet and used it as a handle to pull Massie's arm away. One of the charms fell off in Alicia's hand and she quickly dropped it in her boot.

Alicia saw a sudden flash of light and thought she might be dying until she heard Paolo say, "I love it. Give me more drama."

Big flakes of white powder fell from the ceiling while stage-hands tested the snow machine. Alicia tried to wipe them away from her eyes, but Massie's knees were digging into her arms.

"Stop it, you're hurting her," Faux-livia said as she jumped on Massie's back and pulled her off Alicia.

"Get her, Faux," Alicia yelled.

"Stop calling me FAUX," Olivia wailed, then slapped Alicia on the thigh.

"Ouch," Alicia said before she pushed Olivia's nose.

"Not the nose!" Olivia pushed back hard just as Kristen was coming over to watch and Alicia fell against Kristen's shins.

"I need those for soccer, you know," Kristen said to Olivia before charging her. They fell against Santa's throne and squashed the prop presents that had been placed beside it.

"Did you wrap this one *at work?*" Olivia asked Kristen as she pulled a crushed box out from under her and smashed it over Kristen's head.

"The only job you ever had was the one on your nose!" Kristen said as she whacked Olivia across the back with a satin ribbon.

"Stop it before you destroy my set," Lucinda said, racing to drag the fake presents out of the way.

"Move," Paolo shouted at Lucinda. "You're blocking my shot."

"How's this for a shot?" Lucinda said, snapping his leg with her coin-covered scarf.

Alicia rolled away from Massie and quickly jumped to her feet. She caught her reflection in one of the round silver ornaments on the tree beside her. Her lip was swollen and her hair looked like a bird's nest. She looked around to see how the other girls were holding up.

Kristen and Olivia had each managed to squeeze one of their butt cheeks on Santa's throne and were clawing at each other's necks, fighting for complete domination. Dylan was pulling Kori across the floor by the tips of her rubber snow boots, a big pile of fake snow gathered between her legs. The elves were chasing Strawberry and Claire, trying to pull their pants down, and Lucinda was shouting, "Security!" to no one in particular.

"*You're* calling *me* hearty?" yelled Dylan. Everyone stopped fighting and looked up. Before anyone could stop her, Dylan tackled Santa and they both smashed into the blue Christmas tree.

"*Tim-ber!*" Kristen shouted when the tree started to sway.

Dylan and Santa looked up at the tipping tree and screamed. They rolled away one second before it came crashing down onto the studio floor.

Everyone raced over to Santa and Dylan's side, except Massie. She stood across the room with a half smile on her face, watching the drama from afar. Alicia didn't want to get caught staring at her but found it hard to look away. It felt like there was some mysterious magnetic force at work, drawing her in. And then, as if Massie had felt it too, she turned her head and looked right at Alicia with her fiery amber eyes. A sudden rush of prickly heat shot up Alicia's spine and made her feel intensely alive, like a cell phone that just had its battery recharged.

Suddenly, for no reason and every reason, they both started laughing. And once they started, they couldn't stop. They held their stomachs, slapped their thighs, threw their heads back, and let the tears spill down their cheeks.

Until, without warning, Massie's smile faded. Her eyes became wide with fear and her mouth hung open. She grabbed her wrist and dropped to her knees.

Was she having a heart attack?

Alicia raced across the studio and knelt by her side.

"What's wrong?"

"My crown is gone." Massie ran her fingers along the studio floor, sifting through the fake snow, blue pine needles, and broken ornaments.

"When was the last time you saw it?" Alicia looked around the destroyed studio.

"I dunno." Massie's eyes filled with tears.

"I'll go look on the other side." Alicia stood up. "Don't worry, we'll find it."

"'Kay." Massie sniffed.

When Alicia got to the middle of the studio, she felt a sharp pain in her foot and dropped down to the floor. She unzipped her boot and massaged the sore area until the throbbing eased up. She quickly pulled up her sock and heard a faint *ping* sound. She looked down and there it was, right beside Alicia, in a tiny hill of fake snow. A piece of yellow sock fuzz was tangled around one of its points.

Alicia giggled to herself as the memory of her tugging on Massie's bracelet and stuffing it in her boot popped back into her head. "I found it!" she shouted once she was back on her feet. "Massie, I have it."

Massie was crawling around on her hands and knees, occasionally wiping tears away with her shoulder.

"I found it," Alicia shouted again.

Massie jumped to her feet.

"Where was it?" Massie asked when Alicia put it in her hand.

"Uh, just sitting on the ground. I almost stepped right on it."

"You're the best," Massie said, wrapping her arms around Alicia.

"Thanks, you are too." Alicia hugged her back.

"This shoot is over," Lucinda announced. She was kneeling on the floor, icing Santa's forehead, and he lay motionless beside her. The other girls were fanning him and looking concerned.

"Why?" Massie let go of Alicia.

"Why?" Lucinda shrieked. She stood up and walked over to Massie and Alicia, pointing at them as she spoke. "Because I have no set, no Santa, no presents, no tree, and very little holiday cheer."

Alicia couldn't help feeling disappointed. She had been so looking forward to this day and it was ruined.

"Great idea!" Massie said. "Lucinda, you're a genius."

"Huh?" Lucinda and Alicia said.

"No other magazine would have the guts to show how stressed out people get around the holidays, but it's something everyone can relate to."

"That *is* a great idea," Alicia said. "You can call the piece 'Santa's Little Hell-pers.'"

"That's *perfect,* Leesh," Massie said.

Alicia felt warm and happy inside. Massie hadn't called her Leesh in weeks.

"I heart it," Lucinda said.

"Well, you should." Massie's eyes sparkled. "It was your idea."

"It was?" Lucinda said.

"I thought I heard you suggest that, but maybe I was wrong." Massie glared at Alicia, silently begging her to play along.

"I thought I heard that too," Alicia said.

"You did," Lucinda said, twisting an oversized emerald ring around her index finger. "You did."

"Thought so," Massie said with a satisfied smile.

"I need all stagehands, models, elves, and Paolo to meet over by Santa for a quick meeting," Lucinda shouted. "The show will go on!"

Everyone cheered.

"What was that all about?" Alicia asked Massie once Lucinda left.

"*How to Win Friends and Influence People.* Principle number seven," Massie said. "Let others think the idea is theirs."

"Spoken like a true alpha." Alicia nodded with sincere admiration.

Massie clipped the crown back on her bracelet.

"It's hard doing what you do," Alicia said, wiping her eyes.

"Why do you think I'm so moody?"

"Massie." Alicia heard her voice quiver. "I'm really sorry for everything I did to you. I promise I will never do anything to hurt you guys ever again." She offered her pinky. "Friends?"

"On three conditions," Massie said, holding her pinky slightly out of Alicia's reach.

"Anything."

"One: Claire is the only new addition to the Pretty Committee this year. That means Olivia can't sit with us during lunch anymore, but you can still be friends with her."

"Fine," Alicia said. "Next."

"Two: you have to get rid of those knockoffs."

"But *my* scarf was real." Alicia winked. She untied it from her belt loop and held it out for Massie to feel.

"Not *that,*" Massie said. "I'm talking about Strawberry and Kori. Those girls have *no* soul."

"Done," Alicia said. "And third?"

"Third is do it NOW," Massie said.

"Done." Alicia quickly pulled out her cell phone and used her family account to order a Town Car before Massie changed her mind.

Alicia found Kori and Strawberry standing in the far corner of the studio by the food table while Lucinda met with the rest of the group in a private huddle thirty feet away.

"Why are you all the way over here?" Alicia asked.

"She doesn't want us to listen." Strawberry sneered at Lucinda. "We're not models."

"I'm so canceling my *Teen People* subscription," Kori said. She dropped her shoulders and shot her pelvis forward.

Alicia checked her watch. "Wanna go outside for a minute?"

"Sure," Kori said.

"You may want to grab your stuff."

"You mean you're letting us go home early?" Strawberry asked hopefully.

"Yeah." Alicia sighed. "I'm sorry."

"Don't be sorry—we've been dying to go home. This has been the worst weekend ever," Strawberry said.

"It has, hasn't it?" Alicia agreed.

"Beyond," Kori said.

When they pushed open the heavy studio door and stepped outside, all three girls squinted while their eyes adjusted to the light. The sun had burst through a break in the clouds and the air smelled like clean sheets. The falling snow had started to accumulate and the hectic city was silent and peaceful.

The burgundy Lincoln Town Car pulled up in front of the studio door fifteen minutes later. The driver rolled down his window and held out a sign that said Kori, Strawberry.

"Here's your ride," Alicia said.

"Thanks." The girls hugged Alicia good-bye and practically dove into the car when the driver opened the back door. They waved as they rode away and didn't stop until they were far down the street. Alicia couldn't help smiling as she waved back. It was the perfect end to a perfectly awful day.

Alicia rubbed her cold hands, then glided back into the studio. She was ready to apologize to the others and start making up for lost time.

"Brilliant," she heard Lucinda say when she got back upstairs. "That's a wrap." Everyone started clapping and cheering.

Alicia froze. They had finished the shoot without her.

When Massie saw Alicia, she marched straight up to her and looked her directly in the eye. "*Now* we're even," she said with a cocky half smile.

Alicia opened her mouth to protest, but no words came out. There was nothing left to say.

```
┌─────────────────────────────────────────────┐
│                                               │
│      OCTAVIAN COUNTRY DAY SCHOOL             │
│              THE CAFÉ                         │
│             12:39 PM                          │
│           December 19th                       │
│                                               │
└─────────────────────────────────────────────┘
```

Ever since the *Teen People* shoot, Massie had given Claire permission to eat at number 18. But most days Claire chose to sit at number 2 with Layne, Meena, and Heather. It was the only time she got to spend with Layne now that she carpooled with the Pretty Committee. But this was a special occasion and Claire didn't want to be late.

"Layne, if you don't hurry up and finish your chicken fingers, I'm going to Massie's table without you," Claire said, feeling extra-springy in her new Keds. They had a cluster of star and moon charms dangling off the tongue, which was probably why Massie said, "They're a little better than the old ones," when she saw them.

"I'm coming," Layne said, taking one last bite of her lunch before dumping the rest of her chicken in a Ziploc. She zipped it up and dropped the leftovers in her Sunshine Tours bag. Meena and Heather shrieked.

"Happy?" Layne asked Claire, pulling the fake Louis Vuitton scarf out of her pocket and wiping her hands.

"I thought you left that in the parking lot," Claire said.

"I went back and got it when you guys drove off." Layne shrugged. "It's surprisingly absorbent."

Claire, Meena, and Heather laughed. Layne shook the crumbs off the scarf and stuffed it back in her bag.

"Can we *go* now?" Claire hardly ever reacted to Layne's weird eating habits anymore. She accepted them along with the rest of the quirks that made her best friend so much fun to be around.

"What's the big hurry?" Meena asked. She lowered her wide hazel eyes and admired the henna tattoo on her own hand.

"I told you," Claire said, half knowing the girls were just giving her a hard time. "Lucinda sent copies of the pictures she's putting in the magazine and Massie is showing them to all of the models at 12:40 PM."

"Who's Lucinda again?" Heather smiled, flashing her new multicolored braces.

"Shut up." Claire threw her napkin at Heather and they all laughed.

"When do the lowly non-models get to see the pictures?" Meena raised the back of her hand to her forehead and turned her head to the side.

"They are open to the public at 12:50 PM sharp; that's why I have to go *now*," Claire said, checking her pink Baby G-Shock watch. "I would have invited you, but I'm only allowed to bring one *non-model*." Claire made air quotes when she used Meena's word.

"Eat your hearts out." Layne wrapped her nubby Hello Kitty scarf around her neck and flicked the tip of her nose before she turned to leave. "Let's go, Claire."

Meena and Heather shouted, "Sellout," and threw napkins at Layne's back.

A line of curious students was already forming behind Massie's table when Claire and Layne showed up. Massie's expression was one of pure joy.

"It looks like you're selling Justin Timberlake tickets or something," Claire said to her.

"I know, they've been lined up since the beginning of lunch," Massie said.

"Come on, let's see 'em already," Dylan said, reaching for the white cardboard envelope in Massie's hand. But Massie quickly pulled it away.

"Okay, is everyone ready?" she asked.

"YES!" Kristen, Dylan, and Olivia said.

Everyone leaned in toward the center of the table except Alicia.

"What's wrong?" Massie asked her.

"It's not like I'm in any of them," Alicia said lightly.

"Not true," Massie said. "You're in one."

"You already looked?" Kristen said. "I thought this was the *first* showing."

Massie opened her mouth to protest but let out a laugh instead. "Busted," she admitted.

She opened the envelope and started passing out the photos. Every single shot showed the girls fighting.

"These are hilarious." Dylan was looking at an image of herself with an elf on her back. His little finger was hooking the side of her mouth and pulling it back toward her ear.

"What about this one?" Kristen laughed and passed the picture to Olivia.

"Oh nooo," Olivia said. "I'm so sorry." It was a shot of her stuffing Santa's fake beard in Kristen's eyes while Claire tried to pry them apart.

By now the entire cafeteria was watching table 18—even some of the teachers were hovering. Claire finally lifted her head. "No way. The general public line goes all the way out the door."

"Yes!" Massie threw her fists in the air when she noticed the hordes of people that were waiting to see her pictures.

"They've been standing for almost an hour." Layne shook her head in disbelief as she glanced at the line, where several girls were eating their sandwiches. "They'll do anything for a peek into the fabulous life of Massie Block. It's shocking."

"You're here, aren't you?" Kristen said to Layne.

"I'm supporting Claire." She lifted her chin. "That's the only reason."

"Yeah, right." Claire snapped a picture of the crowd with her digital camera.

"Lemme guess," Layne said. "Another picture for Cam, right?"

Claire shrugged and smiled shyly.

"This is awesome," Olivia said, looking around the Café.

Everyone at number 18 nodded in agreement and Claire felt like the natural order of the universe had been finally been restored. Kristen, Dylan, and Alicia surrounded Massie like the planets orbiting the sun, while Claire, Layne, and Olivia were like the stars, standing over them and twinkling with pride.

"I say we open to the public now," Massie announced.

"But it's not twelve-fifty yet," Alicia said.

"Doesn't matter." Massie surveyed the restless crowd. "I don't want them to lose interest."

"Good point. Step right up," Alicia called.

And for the next forty-five minutes they did.

The proud smile on Massie's face was the last thing Claire saw before a mass of curious fans completely surrounded the leader of OCD's infamous Pretty Committee.

Suddenly Claire had a tiny idea of what being Massie Block must feel like. Every day she had to make people *want* to be her and every day she had to somehow show them that it was a lot harder than it looked. And that was the one thing about Massie that Claire didn't envy.

```
┌─────────────────────────────────────────────┐
│                                               │
│        OCTAVIAN COUNTRY DAY SCHOOL            │
│           TREE-LIGHTING PARTY                 │
│                                               │
│                 6:00 PM                       │
│              December 21st                    │
│                                               │
└─────────────────────────────────────────────┘
```

The dark winter sky was filled with thousands of shining stars and the hickory smell of the bonfires was putting everyone in the holiday spirit. Massie didn't even mind the sound of the OCD choir. In fact, she even walked toward them so she could hear them sing "Jingle Bells" under the tree.

She stood with Claire below the massive pine and looked up. Blue and orange lights flashed for Briarwood, and navy and burgundy glowed for OCD. A copy of every student's ID card hung off the branches, and gifts for the poor, wrapped in shiny paper and fancy ribbons, surrounded the base.

Usually Christmas trees made Massie feel sad because they reminded her of that terrible feeling of being all dressed up with nowhere to go. But tonight the bright dangling ornaments filled her with excitement. She had a feeling the new year would be the best one yet.

"How are we ever going to find Cam in this crowd?" Claire asked Massie.

"He told me he'd call when he gets here. How many times do I have to tell you that?" Massie didn't mean to sound impatient, but it was the third time Claire had asked her about Cam and it was starting to get ah-nnoying. "I hope you don't act this desperate around *him*. It's a total turnoff."

"You're the only one who ever sees me like this."

"I must be blessed," Massie said. "It's freezing out here." She loved her new fur-trimmed Anna Sui Eskimo minidress, but it was doing a lousy job of keeping her warm. How did Derrington do it? Massie felt her heart flutter when she thought about him and couldn't believe she was cursed with liking a boy who only wore shorts. "Where are those kiss-butts with the hot chocolate?"

"Who?" Claire asked.

"Every year a few loser students dress up as angels and pass out warm drinks," Massie explained.

"One kiss-butt at your service." Strawberry seemed to appear out of nowhere.

She wore a white snowsuit with huge angel wings sewed to the back. Her face and hair were covered in silver glitter and she held a tray filled with plastic foam cups. Each cup had tiny angel wings of its own.

Massie busted out laughing and turned away.

"Uh, she's sorry," Claire explained, fighting a smile. "She didn't mean it."

"Whatever," Strawberry said. "Just take one before I whip this tray at her glossy new blowout."

"You noticed." Massie smirked.

Claire helped herself to two steaming cups, automatically handing the marshmallow-free one to Massie. "Thanks, Strawberry. Happy holidays."

Strawberry snorted, then turned and walked away.

Claire turned her back to Massie and took a sip.

"How are the marshmallows?" Massie asked.

"How did you see that?" Claire turned around and faced Massie.

"Why didn't I get any?" Massie whined.

"SUGAR!"

"Please," Massie said. "Do you know how much sugar is in those Dr. Juice drinks I was downing? Did you know that fruit *is* sugar?"

Claire shook her head.

"So I might as well have one of those." Massie pointed to Claire's cup. "It's practically the same as eating an apple."

Claire pinched a marshmallow and handed it to Massie.

"Thanks," she said with her mouth full. "I wonder where everyone else is?"

"Maybe you should check your phone to see if anyone called," Claire said.

"You're brutal." Massie tried to open her brand-new Samsung picture phone without spilling on it. "Weird, it says I have two messages." She secretly hoped one of them was from Derrington.

"Oh my God, check them, check them."

"Hold," Massie said, giving her cup to Claire. "It's Alicia. They're over by the cookie table."

"And the other message?" Claire asked once Massie closed her phone.

"Wrong number."

Claire's face dropped and she looked like a sad puppy.

"Kidding, okay? Cam wants me to tell you he's at the cookie table with Derrington and the girls."

Claire tossed their hot cocoa in the trash and took out her vanilla Softlips SPF 30.

"I don't care what your dad says; I'm getting you a cell phone for Christmas," Massie declared.

On their way to the cookie table Massie and Claire checked in with their parents, said "happy holidays" to at least a dozen teachers, and even waved to a few of the losers. By the time they got to their real friends, Massie's face hurt from fake smiling so much.

"I thought you'd never get here," Cam said to Claire, handing her a CD.

"Thanks." Her face lit up when she accepted his gift. "Sorry I'm late. I was just talking to my boyfriend in Florida." Claire giggled. "He misses me so much around the holidays."

"I can't imagine why." Cam tossed his half-eaten cupcake at her face.

Massie laughed at the glob of brown icing on Claire's nose.

Claire wiped the icing off and smeared it on Massie's cheek.

"Very funny," Massie said with a smile, hoping Derrington would notice how good-natured and fun she was.

Alicia quickly handed Massie a napkin. "So what do you think?" She slipped her gray coat off her shoulders.

"You look ah-mazing," Massie said.

Alicia was wearing the turquoise Greek goddess dress with a pair of skinny black jeans and metallic gold boots.

"Thanks again for my early Christmas present," Alicia said. "Wait until you see what I got you."

"I'm psyched," Massie said before focusing her attention on Dylan. "That DKNY dress is so slimming."

"Thanks." Dylan turned and smiled.

"Cam, that emerald sweater really brings out the green in your eye," she said.

"And Kristen, uh—" Massie searched for something nice to say about Kristen's outfit but couldn't find a thing. Her parents were at the party, which meant Kristen had to wear her dowdy navy church skirt with a yellow knit cardigan. "You look so warm."

"It's okay; I know my clothes suck," Kristen said. "Why do you think I'm wearing this big coat?"

They all laughed.

"Where's my compliment?" Derrington mumbled.

Massie was so nervous around him, she'd accidentally left him out.

"Uh, I like your . . ." Massie could have said Blond hair, big smile, sense of humor, or knees, and she would have meant it all. She just didn't know which one to choose.

"That's okay," Derrington said. "I like you too."

Massie felt that rush of warm tingles on the bottoms of her feet again. The exact same ones she felt at Sushi Samba. She looked over at Claire to see how she acted around Cam and instantly envied her for seeming so comfortable. They were laughing and scrolling through all of the pictures she had stored on her digital camera.

"Where's Harris?" Massie asked Alicia.

"At the Strokes concert," Alicia said.

"Why didn't you go?" Massie asked.

"Uh, long story." Alicia rolled her eyes. "I'll tell you later. It's a total PC."

"Yes!" Massie said. They hadn't had a *private conversation* in what seemed like forever.

Suddenly the sound of teachers and parents shushing the crowd was everywhere.

Massie was standing between Derrington and Alicia while Principal Burns and Headmaster Adams walked up to the microphone on the platform beside the Christmas tree.

"Awww, awww," someone bird-called from the crowd the instant Principal Burns's birdlike face came into view. She ignored the jab as she always did and waited for the crowd to settle down before she spoke.

"On behalf of Headmaster Adams and myself, happy holidays to all of the students and parents who have been part of the OCD/Briarwood Academy family for another wonderful year," Principal Burns said.

The crowd started cheering. She quickly raised her hand.

"I'm not done." She smirked. "I have a very special announcement to make."

"Awww, awww."

Principal Burns exhaled sharply through her nose before she continued. It sounded like a gust of wind. "Many of you know OCD's wonderful DJ, Deena Geyser."

"Hey, Comma Dee," someone shouted. "You're not funny!"

"You suck!"

"Well." Principal Burns cleared her throat. "She's going

to start making very tiny contributions to *The OCD Times* and will no longer have time to DJ."

The crowd exploded with applause.

"So thank you, Deena, for you hard work, wherever you are." Principal Burns acted like she was scanning the crowd looking for Deena and quickly moved on. "And without further ado, I would like to introduce our new DJ, or should I say, our *news* DJ. Every day she will deliver important school news and celebrity gossip. . . ."

Massie looked around, wondering who this new girl could possibly be.

"And she's going to start by giving you the facts on this year's nondenominational holiday tree. Ladies and gentlemen, Miss Alicia Rivera."

Massie's jaw dropped. She had no idea. But when she saw the huge smile across Alicia's beautiful face, she knew it must have been something she had wanted for a long time.

"Congrats," Massie said, hugging her friend.

"Thanks," Alicia shouted above the applause.

She took her time walking to the front of the crowd, her silky ponytail swinging in perfect time with her hips.

"You're hot!" someone shouted.

Alicia didn't flinch. She looked more beautiful and poised with every step she took.

"Thank you," Alicia said when she took the microphone from Principal Burns. She pulled a pink index card out of her back pocket but didn't refer to it once. "Thank you, Principal Burns and Headmaster Adams, for this honor.

This year's tree stands sixty feet tall. It came from deep within the Hudson Valley and it took seven men to chop it down. It is covered with four hundred lights and eighteen hundred photos and the star is made of homemade marzipan from Marion Foley's kitchen. Thanks, Marion. Three hundred and twenty gifts have been left for poor kids and the hot chocolate is free, so drink up! Have a happy holiday season and an ah-mazing new year. This has been Alicia Rivera for OCD."

The crowd exploded and the choir started singing "Silent Night." By the time they got to the chorus, everyone had joined in.

Massie's heart swelled with pride. She had the coolest friends in the world. And she would do everything she could from now on to let them know how important they were to her.

"Hey, Massie," she heard someone say. She lowered her head and saw Todd and his tiny friend Nathan. Normally Massie would have sent them away with a flip of the hair and a snide remark, but this was a special occasion.

"What's up, Todd?"

"Nuthin,'" he said, kicking the grass.

"Liar," Massie shouted over the final chorus of "Silent Night." "What is it?"

"I just heard my parents talking," Todd said to his L. L. Bean boot.

"Shocker." Massie rolled her eyes.

Tiny Nathan covered his mouth and giggled into his palm.

"It's not funny, Nathan," Todd said. "This is bad."

"What?" Massie leaned down so he could whisper into her ear. He looked close to tears.

"We're moving," he said. "My dad bought a house."

"Really?" Massie straightened up. "Are you sure?" She suddenly remembered all those times she prayed the Lyonses would leave her estate and felt a sinking sensation in her stomach. "Maybe you misunderstood." Massie felt a chill in the air and folded her arms across her chest.

She loved having a friend to come home to every night after school. It was like having a sister. Someone she could trust and confide in and even fight over the remote with. The estate was way too big for three people! There was more than enough room for everyone. Why did they have to go?

She saw a tear form in Todd's eye and Massie searched her mind for something positive to say. She had to stay strong. . . .

"At least we'll still see you after school and on weekends, right?" Massie's voice started to quiver.

"I dunno," Todd said. "How far is Chicago?"

"WHAT?" Massie shouted. The singing had stopped and a few parents looked back at her.

She smiled innocently until they turned away.

She leaned down and whispered in Todd's ear again. "Are you sure?"

"Yeah."

"Does Claire know?" Massie glanced at her friend and fought to hold back her tears.

Claire was helping Layne and Eli hand out Santa hats to all of their friends. They stuck one on Massie's head, but she just stood there, stiff, barely aware of the cozy fleece against her cold ears. Layne snapped a picture of Claire and Cam with their arms around each other. They looked so happy.

"Todd," Massie said, placing her hands on his skinny shoulders and turning him to face her. "Don't tell Claire."

"But I have to."

"You can't," she pleaded. "Not tonight."

"Why?" Todd whined. Massie noticed that for once, he actually sounded like a ten-year-old.

"Because tonight," Massie said, "everything is finally perfect."